DEATH AT ASHFORD CASTLE

A STAR O'BRIEN MYSTERY

MARTHA GEANEY
TURLOUGH, NOLAN PUBLISHING

This is a work of fiction. All of the characters, organizations, and events portrayed in this novel are either products of the author's imagination or are used fictitiously.

DEATH AT ASHFORD CASTLE

Copyright © 2019 by Martha Geaney

Library of Congress Cataloging- in-Publication Data (TK)

Produced in the United States of America

10 9 8 7 6 5 4 3 2 1

First Edition

ISBN: 978-0-9600567-2-9 (print)

For requests and information, contact:—

Turlough, Nolan Publishing

PO Box 193

850 Teague Trail

Lady Lake, FL 32159

Email: marthageaney@icloud.com.

Website: www.martha-geaney.com

Facebook, Instagram, Twitter: mgeaneyauthor

ACKNOWLEDGMENTS

Many thanks and shout outs to family and friends who continue to support my career as an indie writer.

In Ireland, there are my cousins who continue to amaze me with their abundance of love and support.

My lifelong friend, Reverend Chas Guthrie, who is always there with an encouraging text.

My cousin, Anne Hughes Kenny, who serves as my "reading detective." Anne goes through my manuscript looking for all kinds of errors, especially geographical ones.

The map depicted in this book is provided with permission to use by Ireland's Coillte (meaning forest) Service. More information may be found at: *https://www.coillte.ie/site/cong-forest/*.

In the United States, special thanks, again, to Nick Johns, fellow indie author, who read and made suggestions that made Star's story that much stronger.

Huge thanks to my friend, Jim Hipple, who continues to allow me to use his name. He provided valuable insights into police and private detective work.

Of course, to the Formatting Fairies, who continue to amaze me with the editing and formatting talent at their firm.

Finally, to Bill, who is my forever cheerleader. I love you.

This book is dedicated to my mother, Mary Geaney, who introduced me to her home and family in County Mayo when I was four years old. I am forever grateful.

CHAPTER 1

Tendrils of fog floated along the path that twisted through the woods at Cong. The mist, rising from the River Cong's depths, materialized as the spectral shape of a gnarled finger, curling around dead tree stumps.

Jane Doherty paused to remove the anorak she'd worn to the pub. The close-to-freezing daytime temperatures had unexpectedly risen a few points after sunset. Jane remained still for a few minutes and then flexed her long thin legs. She relished this night-time jaunt. The labyrinth of narrow paths, rutted from horses' hooves, meant she had to glance down every few seconds to keep from tripping over vines, fallen oaks, and mature, deformed roots brimming through the wet earth. Sometimes the ground was so wet it could suck the runners from your feet as if to envelop you in its dark, twisted environment.

Tying the jacket around her slim waist, she smiled at the simple pleasure that lay ahead of her. The strenuous exercise would burn at least three hundred calories. But then the corners of her mouth shifted downward when she thought of her husband, Dan.

Plain Jane was the nickname he dubbed her with when they

first met thirty-five years ago. "My Plain Jane's beauty is inner," he'd say as he grabbed the comb from her hand and smoothed out her tangled curls in the morning light. What had once been an endearment became an emotional battering ram, eroding her spiritual confidence. Now, whenever she glimpsed her pale and undefined features in the looking glass, the latest rumors about her husband's philandering came to mind.

Fifteen years ago, Jane, blaming her appearance for Dan's straying eyes, had taken up aerobics. After several years, she opened a studio at the local fitness center in Cong. She'd managed to build up a steadfast practice. What would her clients think if they discovered her primary motivation was for herself rather than for them? She'd imagined that once she transformed herself from a mousy brunette to a blonde goddess, Dan's gaze would return to her. For a while, this fantasy worked.

But then as the years passed, her confidence that Dan was attracted to her ebbed, and she turned away from the mirror more and more. Why, she asked herself, did she make the same mistake over and over? With the jacket anchored around her waist, Jane wondered again why she continued to love her husband. His unexplained, in-the-dead-of-night absences increased with each passing day.

Ahead of her, the dark woods promised to sweat out her obsessive, wasteful, and poisonous thoughts. The earlier ground fog had risen to eye level. She heard the slapping of the Cong's water striking the shoreline. Determined to burn energy, she took short strides over the ground, drowning out the sound of the footsteps that trailed behind her.

FOR A FEW MINUTES AFTER THE FINAL AIR BUBBLE BROKE THE water's surface, the killer's hands remained around the woman's throat. Bending close to the woman's ear, the killer rasped, "Whatever you do in life, you have to pick up the tab." Ready now, the killer seized the woman's hair and hefted her over a shoulder like a sack of potatoes. Then, satisfied that the rope and can of spray paint still remained in the overcoat, the killer proceeded to complete this masterpiece.

CHAPTER 2

EARLIER THAT EVENING

The Old Forge Restaurant and Gibbons' Pub sat on the edge of the Headford Road in the village of the Neale. The pub, its restaurant, and a church were the sole occupants of Neale's quarter stretch between Ballinrobe and Cross. Tonight, parked cars jammed both sides of the single lane in front of the pub. Two picnic tables accommodated the smokers who drank, laughed, and puffed tendrils of blue haze into the atmosphere. Specks of ash floated through the air—some getting too close, in my opinion, to the establishment's thatched roof.

I entered through the pub's painted red door, sandwiched between signs for Paddy's Whiskey and Player's Cigarettes. Once inside, I was amazed that a pub the size of a postage stamp could hold musicians, their instruments, the crush of people at the bar, and still boast a dining room. Nevertheless, I elbowed my way toward an amber neon sign that flashed HOT FOOD SERVED HERE.

I hadn't expected a crowd at 9:30 p.m. After a day of lengthy conference calls with Philomena Spring, my part-time technical guru, I'd left Castlebar later than planned. But I'd forgotten that traditional music and dancing were popular on Tuesday and Thursday evenings in Ireland's pubs.

Isn't it ironic? Here I was in Ireland, searching for my birth mother while managing my business, which was three thousand miles and an ocean away in Ridgewood, New Jersey. I'd expected the Consulting Detective's portfolio might suffer during this second trip to the Emerald Isle. Instead, requests for my information brokerage services remained steady. I guess I shouldn't have been surprised. After all, not everyone wants to spend tedious hours scouring databases searching for family information, missing marriage licenses, and adoption papers.

My profession as a researcher and information broker involves me in people's lives, and more often than not, disappearances and deaths. I've found myself at the heart of a mystery more times than I'd like to count. But it's a mistake to label me a private investigator. While occasionally my research points the way to a murder, I am most definitely no Miss Marple! Nevertheless, six months ago, I found myself looking into the eyes of death when I investigated the demise of a young artist on Clare Island, County Mayo. I couldn't help myself. I just had to get involved when the police wrongly branded him as a low-level drug user.

"How do you like the music?" shouted the lanky, smooth-faced man. His curly, salt-and-pepper hair swept his collar. I paused to peruse his mud-splattered work boots, dusty jeans, and knobby sweater.

"Noel—Noel, man, get over here. Remember, you've got to keep yer nose clean, boyo," shouted one of his pals.

My nose wrinkled at the heightened aura of alcohol wafting from his body. Then, I nudged him out of my way and focused again on reaching the promised food oasis ahead. *What is it with men?* I wondered as a throng of couples came through the front door, and the surge pushed me forward. Why do guys believe music and a few beers in a tight bar are attractive to women? This wasn't going to work for me—Star O'Brien. I'd sworn off men for good since I'd fallen for one who'd turned out to be a liar.

At that moment, a gap in the crowd opened, and I spotted my landing site, two tables surrounded by a few stools. I picked up the pace, turning sideways, using my shoulders to propel myself through the human milieu. *Damn!* The moment I neared my destination, a couple and three women took possession of the spot.

Frustrated, ravenous, and itching to get back to the bed-and-breakfast to review today's notes, I felt my fingers twitch to have something to do. But when another table opened up, I strode over and planted my butt in a chair. Then, I pulled my iPhone out of its holster on my Capri pants and searched the display for any messages.

"Ready to order?" the server asked. "It's bar food and snacks tonight." Glancing around at the packed room, she added, "We can't do much more with a gathering this size."

I'd hoped for homemade vegetable soup and brown bread. But when my stomach growled, "Feed me," I settled for a basket of ham sandwiches and a Coke. So much for hot food.

While I waited for the server to return, I rechecked my cell phone for an update from Phillie. Phillie was also the blogger behind *Bits, Bytes, and WITs*. The *WIT* stands for women in technology. Phillie was on a mission, along with other women who worked in the computer industry, to increase the number of females in technology-related jobs.

The digital display had nothing to say. So, instead, I ruminated on the events and months since I'd first set foot in Ireland. In a short span of time, my life had changed forever. It had begun almost a year ago when the love of my life—Dylan Hill—suffered a fatal cardiac arrest. He'd left me with his assets and the stunning revelation that he owned a cottage in Ireland. He had secrets that included a living relative, a former friend, and a tragic love story—none of which he'd ever mentioned.

As shocking and hauntingly sad as it was to lose Dylan, I didn't have much time for grieving. Instead, I had to come to Ireland to settle the estate. I'd arrived sad, alone, hurt, and ready to sell French Hill Cottage. When I reached Mayo, I met Dylan's aunt, Georgina Hill, and his former friend, Lorcan McHale. Then, just when I'd decided to sell the cottage, Georgina got me involved in a tragic love story turned murder.

But the real reason I came to Ireland was the opportunity to scour the countryside for information that might lead me to discover what had happened to my mother, Maggie O'Malley— missing for almost twenty-two years. It bothered me that I spent so much time discovering loved ones in other families, but I couldn't locate my mother. The only solace in this quest was that I was becoming better at what I did. I knew I'd find her, or, at the very least, what happened to her.

She'd vanished two days after my sixth birthday without a word, a note, or a goodbye. I remembered the silence that had greeted me that morning when I raced out of my tiny bedroom, eager for her daily dose of hugs and kisses. But she hadn't delivered any embraces that day or ever since. Instead, I sat at the kitchen table most of the day, listening to the recurring clicks of the clock grow louder in the dark silence that engulfed me. The hours beat away until the shadows cast by our few belongings merged into the darkness. When I couldn't see anymore, I rose, walked to our apartment door, opened it, and rang Mrs. Mueller's bell just across the hallway.

Abandoned. That was what the police had said! I was out to prove that wasn't true.

I picked up my connection to the virtual world from the table to check for messages again, but instead, the sounds of the musicians tuning their mandolins, flute, and bodhrán captured my attention. Although reluctant to linger for too long, I wanted to hear the traditional Irish melodies and come all ya's that echoed throughout Ireland's pubs and dance halls. I had few memories of my missing mother, but one I'd never lost was how she'd sing, "Come all ye fair maidens and list while I sing," at dusk when she'd tuck me into one of the twin beds in our cramped apartment bedroom.

How I longed to feel her arms around me once again and hear her voice whisper the name she'd given me—Star.

"You're my shining star," she'd say when we sat at our apartment window, gazing out at the summer sky.

"Yes." I'd hug myself with the joy in my mother's voice. "I'm your Star."

"That's right, little one. A very special Star from Achill."

Veins of a white crystal called The Star run through Slievemore Mountain on Achill Island. Local legend has it that when people emigrated from the island, they took a piece of the crystal with them for luck. I imagined my mother had chosen my name because she believed I would bring her luck.

And, now, for the first time in a long time, I felt close to finding a connection to her. During the summer, using the Consulting Detective's automatic search software, Phillie discovered an inquiry in an adoption chat room about a Maggie O'Malley. The post offered no details other than stating that the woman in question was born around 1962 on Achill Island, Ireland. Someone named Evelyn Cosgrove in Cong, County Mayo, submitted the query. I thought about the message I'd heard when I dialed her landline in August.

"You've reached Evelyn Cosgrove. I'm out of the office on holidays. I won't have access to voicemail until I'm back on the tenth of September."

Repeated calls to Evelyn's phone number on the tenth resulted in endless ringing, no recorded message, and no human picking up to answer. Now, most of September had come and gone. Time is too long for those who wait, and for me, the last few months felt like an eternity. That's why I decided to show up on Evelyn Cosgrove's doorstep. I'd arrived back in Ireland a few days ago.

The server returned with a heaping basket of sandwiches, napkins, and a slim, tiny glass of beverage. Between bites of the thick-sliced, salty ham, I played with my phone, wondering why I hadn't heard from Phillie. Efficiency and coolness under pressure were her trademarks. It wasn't like her not to get back to me with a call or an email before wrapping up her day. I checked the phone's signal strength. Despite the ancient beams that lined the pub's ceiling, cell coverage was good. Finally, the phone vibrated. My eyes perused the display, expecting to see Phillie's name. Instead, it was Aunt Georgina's.

"Star, you left town again without calling." Her voice came in quick, short bursts as it wafted over the cellular network.

"Sorry, the day got away from me," I said. "I had lots of conference calls and emails to take care of for several projects back in the States. Before I knew it, I realized it was almost 9:00 p.m., and I had to get to Cong to check into Lydon's Bed-and-Breakfast. Then, I drove over here for supper. I meant to call you."

"You know you can call me at any hour." An emphatic steeliness replaced the breathlessness. Aunt Georgina was one of the few people who had some understanding of what I did for a living. "People on this side of the Atlantic care about you and want to know you're safe."

Although Georgina was Dylan's aunt, I'd come to think of her as mine. I'd spent most of my life building a tough, feisty, external shell to cover my vulnerability. I protected my independence. But with Aunt Georgina, it was different. With all the losses in my life, I enjoyed the idea that someone cared about me again.

"I drove by the Golden Thread on my way out of Castlebar, and it looked like a fashion convention had moved to your dress store," I said. "You wouldn't have had time to answer the phone anyway."

"It's the Carlyle wedding. The entire bridal party and dozens of their relatives have asked me to consult with them on wedding day dresses." Georgina paused, then went on to say, "But my busyness doesn't excuse you not getting a message to me."

She was right. Sometimes, I forgot that this sixty-two-year-old woman knew everyone in the countryside as well as ran a successful clothing boutique. It wasn't fair not to respect her concerns.

"I'm fine. I'll call you tomorrow. I promise," I said.

"What's all the noise in the background?" Aunt Georgina asked. "Are you at the Old Forge and Gibbons' Pub? Did you have a chance to speak to Jimmy Mahoney about Evelyn Cosgrove?"

"Coming across him in this pub would be like finding a grain of salt in the desert. Sardines have more room in a can, Aunt Georgina." I stopped myself before I uttered another inane idiom.

"Years back, the pub belonged to a Cosgrove family," Georgina said. "Whether or not that fact is connected to Evelyn, I don't know. I never had any dealings with them. But since Jimmy's the current owner, it's a good idea to talk to him. Besides, he's a native of Cong."

Aunt Georgina had broken her six-month relationship with Jimmy. "Something just wasn't right" was all she'd said when I asked her what happened. But still, they seemed to remain on good terms.

"I promise I'll call him tomorrow morning," I said.

"Good, make sure you do that," Georgina replied. "And, whatever happens, don't forget you have your life to live. Now, I've got to go. I'm late for dinner with Lorcan and his mother, Lady Marcella. Talk to you soon, love."

Lorcan! I groaned inwardly. His message, asking me to dinner, flashed through my mind. I hadn't returned his call but for reasons other than my busy schedule. I supposed that at some point, I'd have to make a decision about maintaining the cool acquaintance we'd developed or responding to the inner attraction that bubbled under my crusty exterior. But how could I expect to find another relationship like the one I'd had with Dylan? Didn't that kind of love only happen once in a lifetime? Besides, I'd lost everyone I'd ever loved: my mother, my adoptive parents in a plane crash, and Dylan to a widow-maker heart attack. Why should I take the chance to add another name to the roster of life's fateful and cruel tipping of the balance scale? At that moment, a man and woman jostled the table with enough force to interrupt my thoughts.

"I could kill you!" a male voice said. The couple stopped moving and glared at each other. Didn't they realize they were leaning on my table? Two to four feet is my preferred distance from strangers. I glanced around, wondering if anyone else had heard his threat.

The man shifted his lean body toward the woman, intruding beyond the invisible boundary that separated acquaintance from sexual partner. Muscles rippled under his tight-fitting white shirt and blue jeans, emphasizing his trim physical appearance. Unlike most Irish, his face sported a tan complexion. His eyes narrowed to slits. Salt-and-pepper hair, more pepper than salt, completed his appearance.

"You lost the right to criticize me years ago, boyo." The snarling voice contrasted with the statuesque, lean-muscled blonde who went nose-to-nose with her partner.

I have to get away from these people, I thought. While I considered how to make my escape through the crowd, the couple disappeared when space at the bar opened up.

I looked around for the server but soon realized this was a hopeless quest. I decided to pay up with the bartender. I rose from the table and grabbed my iPhone. I wouldn't want to lose my connection to the world.

When I arrived at the bar's countertop, I attempted to catch the bartender's eye. Too late, I realized that I stood next to the arguing couple. This time, the musical crescendos, the singing, and the voices at the bar kept me from hearing their conversation. But it didn't take long to figure out the discussion's drift because the woman reached across for his glass and hurled its contents at his face. With that, she jumped from the barstool, turned, and shoved her way to the exit. Her partner grabbed for the cocktail napkins piled along the bar, wiped his face dry, and winked at me. The bartender cleaned up the mess. Then, he pointed at me in expectation of a drink order—all as if nothing had happened.

I'd had enough for one night. I paid my bill and left. The moon hung full, lighting my way as I drove along the narrow, stone-walled roads to Lydon's. While I drove, I couldn't help wondering why people stayed in toxic relationships. Why did some people yearn for what they couldn't have? Did every relationship exact a price that was too dear to pay? I thought about the relationships I'd experienced in my life and the pain of losing everyone I'd ever loved.

I just don't get it. Sometimes, I wished I'd been born without the capacity to love. Because I loved my mother, I'd spent my life searching for her. And now, it seemed like I was close. Did I want to know the truth? Was I ready to accept the pain of knowing what happened the day she vanished? Was I ready to leave the past behind? I thought about Evelyn Cosgrove. Would she have the answers? If so, would they change my life? Perhaps tomorrow would make that determination.

CHAPTER 3

By the time I stationed myself across from Evelyn Cosgrove's house, the morning's fair weather had changed. Puffy, dark clouds diminished the earlier brilliant sunshine. I tightened the drawstring on my pink sweatshirt and plunged my hands into its pockets to keep the brisk air at bay. Who or what would I find when I rang that doorbell?

Draped in ivy, the house's stone walls looked almost as old as the Augustinian abbey ruins situated across from it. White lace curtains graced the two narrow front windows. Potted geranium plants elbowed each other for space on the inner window ledges. A tiny, painted green door served as sentry between the windows. There were no lights, no signs of movement, and no newspapers tossed on the front path. The house sat up against the River Cong. Strangely, Number One Abbey Street was the sole occupant of the short lane. Just past the cottage, the lane fed into a winding driveway, which crossed a bridge and disappeared into the woods toward Ashford Castle.

I touched my iPhone, debating whether to call the telephone number again. Instead, my feet impelled me across the street. My hands opened the gate. My fingers pressed the doorbell, and I waited. In the minutes that trickled by, I heard cars passing through the street at the top of the town, church bells rang nine times, and school-age children called out to their friends. But the house kept its peace.

I moved closer and knocked this time. Then, I waited and listened. The river water rushed along the side of the house while car tires whooshed on the cobblestones. The wind rattled a rusted chime hanging from the gable. But there was no human presence. Finally, when the clouds won their battle with the sun, I shoved my numb fingers into my pockets and turned my back to the cottage. A few people wandered down the lane, paused to look at me, then disappeared into a church —St. Mary of the Rosary, a one-story, squarish building, it seemed built to be subservient to the ancient abbey grounds and cemetery.

A moment later, I stood in the darkened vestibule of the church. I lingered near the door while my eyes adjusted to the darkness and remembered when my mother and I attended Our Lady of Angel's Church in the Bronx. The ritual lighting of three candles capped each visit.

"Keep your eyes on the altar, Star," she scolded me whenever I fidgeted.

"Why do you light three, Mom?" I asked her one time.

She smiled, her hands pausing for a moment from the task of removing the taper from the basket of sand and lighting it from the fire of another candle. "It's a light for the one who's not here," she replied.

I didn't know what she might have meant by that. I'd held what she said in my mind for a long time, imagining and believing that the light was for my father—that we were separated for good reasons. But she never explained.

Foster care put an end to my church-going until the O'Brien's adopted me. We attended 7:00 a.m. Mass every Sunday at Our Lady of Mt. Carmel Church in Ridgewood. But once they were gone, I stopped. It wasn't that I didn't believe in

God; it was that I didn't think God was in churches. I liked to think he or she was in the people we met.

Leaving my memories behind, I ventured farther into St. Mary of the Rosary Church, looking for someone to ask about Evelyn Cosgrove. A woman sat in one of the back pews. Turning toward me, she tilted her head to one side. I approached her.

I kept my voice to a whisper. "Excuse me; I'm looking for Evelyn Cosgrove. Is that her house across the street?"

"Evelyn? It's Evelyn Cosgrove you're looking for?" The woman's fingers never stopped moving along the rosary beads she held in her hands. Her eyes blinked as she perused me from head to toe and raised her eyebrows in question.

No, I thought to myself. *I'm looking for my mother*. Instead, I nodded. "Yes, I understand this is where she lives."

"Aye, you're right. But Evelyn's been gone for months, ages really. Where she's gone to now, I don't know." A bell rang, and a priest entered from the sacristy. He carried his chalice and placed it on the table facing the congregation. "Try the bookstore. Ben might know." The woman's eyes turned away to fix their gaze on the altar.

I was dismissed.

"Good morning," the priest's voice boomed throughout the room.

I bent my head and fled out the back door.

Who goes away for months without updating his or her away messages? What happened to the message I'd heard? I'd scoured the Consulting Detective's databases but hadn't turned up any other information about Evelyn other than the one query she'd made. I wouldn't rest until I spoke with her and determined why she'd been looking for a Maggie O'Malley.

Once outside, I looked around, wondering about the location of the bookstore. The church lady hadn't said. Still cold, I put my hands back into my pockets and walked along the pave-

ment to the building that served as the local tourist information center. A quick survey of the visitors' map indicated the
town's one bookstore. Five minutes later, I peered through a
glass window that boasted rare books for sale. Crushed
between a butcher shop and a bakery, Ben's Rarities didn't
open until 10:30 a.m. *What now?* I fidgeted with the phone in
my holster and considered calling Jimmy Mahoney. No, I
decided; it was too early for a pub owner to be up. And, I
couldn't call the States because the Consulting Detective team
wouldn't be at work yet either. But then, my stomach reminded
me I hadn't eaten breakfast, so I walked across the street to the
Quiet Man Café.

The steaming mug of tea warmed my hands in seconds.
Then, I turned my attention to the basket of homemade brown
bread the owner of the café set on the table beside a pot of jam
and a butter dish.

"Visiting, are ya?" she asked when she came back to
replenish the empty basket.

"I've got some business with Evelyn Cosgrove."

"It's Evelyn you're after, is it?" She stepped back and used
her hands to smooth her apron before she continued. "Well, I
don't think you'll find her. She's not one to let the sod grow
under her feet."

The image of the healthy-looking geranium plants outside
Evelyn's cottage flashed through my mind. "Who waters her
plants while she's away?" I asked.

"Oh, probably someone at the church. We all do our best to
keep the town looking fresh." Her eyes shifted to the phone
holstered at my waist. "What kind of business?"

"I'm not at liberty to say," I replied. "Do you know how to
reach her? It's an important matter."

"No, now I don't. But you might try Ben O'Malley's
bookshop."

"Is that the place across the street?" I asked. "The one called Ben's Rarities?"

She nodded. "I've seen her going in and out of his shop quite a bit. Always have their two heads together, they do. You'd think they manage the future of the world economy the way they clam up whenever anyone gets within hearing distance." Just then, the bell over the café's door rang. "I've got to get to my other customers. Give a shout if you need more tea." She hurried off to tend to her guests.

Ben *O'Malley*? Now, this was interesting. Could he have something to do with Evelyn's interest in my mother? And why did my mother have to have one of the most proliferated names in Irish history instead of a name like Gunshannon? Right from the beginning, the search for a Margaret O'Malley was like looking for a drop of water in an ocean.

Realizing ten-thirty had come and gone, I looked around for the café owner, but she seemed to have disappeared. Impatient for action, I calculated the bill and deposited several euros on the table. Then, I walked across the street to the bookstore. Its glass panel door sat between two full-length windows. Each window bore stenciling that read *Rare Books*. I couldn't see much into the store because of the book posters that covered every inch of glass. I strode through the door. I began to weave a path around shelves and piles of old manuscripts, maps, papers, magazines, books, and other collections of detritus.

"No, I need more time. Yes, yes. Next month." The disjointed words from a man pierced the powdery air and guided my way through the paper maze.

When I came around the final towering stack of books, I expected to see the wizened proprietor of this mausoleum. "Oh, sorry. I'm looking for Ben O'Malley."

The object of my inquiry turned away, lowered his voice, and said, "I have to go. Someone's in the shop." Thrusting the cell phone into his jacket pocket, he turned his gaze to me. "I'm Ben. How may I help you?"

Boy, was I surprised! I hadn't expected to find someone who was at least thirty years younger than what I'd imagined. Ben O'Malley's physical attractiveness—the ready smile, green eyes, and jet-black wavy hair—made him a candidate for the cover of a historical romance rather than the purveyor of old books.

"Good morning. My name's Star O'Brien. I live in Castlebar. I'm looking for Evelyn Cosgrove. I understand you may know how to contact her."

He nodded by way of beckoning me over to a desk and two chairs, where he indicated I should sit. The fabric covering the seat cushions was frayed and shedding threads. But in contrast to the rest of the shop, they were devoid of dust and papers. I sat down.

"And, what do you want with Evie?" he asked. "You say you live in Castlebar. I'm sorry, but I detect a fresh Yank accent." His fingers drummed a rapid beat on the mahogany secretary.

When I finished explaining about my mother and the inquiry from Evelyn, there was a long silence.

"Ah, Evie." The desk drumming began again. "I've never known a woman with such a lust for travel and adventure. She's gone off on one of her trips to God knows where." Ben's bright smile lit up this dark corner of the shop. "I'm sorry, I can't help you. She doesn't check in with me."

My hand clenched my phone to hide my disbelief. After all, he must know her well enough to have shortened her name from Evelyn to Evie. "Has she ever left a cell phone number or email address that she uses for contact when she's away?"

"Not that I know of." He shrugged. "We both have an interest in rare letters and manuscripts. But she's mysterious about her comings and goings. I wouldn't know how to reach her."

I thought of how tethered I was to the gadgets that keep me

connected. How someone could survive without being able to communicate at light speed to anyone in the world was a mystery to me. Looking around, I remarked on several antique frames that held tattered and yellowed letters captive. "You must have a thorough grasp of history to recognize famous signatures and missives," I said. I wanted to draw him out.

The drumbeat slowed, paused, and recommenced.

"Aye, I've developed a knack for it." His eyebrows rose as his green eyes held mine briefly before he glanced away toward the front of the shop. "Are you interested in a particular period or historical figure?"

"I imagine that bearing the O'Malley name, you've researched its history. I'm interested in old papers, books, or diaries from Achill Island. Specifically, from the nineteen-sixties, when my mother might have lived there."

"Hmm." He glanced at his watch. "Look, sorry, I don't mean to rush you, but I'm expecting someone here soon. If you don't mind, I have some work to do before my appointment. You came in just as we were finishing up our call." Ben rose and led the way to the shop's door. "Why don't you stop back later when we can discuss the details? Oh, and you should know that I work on retainer."

The door swung shut behind me. What now? I looked at the time on my cell phone and decided to call Jimmy. It took one ring before someone answered.

"I already told you..." Although the words were whispered, the speaker's tone was harsh.

Taken aback, I took a quick glance at the phone's display to check that I'd reached the right number. I had. "Is this Gibbons' Pub?" I asked.

"What the heck? Oh, sorry, I thought you were someone else. Aye, this is Gibbons. Who am I speaking with?" This time, the man's voice was normal.

"Mr. Mahoney?" I asked.

"Aye, 'tis," he responded.

"I'm Star O'Brien. Georgina Hill suggested I call you about a matter I'm looking into. Do you have a few moments?"

"Oh, right. You're the Yank she told me about."

"Yes, I'm looking for—" Before I could finish, a loud bang reverberated from his side of the call. It sounded like he'd dropped the phone.

"I told you to get the hell out of here," Mahoney yelled. In the next instant, he was back on the line with me. "Sorry, love, I have to go now." He hung up.

I hoped he was all right. I thought of calling back but decided against it. I was here to find my mother and nothing else. But I did wonder if this had anything to do with why Georgina broke it off with him.

CHAPTER 4

F rustrated with the morning's lackluster results, I decided
to power walk along the trail through Cong Woods. I
figured the three-mile hike would quell my restless energy. The
wind's sharp tentacles stung my face as I weaved through the
abbey's cramped cemetery. I stepped over crumbled headstones
and walked past the remains of the monk's fishing house. I'd
have liked to walk out along the narrow ledge to take a look at
the stone structure, which sat over the rushing waters of the
River Cong. I'd read that the monks tied a line from a bell in the
abbey to the hole in the house's floor, where the monks could
drop a net. When a fresh catch got caught in the net, the bell
rang in the abbey's kitchen—the sixteenth-century version of a
message alert. But I didn't linger; instead, I crossed over the
narrow bridge that spanned the river to the walking trail.

The damp, musty smells of moss covering the tree trunks
competed with the sharp, crisp air. The sinuous path forged a
labyrinth among the ancient foliage. I kept my eyes riveted to
the ruts from horses' hooves to keep from falling over vines,
dead tree stumps, and gnarled roots bursting through the
sodden earth. Cigarette butts and empty potato chip packages
mingled with the dead vegetation dropped from the rhododen-

dron, boxwoods, and California Redwood trees planted by the
Guinness family beginning with Sir Benjamin and then his
son, Arthur. The travel books note that Arthur—Lord Ardilaun
—and his wife, Olivia, devoted much of their considerable
wealth to developing the castle, walks, forest, and local historical artifacts. What would they say now if they saw the garbage
that marred the beauty of their life's work?

In some places, the soggy ground threatened to suck my
Rocket Dogs from my feet and keep me enveloped in its dark,
twisted environment. The last place I'd heard birdsong was
back at the bridge over the river. Silence marked the air as if the
woods waited and watched.

I paused at the Priest's Hole I'd read about in the tourist
guide—a dim, dank, stone-walled cave in the ground. During
Cromwell's persecution, Ireland's priests and Catholics fled far
from civilization to the country's western mountains, lakes,
woods, and craggy outcrops—the places that only sheep could
navigate. Priests carried their church with them in suitcases
containing altar clothes, a Bible, and the Eucharist. The ritual
celebrations of the sacraments were held in secret places, even
in cemeteries. These hiding places could be anywhere: a hole
in the ground, concealed in the wall of a building, or inside a
chimney. The islands in Clew Bay and the lakes surrounding
Ashford Castle were full of them.

How had the priests survived? Just the idea of getting into a
confined space was enough to frighten me, even if taking that
step was self-imposed imprisonment. I'd lived in my emotional
prison long enough—walled in, trapped by not knowing what
happened to my mother. No father. My bars were the fear of
never knowing. My only escape was to continue believing that
my mother had not abandoned me.

In the blink of an eye, the woods released me from its
narrow path into a grassy field with a panoramic view of the
river, Ashford Castle, and the Connemara Mountains. Still rest-

less, I wandered across another bridge, through the castle's open iron gates, and around the deserted courtyard toward Lough Corrib. Here, the path widened to accommodate walkers, horse riders, and the way to the boathouse where skiffs floated, waiting for anyone who wanted to try their luck in the lake's cold waters.

I jumped as a rush of air and solid muscle mass assaulted me from behind. Whirling to face my assailant, I discovered a black and white border collie, who dropped a branch at my feet. Looking around for the dog's owner, I tossed the piece of wood and continued walking. The collie kept pace with me, running back and forth, picking up sticks, and presenting them to me. A wave of homesickness hit me as I thought of Skipper, my little black Schipperke, at home in Ridgewood.

Naming my temporary companion Ashford, I threw another branch he'd laid at my feet into the woods. He charged after the stick and disappeared. I spent a few minutes waiting, but he didn't return. Oh, well, why should he be any different than the people who'd come and gone in my life? I continued my walk.

Suddenly, frantic barks and howls filtered through the dark foliage. Fighting my way through the branches and sticker bushes toward the sounds, I emerged onto Corrib's sandy shores. Ashford's barks beat a staccato pulse as he tugged on something lying at the base of a stone obelisk, which faced the Connemara Mountains and the lake's beach.

As I got closer, I saw that Ashford wasn't trying to pick up a tree limb. No. It was an arm. I made a quick run toward the body, dropped to my knees, and prepared to perform first aid. Then, I stopped. My heart pounded. Hers did not. As Ashford's cries reverberated against my ears, my eyes cringed to avoid the scene before me.

The woman was bound to the obelisk with a thick rope, her arms spread as if in flight. Red paint unevenly underlined one

of the phrases etched into the monument: *Rien ne m'est plus;*
Plus ne m'est rien. I could see dark bruising and scratches on her
neck just above the collar of her shirt. A windbreaker jacket lay
across her legs. Caked with mud and wet grass, her yoga pants
and sneakers looked fashionable. I didn't take the time to look
any further. Emergency services answered my call, telling me to
remain where I was until the police arrived.

I moved as far away from the monument as I could without
actually leaving the scene. While I waited on the deserted
beach and listened to the water lap at the shore, I looked across
the lake to the Connemara Mountains. Hugging my arms
around my body to counter the chills that had taken hold of
me, I turned away from the view to gaze at her still body. What
was her story? How had she come to this place? Who would
feel loss today? Whose life would never be the same again?

As the initial shock subsided and the adrenaline coursing
through my veins slowed, my eyes widened. I recognized her
clothes and hair. Even though rigor mortis had stiffened the
lean muscles and her hair lay plastered to her skull, I was sure
that this was the woman I'd seen arguing in Gibbons' Pub last
night!

Jumping up, I turned away from the corpse. I had a decision
to make. Six months ago, the Castlebar detectives told me to
mind my own business when I'd gotten involved in solving
Matthew Sumner's murder. They'd even suspected me in his
fiancée's death. I knew they were mistaken about Matthew—
just as the police in the Bronx had been wrong about my
mother. Should I tell the police about the argument in the bar?
If I did, I'd get caught up in the investigation. There'd be
endless hours of explaining why I was in the country, what I'd
been doing at Gibbons' Pub in the Neale, and how I'd come to
find the body.

Oh, why even debate the question? My conscience,
ingrained with the O'Brien's words, *"You have more than others,*

Star, and as a result, you carry more responsibility," echoed in my mind. I had a duty to tell the police everything I knew. And besides, what if this woman were Evelyn Cosgrove? Still, knowing that I had a responsibility to leave the world a better place didn't keep me from wondering about people's responsibility to me and what I came here to do. Not for one moment would I allow any police investigation or the police to keep me from proving the truth about my mother.

CHAPTER 5

"Miss O'Brien, step this way."
I followed Thomas O'Shea and James Keenan away from the staccato radio bursts, hushed voices, and solemn faces in the crowd. Neither man smiled. Was it due to the gravity of the situation or because I'd met these two Castlebar detectives before under similar circumstances? Suspicious of my involvement in the death of a financial investment advisor, they'd refused to listen to me when I tried to tell them what I knew. *"As I said, Miss O'Brien, this is a garda matter. It's not for the likes of you, a foreigner, to question or even know the facts of the case."* Even after several months had passed, the memory of O'Shea's words had the power to raise my bristles.

When we had distanced ourselves from the horrible scene at the monument, they placed themselves between me and the increasing number of onlookers who bunched along the edge of the beach and the path back to the castle. The deep scar gouged over O'Shea's left eye contrasted with his blue eyes and dark blond, wavy hair. Both men wore gray suits, periwinkle blue shirts, and matching ties: the Hardy Boys, Irish edition, all grown up.

"I..."

O'Shea held up his hand.

"This is our investigation, Miss O'Brien," he said. "We'll ask the questions. I gather from the emergency services operator you were the one who found the body. Is that correct?"

"Yes, I was walking along the path when Ashford began barking. He just didn't stop. When he didn't respond to my calls, I went to look for him—and found her."

"Hmm. I seem to recall that you're a visitor in Ireland. But now you claim to have a dog. How is that possible, Miss O'Brien?" O'Shea asked.

"He's not my dog." I shrugged my shoulders at the question and said, "I happened upon him this morning."

"Yeah, right," O'Shea said. "We'll see about that." He nodded at Keenan, who scribbled in his notebook.

I looked over at the crowd. That's when I noticed the guy from the pub who'd fought with the woman—the one who now lay dead. From where I stood, it looked like he was wearing the same clothes he'd had on last night. Except now, they looked more wrinkled than pressed.

"I didn't waste any time. I phoned emergency services. But I want to..."

O'Shea raised his hand again.

"In a minute, Miss O'Brien." He glanced toward the stone monument. "Now, did you touch the body or move it in any way?"

"No, as soon as I got close enough, I knew I couldn't help her. After I made the call, I sat on the beach until I heard the sirens and cars arriving on the path. You know the rest."

"Did you notice anyone else in the area?" O'Shea continued while Keenan scribbled in his notebook. "Did you meet anyone on the walking path?"

"No, I didn't see anyone else. But I'm trying to tell you—"

"What about this Ashford?" Keenan interrupted me this

time. "You're contradicting yourself. Who is this Ashford person?"

"Wait one minute!" I hurled the words at the two detectives. "If you two listened, you'd know that Ashford is a dog. He began following me while I was walking. He's the one who found the body."

"That's enough for now, Miss O'Brien." O'Shea's cold, hard eyes bored into mine.

"No, it's not enough." I stared back at him. "Listen to me; I recognize this woman. I saw her last night. She fought with a man in Gibbons' Pub."

O'Brien and Keenan exchanged glances.

"Miss O'Brien, I have to advise you that you'd better not be meddling in garda business." O'Shea's scar deepened as he narrowed his eyes and lowered his voice to deliver this warning. "The consequences are serious."

"I'm trying to help you." I kicked the sand to emphasize my point. "I'm not interfering. I overheard this woman arguing with a man last night."

"And I'm sure you have some theories, Miss O'Brien." O'Shea smiled at Keenan.

"I'll leave that to your brilliant minds." I gave another glance at the crowd on the beach before turning back to the detectives. "Meanwhile, if you want my advice, you'll talk to that man hovering on the beach area closest to the body. He's wearing a white shirt with blue jeans. He's got a tan. He's the one I saw with her in the pub."

They didn't listen. Instead, their heads swiveled toward the growing crush of people pressing onto the scene and the flashing lights of a white van emerging through the trees. A man, exiting from the van, called out, "What have we got?"

"Thank you for your time, Miss O'Brien," O'Shea said. "We'll be in touch if we think of anything else to ask you. We have your contact information."

I shoved my clenched hands into my sweatshirt pockets so that I wouldn't punch him for ignoring my attempts to provide relevant information. Dismissed, I joined the silent crowd near where the man from the pub stood. No one spoke as everyone watched the rising of a tent shelter over the body and the cordoning off of the sandy perimeter.

"Let me through." The words pierced the silence. The crowd parted to allow the person shouting the words to come forward. He walked up to the individual I'd just identified to the police. I assumed there must be some kind of family relationship because the newcomer, although younger, bore a strong resemblance to the older man.

"This is your fault!" The words erupted from the younger version. The thirty-something's shoulder-length dark curls, smudged glasses, and untucked shirttails contrasted with the other man's classic hairstyle and tight-fitting shirt and jeans. But they shared the same black hair, brown eyes, and dark brown skin.

"Goddamn it, Paul, hold your tongue," the man from the pub hissed, scanning the area as if to verify that no one had heard the harsh words. "I have no intention of explaining my relationship with your mother to you. Now or ever. If you can't keep your mouth shut, I won't be responsible for the consequences." His gaze settled on the tent that sheltered everyone's eyes from the lifeless form within.

"Oh, yeah, I forgot. You're the great Dan Doherty. You don't answer to anyone—not even your own son." The younger of the two jerked the person he'd called Dan by the arm, spinning him around to face him. "If you'd paid more attention to Mom, she might not have ended up like..." Paul gasped, sobs overcoming his words.

"Dan, what's going on here?" The wind telegraphed the woman's words through the air. Searching for their source, I glimpsed a female elbowing her way to the front. For one instant, her lips arched upward as her eyes focused on the activities going on around the tent. "Jane." The word was uttered as a statement, not a question. The newcomer was fastidiously dressed in a navy business suit, heels, and expensive-looking rimless glasses. I couldn't help wondering if the tall, thin, salt-and-pepper brunette was a family member, perhaps a sister to Dan. Then she stepped forward, rested her hand on Dan's shoulder, and gazed up at his face. With the way she looked at him, I changed my opinion about her being a sibling. She took charge of both men, marshaled them away from the crowd, and commanded a blanket from one of the police. She draped it around Paul's shaking body.

"Thanks, Ann," Paul said gratefully, wrapping himself in the blanket.

While both men continued to glare at one another, the police made their rounds of the crowd, asking questions, writing down names and contact information. After more than an hour, O'Shea and Keenan approached the trio, exchanged a few words, and led Dan and Paul to a waiting police sedan.

"I'm going with you." The brunette's heels spiked up the sand as she ran to a car with an advertisement for Ann Ryan's Auctioneers pasted on the driver's door.

When the man who'd arrived in the white van emerged from the tent, one of the police shepherded the remainder of the onlookers away from the vicinity. "There's no reason to remain, folks. Please, go about your business. This is a garda affair."

Yeah, a police affair. They hadn't even given me a chance to describe the fight. I had to find a way to get them to listen to me. How strange that today the scene that played out here was similar to what had played out when my mother disappeared. The police wouldn't listen then, and they weren't listening now. It was what inspired me to become an information broker. I was tempted to thank the detectives for that but suspected they wouldn't get the irony.

Ashford's reappearance at my side—while I'd made the call to emergency services, he'd disappeared into the woods again —kept me from dwelling too long on my relationship with the police. Bending to rub the dog's ears, I noted the absent collar or any kind of identification.

"Looks like it's you and me until I find your owner," I said, patting him on the shoulder. "Let's go."

A half-mile later, the wooded path reopened to Ashford Castle's grounds. The castle stood on a rise, set amidst the untamed landscape, protected from nature by manicured lawns, shrubs, and flower beds. The structure's stone façade was a dull gray rather than the darker stone that had become popular in Ireland's new homes. Its turrets, chimneys, and orioles brooded over Lough Corrib's three hundred sixty-five islands—all under the scrutiny of the Connemara Mountains. Lord Ardilaun and Lady Olivia created a legacy that outlasted their family lines. Although they'd died childless, their roots were as deep and strong as the four-hundred-year-old redwoods growing in the castle forest. I felt the enormity of what these two lovers contributed to each other and those around them.

Suddenly, Ashford bounded off the path toward the castle and rounded the side of the building. I followed along and found him at a back door, where a man sat on an empty milk crate, taking deep drags on a cigarette. When I got closer, I noticed he wore a black jacket with the letters *AC* mono-grammed on its lapel.

"I see you've found the castle dog," the man stated, grinding the end of the cigarette beneath his shoe.

Ashford seated himself at my side as if to contradict the man's words.

"Are you his owner?" I hoped not. I couldn't see Ashford living a life of second-hand smoke.

"That creature?" The man nodded his head toward Ashford. "He's been around here for months. I've seen him walking beside a couple some afternoons. I thought maybe they owned him, but I haven't seen them for over a month. Matter of fact, I think one of them ended up dying sudden-like. They say a heart attack took him." Shaking his head, he looked toward the path leading to the lake. "And now, today's event. It's gonna queer people from being alone in the woods." Then, he turned his attention to me. "Tourists don't usually come around to this side of the castle. Can I help you with something?"

"Yes, maybe you can. I'm looking for someone named Evelyn Cosgrove. I believe she lives in the cottage at the end of the castle's driveway."

"Hmm, is that so? No, I can't say that I've ever heard of her," he said. Then he glanced at his watch and rose from the crate. "I have to get back to work." He bent to pick up his cigarette butt, threw it into a cigarette receptacle, and walked into the castle.

I stood in the courtyard and listened to the silence. It began to mist again. I shivered and pulled the drawstring on my sweatshirt tighter.

"Come on, Ashford," I said. Then, we proceeded solemnly through the quiet landscape and woods back to my car.

CHAPTER 6

My Renault rumbled along Cottage Road. French Hill Cottage was situated at the end of the one-lane byroad between the villages of Breaffy and Errew. I'd come here a few months earlier with the intention of selling the place. But, for now, locating Evelyn Cosgrove and figuring out if she had any connection to my mother outweighed my intentions.

In the hour it took to drive from Cong to Castlebar, the clouds cleared. The air was cooler now. A gentle breeze ruffled the branches of the Hazelwood and ash trees that surrounded the cottage grounds, creating a welcome shelter from the outside world. Inside the cottage, the three bedrooms, kitchen, bathroom, and living room were a modest alternative to my home in New Jersey, but surprisingly, I felt most cozy here. Maybe the feeling came from the sense of continuity I got from knowing that the antique mahogany, oak, and pine furnishings had belonged to earlier generations of Dylan's family. Whatever the reason, I sensed a connection to him when I was alone here at night—safe, secluded, and far from the worries of the world.

I let myself and Ashford into the cottage. Then, I checked for voice messages and emails. For once, I was relieved to discover an empty inbox. A quick search of the refrigerator revealed the last few slices of Aunt Georgina's homemade brown bread. Unlike the yogurt, fruit, and vegetables that often turned moldy from my neglect, Aunt Georgina's home-cooked meals vanished within days. After I slathered the slices with a mound of Irish butter, Ashford and I feasted, enjoying the companionable silence. Then we returned to the car for a drive into Castlebar.

"SORRY, I DON'T DETECT AN IMPLANT, AND I'VE NEVER SEEN THIS dog in my practice before." Dr. Kelsey Krause placed the radio frequency identification scanner on her desk. Ashford stretched out on the stainless-steel examination table, chomping on a large Irish Rover biscuit. She ruffled his hair. "We work with a local shelter. I can get him placed today if you like."

For a moment, I considered my workload and my comings and goings between the U.S. and Ireland. I knew the dog probably wouldn't be able to cross the Atlantic with me. But the thought of relinquishing him to strangers made my gut clench with a sick feeling. I knew how it felt to be passed around from family to family.

"No, he stays with me," I said.

"Fine. Then I'll set you up with the proper food supplies and an appointment for his next exam." She shook my hand. "I understand how you feel. I've had a few rescues in my life. There's no greater love bond."

On the way home, I headed toward the Golden Thread. Ashford lazed on the back seat of the car while I wound through the maze of the town's one-way streets. Finally, I found a parking space behind the shop.

"A dog! Jesus, Mary, and Saint Joseph! What were you

thinking?" Aunt Georgina's hands moved from the dress she was working on to her hips. Her brown eyes bored into mine.

Today, Georgina's five-foot four-inch frame wore another of her olive-green shirtdresses. A gold silk scarf tossed around her neck completed the ensemble. The colors highlighted her dark olive skin and brown eyes.

"I couldn't leave him with strangers." I plunked my body down onto one of the two leather chairs that sat inside the shop's front window. "Not after what we've been through today."

"What in heaven's name could justify getting a dog?" Georgina asked.

"This dog and I found a body on the shores of Lough Corrib this morning."

"What!" Georgina exclaimed. "You know I called Gibbons' Pub this morning. I wanted to know if Jimmy spoke with you about Evelyn. He said he'd had an emergency and hadn't had the time. But he never explained."

"Well, that's not all." I shuffled my feet into a more comfortable position. "It might have been a coincidence, but I saw the dead woman last night at Jimmy's pub."

Ignoring my previous refusal of a cup of tea, Georgina whirled around to the back of the shop, where she kept a hot plate. In no time at all, she returned with two cups of peppermint tea. She handed one of the steaming mugs of liquid to me and perched herself on the shop's window seat. "Now, start at the beginning. I want to know everything."

I stirred the hot brew, took a sip, and spilled my guts.

"What are you going to do?" Georgina asked when I'd finished.

"For now, nothing." I took another sip of tea. "The police made it clear they don't consider me a reliable witness."

"That's a shame. But after what happened the last time you

were here, I have to admit that I'm relieved. This information broker business is dangerous."

"You're somewhat right about that." I nodded and placed the empty teacup on the window seat beside her. "My work does sometimes lead to finding a missing person and why they disappeared to begin with."

"But you're not totally comfortable doing nothing, are you?" Georgina asked.

I shook my head in agreement, confirming for myself the uneasiness I'd had since leaving Cong. "Frustrated is more like it. Why won't the police listen to me?"

"Some things just aren't worth worrying yourself about, girl." Georgina straightened her scarf, shook her lustrous head of hair, and smiled over at me. "Besides, you need to focus on what you came here to do, like speaking to this Evelyn Cosgrove."

Realizing how much I had grown to love Georgina in the months since I arrived in Ireland, I couldn't help smiling back. "Yes, there's that," I admitted.

"I'm sure you'll find her. But where does the dog come into all of this?"

"It just didn't seem right to leave him," I said.

"Hmm. I thought you didn't want any attachments in your life?" Georgina asked.

"I don't. And, this isn't a permanent commitment. I'll just take him until his owner shows up. That's all," I said, ignoring the slight smile that lurked on Georgina's face.

"Well, I've got to get back to work." She placed her mug on the window ledge. "That dress I was working on when you arrived has to be ready for pick up this evening. I'll see you later, Star," she called over her shoulder as she bustled to the back of the shop and her assistant.

Before returning home, I stopped at Mulroy's shop. I left with cooked chicken pieces, tomatoes, and a mashed potato salad. A short time later, Ashford and I entered the cottage. Then, we locked the door on the world.

"That's that," I said to Ashford, picking up the empty plate he'd licked clean. "It's time for you to explore the garden while I do some work." He followed me onto the cement patio at the back of the cottage. I secured the collar and leash the vet provided to a long clothesline I'd found in the barn—I wasn't taking any chances. Sitting at my desk, emails answered, I called home. My office manager answered on the first ring.

"The Consulting Detective, Ellie Pizzolato speaking."

"Hey, Ellie, it's Star."

"I'm glad you called. We miss you. It gets a little crazy working in this treehouse when you're not here."

Part of my old colonial house was given over to my business. Our office space occupied the top floor, a few feet below the treetops. I'd designed the workspace with ceiling-to-floor glass windows, and a deck along the back side overlooked a brook. In the summer, when the trees bloomed, we lived in a jungle, or as I called it, our treehouse.

"How did your meeting with Evelyn Cosgrove go?" Ellie asked.

I twisted the phone cord, hating to tell the team what had happened. Ellie and Phillie were more than loyal employees. They were fully invested in wanting to help me find my mother.

"It didn't go well. In fact, we didn't meet at all." Glancing down at the tangled mess I'd made of the telephone wire, I felt my stomach knot in a similar manner. "No one's seen her for months. She's vanished."

"No, it can't be. This seemed like such a good lead," Ellie said.

I refused to allow Ellie's sympathy to fuel my tears. "Don't worry, Ellie; I'll find her." My words echoed my persistence. "Listen, is Phillie available? I want her to follow up on this for me."

"Yes, she is," Ellie replied. "Hold on."

"Hi, boss. Ellie says this Cosgrove woman is a no-show."

"Everyone here seems to know her, but they don't know where she is or how to reach her. That's what they say anyway. Can you recheck the database where you first saw her query? Maybe she's reached out again." I wasn't optimistic that this was the case. Phillie would have been monitoring the message board.

"Sure, boss," Phillie said. "I've been checking but will drop back into the site again and see what's going on."

"Oh, and see if you can find an employer. She seems to travel quite a bit. Maybe she's a consultant."

"Do you think she got married and changed her name?" Phillie asked.

Because Evelyn's voicemail said she'd be back by September tenth, we hadn't searched for marital data. After all, we had her phone number and an address. Now, I realized that it might have been a mistake. Pulling the phone cord with me, I slumped down onto one of the kitchen chairs.

"Go ahead and see what you can learn from public information," I said. "See if you can find an employer. Maybe they know where she is."

"Will do, boss. And Ellie wants to talk to you again."

Ellie's voice came back on the line to tell me about a request for our services. "It's Southern Aircraft Corporation, Star. Someone is claiming that he's related to the founder, Igor Southern. Southern wants us to investigate the relationship claim."

"Did they ask to meet with me?"

"Not yet," Ellie continued, "I told them you're away. But, they're anxious for us to get started."

"Okay, ask Phillie to begin gathering any information she can from the internet. And, Ellie, one more thing. How is Skipper doing?"

"Oh," Ellie laughed. "He's getting lots of attention. Your friend Joanne brings him treats every day. Don't worry. We're keeping him busy."

After the call, I sat at the kitchen table, thinking about my mother and now Evelyn. Some people, like my mother, don't leave much. I had few clues to follow in my search for her: a letter from Clare Island, her story about the origin of my name, the lighting of the church candles, and a Bible with ripped out pages. Two things were clear in my mind and my soul—the memory of her love and the certainty she hadn't abandoned me. And now, another person seemed to have vanished quietly without any trace.

I got to my feet, squared my shoulders, and went in search of Ashford. I found him curled up on a mat outside the kitchen door. As we settled in for the evening, I knew two things for sure—I would find Evelyn Cosgrove and my mother.

CHAPTER 7

"D on't you return messages?" Lorcan asked as he glanced down at a paper in his hand. His thick blond hair scraped the top of his shirt collar as if challenging me to touch it.

From the first moment I'd met him, I thought Lorcan McHale was one of the most handsome men I'd ever seen. Yet I did everything I could not to gaze into the blue eyes that drew me to him and threatened to make me lose control. He stood at the fence that separated French Hill Cottage from his estate. At one time, the cottage had served as the McHale estate's lodge. Now, the cottage was mine, a tiny oasis amidst his sprawling one-hundred acres.

"I've been busy." I caught the scent of *my* sweat from jogging and just knew my short cowlicks probably stuck up like porcupine needles. *Why does he always materialize at my most embarrassing moments?*

"Is there any chance you're avoiding me?" Lorcan chuckled. I watched him fold the paper into symmetrical parts. Then, he placed it into his left breast pocket. His eyes studied me over the rim of his John-Lennon-style, pewter-framed glasses.

Before I'd ever met Lorcan McHale, I had been prepared to

hate him. Dylan had made a passing comment once about someone called Lorcan, and then, with a curious roll of the eyes, said, "That guy's trouble." When I'd first arrived in Ireland and met this Lorcan person, I imagined that Dylan must have had a good reason for never discussing him with me. But then Dylan had kept many secrets from me, including his family and Irish cottage.

Lorcan had explained the reason for their falling out and why Dylan had protected me from his past sorrows. Before I'd come into his life, Dylan had an Irish lover. Her name was Caitlin May. A botanical researcher, she contracted a virus in the lab and died within hours. Poor Dylan! He had suffered losses too! The issue between Lorcan and Dylan arose when Dylan met me. Lorcan advised him to tell me about Caitlin. But Dylan had refused. He said he wanted a clean break from the past. Lorcan also revealed that Dylan worried about my obsession with finding my mother. He didn't think it would come to any good. So, he'd kept Ireland out of our relationship. Lorcan hadn't agreed with him. That's the last time the two friends ever spoke with each other.

"No, that's not why." *Coward*, I said to myself. *You're afraid to have dinner with him.*

"I understand. Georgina told us you'd gone to Cong to speak with Evelyn Cosgrove in person." Lorcan paused as a tractor rode by and waved to the driver. "How did it go? Any more information about your mother?"

Realizing he might not have heard about the body on the beach, I explained what had happened and the police's decision not to listen to me.

"The garda don't mean anything by it, I'm sure. Do you want me to speak with them?" Lorcan asked.

"No. I don't think they take anything I say seriously. Besides, Evelyn wasn't at home." I paused, wondering if I should share my concerns about Evelyn with him. "It seems she travels quite a bit—often without leaving forwarding information. I'm going back to Cong this morning. I intend to find anyone who might know where she is."

At that moment, Ashford came bounding up the road toward us and settled himself at my feet. Laughing, Lorcan bent down to rub the dog's ears, saying, "Where did this fella come from?"

"Oh, he's mine," I said. Then, I added, "Temporarily. He followed me on the path around Lough Corrib at Ashford Castle yesterday. I checked with someone at the castle, and he didn't know who the owner is. I decided to bring Ashford home with me."

"Temporarily?" Lorcan's eyebrows lifted as he smiled up at me. "I've never known anyone who owns a dog temporarily." Turning his attention back to Ashford, he added, "Well, Ashford, welcome to French Hill—temporarily."

"Okay, okay. You've made your point. I checked with the vet, and he's not chipped, but when I get back to Cong today, I'll ask around again about whom he might belong to."

"I know you want to find Evelyn, but is it a good idea to go back to Cong while the garda are investigating the murder?"

"I need to know more about her. Don't worry; I'll have Ashford with me."

"What about the meeting with the director of the national records?" Lorcan asked.

"He's still away, but I'm on his calendar for when he returns." I glanced down the road before looking back at Lorcan and said, "Thank you for making the introduction."

Lorcan, who knew the director, had spoken to him on my behalf to get me access to the national archives in the hopes I'd find some information about my mother.

"It's a long shot, but who knows," Lorcan said. Then he turned his attention to his ringing cell phone.

LATER THAT MORNING, ASHFORD AND I ARRIVED IN CONG AMIDST a half-dozen tour buses and tourists snapping pictures and referencing guidebooks. I found the post office on the outskirts of the village, perched on the banks of Lough Mask, in an area rich with overgrown trees and bushes. Another of Lord Ardilaun's work projects, the granite structure, which now served as the post office, began its existence as a granary. Its water wheel still cupped the fluid from the river stream during each revolution.

Ashford leaped out of the car right behind me. I expected him to bolt as soon as he recognized his surroundings. Instead, he ran circles around me, kicking up stones as I crossed the narrow bridge and went up the walkway to the post office's green door, where he parked himself. I went inside.

The neon display over one of the postal worker's windows flashed the number stamped on my ticket, and a computerized voice prompted for the "*Next customer, please.*"

"Yes, may I help you?" Silver-gray eyes peered at me through the bars of the customer window. The eyes belonged to a woman whose nametag identified her as Ellen Flynn.

"I'm looking for Evelyn Cosgrove's forwarding address." I held my breath as I waited for the response. Years ago, the U.S. Postal Service used to provide someone's forwarding address in exchange for a few dollars. But privacy laws have claimed another victim. All you can get now is the person's box address from when the box was opened, but only if a subpoena has to be served.

The clerk's eyes blinked as if processing my request. I rushed on. "I'm in Ireland researching my mother's family. Evelyn contacted me several months ago. I thought, while I'm here, I'd get to talk to her. But I've phoned several times and stopped by her house and haven't been able to reach her. The woman who runs the Quiet Man Café says Evelyn travels often." I stopped talking, hoping interest in my Irish roots dispelled any hesitation to keep Evelyn's forwarding address private. Although a postal worker shouldn't disclose personal information, sometimes he or she will tell you where, should you write a letter to the person in question, the mail will be forwarded.

"Where was your mammy from?" Ellen asked.

"Achill Island. She's a Maggie O'Malley. Evelyn posted a question about her on one of the online family databases." My hands gripped my iPhone as I leaned forward, closer to the window. "It could be nothing, but I've just got to ask her why she was looking for Maggie O'Malley."

"Well, let's see if I can help you. Hold on now a minute." Ellen swiveled her chair, bounced down onto the floor, and swung open the door to the back of the building. "Tom, could ya come here a minute?" she called into the space created by the open door. Tom appeared, and the two of them had a short conversation, which ended with Ellen nodding her head in my direction.

"This here's Tom. He knows the area better than me. He'll help you now." Ellen positioned herself back up onto her stool, called for the next customer, and winked at me. "I hope you find your family."

"Yes?" Tom asked. His over six-foot frame and wide shoulders towered over me. His identification badge carried the title Postmaster.

"I'm looking for Evelyn Cosgrove's forwarding address," I stated. "I've been unsuccessful in my attempts to reach her, and, at this point, I'm worried for her safety."

"And why is that?" Tom asked.

"For one thing, she doesn't answer her phone. For another, her house looks abandoned."

Instead of responding, Tom bent to pick up a slip of paper

from the floor, which he then folded into a triangle. Sensing what I thought was his deliberation of my request, I persisted. "I'm really concerned. I don't know too many people whose phone just rings for days on end."

"Wait here," Tom said. He moved back behind the postal area and logged onto a computer. "I'm sorry. I cannot divulge anything more than she used a local box for her mail."

Disappointed, I asked, "Is there anything else you can share with me that might help me get in touch with her?"

"Have you looked around Rose Cottage?"

"Rose Cottage? Where is that, and what's the connection?"

Tom chuckled. "Evelyn's one of those archaeologists. You know, someone who's always digging up things. She travels all over the world. I guess that's why she doesn't leave a forwarding address. Before this last trip, she spent a lot of time over at Rose Cottage—the one that's haunted." Tom's voice fell to a whisper as he glanced around at the people waiting in line.

Did he lower his voice out of respect for the customers or because he didn't want anyone to know he believed in ghosts?

"Evelyn's an archeologist?" My mind raced as I thought of the associations and universities that might put me in touch with her. Phillie was going to enjoy this assignment.

"Well, she's some kind of a digger." Behind him, another postal worker peeked his head around the door and shouted out to Tom that he had a call waiting on the line. "Always finding old maps, letters, and wills. Anyway, you take a walk over to Rose Cottage. It's back in the woods a bit. Better take some boots with you," he said, glancing down at my Capri pants and flats. "Someone there might know where she's gone to this time."

Tom returned through the door to the back of the building, and I raced outside to collect Ashford. By the time I arrived at the tourist office to buy a map and get directions to Rose Cottage, I'd texted a message to Phillie, telling her to generate a

search of archeological digs conducted by universities, muse-
ums, and foundations all over the planet.

"Damn!" The Closed, Back in An Hour sign dangled from
the tourist office door. *Where do I go from here?* I decided to buy
a pair of boots. I made my way around the town to one of the
local shops that sold farm supplies, including wellingtons.
While I waited in line to ask for a pair in my size, the man in
front of me purchased an ordnance survey map. I realized then
I wouldn't have to wait for the tourist office to open to buy a
map. At that moment, the bell over the shop door tinkled, and
the man's head swiveled toward the woman who burst through
the door.

"Do you have to follow me everywhere I go?" he shouted.
Clutching the map in one of his fists, he stomped across the
floor and glowered over the pixyish blonde who smiled up at
his towering frame.

"Luke, don't talk like that. Your father wouldn't want us to
argue." The smile emphasized the two small dimples she
sported on each side of her face. But I noticed the smile didn't
reach her eyes.

"If my father had any guts, he'd have left the farm to me."
Luke clenched his fists, shoved the crumpled map into his coat
pocket, and slammed the shop door behind him. He glared
back at the shop as he loaded some paint cans into the black
Land Rover parked at the curb. Then he jumped in and drove
away.

"Pat, are you all right?" The shop owner's voice emphasized
his concern for the woman. "I can get..."

"Of course, I'm fine," she interrupted him. "Why wouldn't I
be? He'll get over it." The words bubbled out of her in staccato
shots like a telegraph keyboard dotting and dashing its
message.

For the first time, I noticed her wellingtons and the flannel
man's shirt she wore tucked into the faded, worn blue jeans

that accentuated her tiny waist. In comparison to the man with the map, she was probably twenty years older, maybe in her fifties. The skin around her blue eyes crinkled like someone who spent time laughing or squinting into the sun.

"Are you sure you wouldn't take a cup of tea?" the shop owner said as each of them lifted bags of grain from the floor and walked out the door to a silver Land Rover.

"No. I want to get back." The rat-tat-tat of her voice faded as the door closed behind them.

The shop owner returned in a very short time. While he moved an open can of red paint and a brush from the counter, he asked how he might assist me.

"I'd like one of those maps you just sold to the man who was in here and a pair of wellingtons in size nine." Impatient for action, I pulled my credit card out of my pocket and put it on the counter.

"Well, now, I can help you with the wellingtons, but Luke there got the last map."

I glanced at my phone's digital display. I still had time to get a map somewhere else in town, maybe the bookstore I'd visited yesterday.

"I'll take the wellingtons," I said.

"Righto, I'll just be a minute." He disappeared into a room at the back of the shop. "I'm sure I have your size in here." He reappeared with the boots in his hands.

"It's too bad you don't have any more of the maps," I commented.

"I don't keep too many in stock. Tourists are usually looking for guidebooks. They can get those at the information center." He handed over the receipt for my signature. "I wonder why Luke needed one, though. He must have played in every nook and cranny of this area when he was growing up," he said while he waited for me to return the slip of paper.

"He seemed pretty stoked up about something," I said.

"Those two, Luke and Pat, have been at it ever since Jake died."

"I heard him say something about a farm and his father. Was that Jake?" I asked.

"Yes, Jake Ryan was Luke's dad." The shop owner shook his head. "Poor Luke, I can't say I blame him for being angry."

"And why's that?"

"Ah, now, I'm sure it'll all settle down one of these days. Anything else I can assist you with?"

"I'm planning on visiting Rose Cottage. Is it far from here?"

"Rose Cottage? Are you one of those ghost hunters from the States? I wouldn't go out there if I were you. It's not safe in those woods, not with what happened to poor Jane."

By the time I gathered up the boots and reached the door, he'd stopped talking. Back outside, Ashford reappeared and followed me to Ben's Rarities. *Ben O'Malley,* I reminded myself as I swept through the door, remembering the twisted maze between the front of the shop and the owner's desk, and slowed my pace in time to prevent a landslide of books.

Voices filtered over the tops of the stacks. Damn! I wanted to ask him about the O'Malleys, but a glance at the time on my iPhone warned me I'd have to wait if I wanted to find Rose Cottage today.

"Hello." I raised my voice to warn whoever was back there that someone was in the shop. "I'd like to buy an ordnance map."

When I rounded the last leg of the maze, I stopped in my tracks. The first person I saw was Ben. The glimpse of the second person as she turned to see who interrupted them surprised me. Pat—the woman I'd seen in the store—twisted away from me, but not before I saw her raise her hands to her face and wipe away the tears running down her cheeks.

"I'm sorry; I didn't mean to interrupt. If you have the map, I'll take one and be on my way."

"I thought I mentioned to you yesterday that you'll need an appointment if you're interested in rare books or manuscripts." Ben's hazel eyes bore into mine as he drummed his fingers on his desk.

At that moment, I saw a book with the words *History* and *O'Malley* on a shelf behind him. Reaching forward, I retrieved it and said, "And I'll take this as well."

"It's all right, Ben." Pat's face regained its smile as she reached out her hand and patted him on the shoulder. "Don't mind my son. He's over-protective of his mother right now."

Son! That explained it. She must have been telling him about the incident with Luke in the grain store.

"Didn't I just see you in another shop in town?" She tilted her head as she asked the question, and her eyes perused me from head to toe.

"Yes, you did. They're out of ordnance maps and suggested I come here."

"Ordnance map?" Her brow creased. "You're not one of those explorers of hidden underground chambers, are you?"

I laughed. "No, I'm looking for Evelyn Cosgrove, and I heard someone at Rose Cottage might know how to get in touch with her. I understand I need a map to find the trail through the woods to the cottage."

"I'm glad you're not one of those daft people who come here to go spelunking. We lose someone every year who gets trapped underground." Pat's face relaxed, and the dimples reappeared, but her eyes continued to take an inventory of my face.

"Nothing so adventurous," I assured her as I thought to myself, *She's worried about something*.

"I haven't seen Evelyn in ages. She's in some of the same aerobics classes with me when she's around the place long enough." Pat paused, studying her rough, reddened hands. "But my son should be able to help you. I think she's one of his friends."

"Pat, I can't help her now," he said. Then he thrust the map toward me, glanced at the book in my hand, and demanded twenty euros.

I wondered why he didn't call her Mom. They didn't share any visual resemblance. His ebony hair and facial features contrasted with her blonde hair and blue eyes.

Ignoring him, she continued. "Be careful. Even if you're not caving, Capri pants and ballet slippers aren't the right gear for taking a walk through the woods, which you'll have to do to get to Rose Cottage."

Just as I exited the shop, I heard Pat ask Ben when he'd be home and if he wanted chops for dinner. Did he still live at home with his mother?

"Come on, Ashford. Let's get changed and go for a walk." I unfolded the map and read the tiny print as we walked along the cobble-stoned streets back to where I'd parked my car. I didn't want to waste another minute.

My iPhone, its case tethered to my pant waist, vibrated, alerting me to an email message. Placing the map and the book I'd bought under one arm, I read the display. *Phillie*. Good, she'd gotten my text. I hoped she had some news for me. A minute later, we were connected.

"What have you got?" I asked. In some ways, Phillie and I were kindred spirits. We never let the subtleties get in the way of focus. Phillie called it "flow."

"Nothing yet. Do you know most of these places don't have any way of reaching their staff when they're out in the field? Do you believe it, boss? We spend our lives trying to find people and information, and they spend their life getting lost miles away from civilization."

Phillie's voice echoed my opinion that anyone who isn't up to date on the latest technology is a Neanderthal. Although I agreed with Phillie, I didn't have time to discuss the perils of being unversed in technology with her.

"Thanks. I'll call you later." I rushed off the call and picked up the pace.

Just as I holstered the phone, it chimed. Sighing, I checked the display. *Aunt Georgina.* I hesitated but decided to answer. I'd promised to check in with her.

"I don't have much time. Can I call you later?" I asked.

"Where are you? I called at the cottage. Listen, Star, I need to tell you something about the woman you found on the beach..."

"We'll have to talk about it later," I interrupted. "I'm in Cong and on my way to someplace called Rose Cottage. I have to go before it gets too dark."

"Cong? Did you take that dog back? I hope so. And where is this Rose Cottage? Call me when you get home." *Click.* She was gone.

As I opened the trunk of my car to grab a sweatshirt, the history book slipped out of my hand to the ground, and a folded piece of paper fell out. Curious, I opened the paper to find a handwritten note. The first words I read were *Dear Jake.* Seeing this was a personal letter, I hesitated to continue. But then, my eyes moved to the bottom of the page, where I read the words, *Love, Jane.* My curiosity got the better of me.

Dear Jake,

The lies have to stop. When I saw you with Pat at the gala dinner, I wanted to scream. The way you draped your arm over her shoulders. And, there I was. Sitting next to a man, my husband, whose eyes avoid mine. It's become too unbearable. I want to touch your hair, your skin. Feel your lips on my body. If you don't tell Pat, I will. Meet me near the priest's hole. You know the place. If we tell the truth, it will all work out.

Love, Jane

--

I refolded the letter, taking care to use its original creases. I'd already heard the name Jake in connection with Luke and Pat. And, I'd be willing to bet the Jane in this letter was the dead woman. If I was correct, how had this intimate missive ended up in a book in Ben's shop? I dropped the book into the trunk and placed the folded paper into one of my pant pockets, intending to show it to Ben the next time I saw him.

Then my phone rang again. What now? I'd never get to Rose Cottage. The workers would be gone. When I saw *Lorcan* on the call display, I didn't hesitate to ignore it. Glancing at the time, I told myself I wouldn't be back to Castlebar in time for dinner anyway. The truth was I didn't want to deal with my attraction to Lorcan.

CHAPTER 8

A light drizzle fell as I headed onto the walking path through Cong's woods toward Ashford Castle, where I crossed over to the Lough Corrib path. According to the map, Rose Cottage was a mile beyond where I'd discovered Jane's body. Ashford tagged along, disappearing in and out of the bramble, sometimes pausing to wait for me. Once more, my thoughts turned to the couple the hotel worker mentioned. Who were Ashford's walking companions? If only he could talk. At that moment, Ashford barked as if in answer to my silent wish. When I turned around, I glimpsed Tom, the postmaster, walking along behind me.

"On to Rose Cottage, are ya?" he asked. "Well, you'd better hurry if you want to catch up with anyone. The crew disappears about this time every day. Of course, there's that ghost everyone's been on about." He laughed, tipped his hat at me, and kept walking, not waiting for my answer.

What a strange guy! He'd sent me in search of an ordnance map when it looked like he knew the way there. Why hadn't he just given me directions?

I continued along the path. Soon, the faint outline of the famous Lord and Lady Ardilaun obelisk, the very place where

I'd found Jane's body, appeared through the mist. Initially, Lord Ardilaun built a one-room chateau here as a shelter for his lady. I read they often walked along the lake to enjoy the view, afternoon teas, and picnics. When he died, she erected the obelisk to his memory. The inscription read, *Rien ne m'est plus; Plus ne m'est rien*—Nothing remains to me any longer; anything that remains means nothing. How sad she must have been to have these words chiseled forever into that granite slab. Did she ever come to terms with her grief? A year ago, my sentiments matched hers. But coming to Ireland changed all that. I'd resolved my feelings for Dylan once and for all.

In a short time, I reached the end of the path and spotted a sign nailed to a tree. The words Rose Cottage and an arrow pointed the way through the woods and bramble bushes. Ashford took the lead and disappeared into the fading light.

Barking erupted. I followed the sounds, running out of the woods onto the grounds of the cottage. The first things I noticed were mounds of dirt, sieves, pails, and a tent littering the area. I ran toward the tent, but when I lifted the flap, I found an empty space.

Damn! *I'd have to come back.* I made my way around the cottage exterior. Perhaps I could find some sign or certificate with a contact for the dig. But that too was a dead end.

In contrast to the backyard, the cottage's front lawn was a labyrinthine maze of thorny rose bushes, dense gorse thicket, and monkey trees. No wonder people thought a ghost haunted the place. Sunshine barely penetrated the tangled greenery. Add some fog, and you had yourself a mystery.

As I walked around the cottage, Ashford's barks continued. I didn't have time to think about why because a sharp pain rocketed through my right foot. Having bent down to peer at what had penetrated my boot, I picked up a jagged white rock —gold streaks ran through it. Curious about how it got here, I dropped it into my sweatshirt's pocket to inspect later. I looked for Ashford and the source of his commotion. After a few minutes of groping around the front yard of the cottage, I discovered a rusted gate. When it wouldn't budge, I stepped over it onto a one-lane dirt road. In the distance, I spotted a barn-like structure. Ashford's barks came from there.

I headed straight across the field toward the sound of the racket. When I got closer, I noticed a derelict No Trespassing sign naming the building as an abandoned sawmill. The barking had stopped. But I still couldn't see Ashford.

"You're on private property." The man's voice leaped out of the shadows of the building before he moved forward into the twilight. His hand grasped Ashford's collar, keeping him at his side.

Dan Doherty. What was he doing here? He must have satisfied the police's questions. Still, this was a strange place to be when his wife's body was either in the morgue or a funeral home.

"I'm just looking for my dog," I said, nodding my head toward Ashford.

"He's not your dog." Frowning, he removed what looked like a pair of reading glasses from his face. He placed them into the pocket of his tailored shirt. "You didn't answer my question. You're on private property. What are you doing here?"

"Is he your dog?" I asked. "He found your wife's body yesterday."

"How do you know that?" Doherty said through clenched teeth. He stepped closer to me.

"I'm the one who called the police." I felt instinctively for my phone and mentally prepared to run.

"No, he's not mine, but my wife had a fondness for him. She used to walk with him through the woods." His voice quivered. Then he peered at me again. "You didn't answer my question. What are you doing here?" He took another step toward me.

I waved my hand back toward Rose Cottage, explaining my

quest. While I talked, I took note of the sawdust that littered his jacket. A light flickered in the mill behind him, and the scent of pine wood assaulted my nostrils. Strange. I thought the sign read Abandoned.

"You'd better stay away from that place." His words exploded through the air as he laughed, adding, "Some people think it's haunted." With that, he released his grip on Ashford, turned away, and yelled, "Now, get the hell off my property."

Ashford and I wasted no time. We crossed the field and jumped the cottage gate. As I crossed the cottage yard, I peered through the darkness for the way back to Ashford Castle. That's when I heard a car engine. I stopped, thinking maybe one of the villagers would give me a lift to the castle so I could avoid walking through the woods. I turned around and went back over the gate. Silence greeted me. The vehicle was gone.

"Come on, Ashford." I patted my thigh to summon his attention only to discover he'd disappeared again. *Where has he gone to now?* Deciding he knew these woods better than I did, I crossed back over the fence and plunged forward into the darkness.

Now, after 6:00 p.m., the light mist had cleared, replaced by ground fog. I pulled my sweatshirt around me as tendrils of cold air penetrated my body. I kept my head bent, focused my eyes on the ground, and attempted to stay out of the bramble. I wished I'd checked the map again before I entered this wooded corridor, which was as devoid of light as a meteorite.

Thirty minutes later, I knew I was lost. It hadn't taken this long to get through the woods earlier. Where had Ashford got to? I could have used him now. Instead, I pulled the map out of my back pocket but quickly realized I couldn't see anything on the chart in this pea soup. I took out my phone and fumbled in the dark to turn on its flashlight. When I finally managed to swipe it on and study the map, my ears picked up the sounds of snapping branches.

"Ashford, here, boy," I called out. The volume of movement increased. The crackling sound seemed to crash around me. "Ashford?"

The crunching and snapping underbrush made noises that sounded like a thunderclap. The sudden and violent sounds rushed at me. I ran, but I tripped over something. When I got up, the din was closer. I ran a bit more when all at once, a hazy, white blur hurled itself at me, shoving me backward. I fumbled for balance, my hands grasped air, my knuckles grated rough stone, and my body plunged down. I landed in what felt like a pile of dead leaves, twigs, and moss.

Frozen in fear, I sat and listened for movement above me. My mind raced. Where was I? Maybe a priest hole or a well. I shivered. No way this was a haunting. After a few more moments of silence, I wriggled my toes and fingers. Everything felt intact. I got to my feet. That's when I realized I didn't have my phone. *Damn!* I must have dropped it along with the map when I tripped. I felt around the murky pit for what I considered my lifeline to the world. Then, the phone rang and rang. My heart sank when I realized the sound came from somewhere above me.

Several attempts to climb out failed. I tried with the boots on and then without them. Either way, my feet slipped on the smooth, mossy, wet stone that lined the walls around me. By this time, I was exhausted, my clothes were soaked, my feet were frozen, and the cuts on my hands stung. I considered yelling for help, but fear of who might be lurking above kept me from calling out.

When I realized I'd need the morning light to see how I could escape this prison, I put the boots back on. I marched in place, pumping my hands to generate body heat. Fighting the urge to sleep, I tried to gauge how long before advanced hypothermia would set in. In the distance, something screamed. From somewhere overhead, scuffling sounds became louder. I froze. My breath caught in my chest. I didn't want to, but I had to. I looked upward. I breathed a sigh of relief when I spotted a pair of glowing eyes—I could deal with a sheep. Then I let it all out. "Help! Help!" I shouted until my voice cracked, and I couldn't muster enough breath. I could feel and hear water trickling through the stone walls. My toes felt numb, and my feet didn't want to move any longer. For the first time, I admitted that I might not make it through the night. Unable now to control my quaking body, I wondered if this was what happened to my mother. Was it some kind of accident? Had she waited for help, only to succumb to injuries in the end?

I heard Lorcan calling my name.

"Help!" I yelled. "Help!" Maybe I was delusional, but I wasn't taking any chances. "Over here!" I screamed as loud as I could. Then, I heard Ashford's bark.

"Star!" Lorcan's voice came from above.

"Down here," I croaked, not bothering to wipe the tears that trickled down my cheeks.

CHAPTER 9

I awoke, wrapped in a blanket as warm air blasting from dashboard vents penetrated my skin. Ashford's tail beat a steady rhythm on the back seat as Lorcan's car turned down the road to French Hill Cottage.

"Don't move; don't talk," his voice warned me. "I'll have you inside soon."

When we pulled up at the gate, Aunt Georgina burst through the cottage's front door. She ran along the footpath toward us. Her scarf billowed behind her.

"Star! My God, you look like you've seen a ghost!" she exclaimed as she ushered us into the living room. "Come along; we need to get some life back into you."

"Something to eat would be nice," I said. Lorcan guided me into the love seat facing the hearth. A blazing fire blasted heat into the room. Ashford settled at my feet, resting his head on his paws.

It didn't take long for Aunt Georgina to rustle up some food. Over steaming mugs of tea and cheese sandwiches, I explained my cuts and bruises to her.

"I've contacted the garda. They'll be in touch in the morning," Lorcan said. His eyes were solemn and unsmiling as he closed his flip phone and pushed his glasses up on his nose.

"Why didn't you call one of us? Where's your phone?" Aunt Georgina demanded.

At that moment, I felt for my iPhone, realized where it was, and shuddered to think of ever being without it again. I had to go back and find it.

"In the woods somewhere. I could hear it ringing." I shivered. "It fell when...I just hope it's not broken."

"You without a cell phone is unfathomable," Aunt Georgina said. "You must have been terrified."

"How did you know where to look for me?" I asked, ignoring the dark circles under her eyes.

"You said you were going to Rose Cottage," Georgina answered. "You didn't explain what you were up to, so I called Jimmy to ask him about the cottage. He brushed it off. Told me the place was nothing more than an abandoned heap of stones."

Between bites of a second cheese sandwich, Lorcan continued the story, "When you didn't answer any of our calls, I drove to Cong. The shops were closed. I tried the Quiet Man Café, but the owner didn't know anything. Said it would be difficult to find the cottage in the dark."

"Then how in the world did—"

"Ashford gets all the credit," Lorcan interrupted me. "He ran toward me just as I left the café. You owe your rescue to him. He herded me through the woods." Lorcan's grin reached his eyes. "He was relentless—like someone else I know."

"Now, then, let's get you cleaned up," Aunt Georgina said, setting her mug onto the table. She rose and headed into the bathroom to turn on the water taps. Shortly after, she shut the front door behind Lorcan with assurances she'd take good care of me. Then, she helped me into the tub.

As I lay prone in the water, soaking its warmth into my

bones, I closed my eyes. Once again, I saw the ghost-like figure whirling toward me. I knew one thing for sure; I wasn't attacked by a ghost. And, it wasn't any wild animal either. Granted, a few sheep or other animals roamed the woods at night, but human hands pushed me into that hole. I considered who might have done it and why. By discovering Jane's body, had I inadvertently gotten in a murderer's way? I ticked off a list of the people I'd spoken with since finding Jane's body: Pat O'Malley, her son, Ben, and Luke Ryan. Of course, Jane's husband, Dan, topped my list. Or, did this have something to do with me asking around town about Evelyn Cosgrove? I opened my eyes. I knew one thing—I'd find the answer.

CHAPTER 10

Lorcan's red and white Piper Super Cub's droning engine roused me from sleep. Although the sun shone around the edges of the window shades, I hugged the silk sheets and planted my feet on the still-warm hot water bottle Aunt Georgina had placed there the night before. My fingers explored my body for swelling but only found some soreness. Closing my eyes, I willed myself to let the airplane's white noise lull me back to sleep. I didn't want to think about last night's events—most notably, how I'd felt when Lorcan rescued me out of that hole. It could all wait another few hours.

When I raised my lids again, cars whooshed along Cottage Road. Reaching under my pillow, I pulled out my watch: 10:00 a.m. At that moment, the door opened, and Aunt Georgina glided into the room, toting a tray.

"I didn't know you were here," I said.

"I used my key to the kitchen door. I've made you breakfast," she said, placing the tray next to me on the bed.

"I'm starving," I responded as the aroma of mint tea filled my nostrils. "This is delicious. Is there any more?" I asked after demolishing the fresh-made brown bread, eggs, and bacon she'd conjured up. "Where did you get this food? It sure didn't come from *my* refrigerator," I said. "It's delicious."

"You can have more after you've gotten up. I'll see you in the kitchen." She scooped up the empty tray and swept out of the room.

She was right. After I dressed for the day, I joined her in the kitchen.

"How about more of that brown bread?" I asked as I positioned my chair to bask in the golden light that streamed through the window in the hopes it would keep me warm. Aunt Georgina had popped a few roses into a broken teapot that sat on the windowsill. The kettle simmered on one of the electric stove's back burners, and Bewley's tea bags were strewn across a kitchen counter. A pot of jam shimmered on the oak kitchen table. As I watched Aunt Georgina bustling around the room, I blinked back tears—what I wouldn't give to have had mornings like this with my mother.

"Of course, there's plenty of it here," Georgina said as she worked the bread knife through the crusty brown log and moved some slices to a plate, which she placed in front of me. As the loaf of bread diminished, Aunt Georgina and I talked about the events that had transpired the night before.

"That part of the country is associated with a lot of old ghost stories" – Aunt Georgina paused between sips of tea – "but even I don't think of them as much more than stories."

"Someone wants people to think a ghost is roaming the woods in Cong, but I know differently. Flesh and bones pushed me into that cave. I have to figure out if I was the intended victim or someone else." I held my mug of tea with both hands, trying not only to warm them but also my insides as my thoughts revisited the fleeting blur of white mist that had hurtled itself at me.

"You're sure you didn't get a glimpse of the person?"

"No. It happened so fast. All I saw was a swirl of white

covering someone from head to toe. That's what makes me wonder if they mistook me for someone else. Seeing through all that material must have been difficult."

"You know what happened to you, Star, sounds like the legend about Captain Webb's Hole." Aunt Georgina shook her head. "A lot of the villagers in Cong probably know the story."

"Just before I walked out to Rose Cottage, I stopped in the post office. One of the workers, Tom, mentioned ghost sightings. But why in the world would someone purposely reenact local legends?" While I considered Aunt Georgina's suggestion, I absentmindedly reached for my cell phone. Then, I realized that both the phone and my car were still in Cong.

"These days, you just never know what someone is thinking or why they do the things they do," she replied.

"All right, go ahead, what is this particular legend?" I felt a smile forming on my lips as I waited for Aunt Georgina to share her vast knowledge of Irish people, places, and things—even those who were imaginary.

"Well, he was a thief with a reputation for cruelty and violence. Headquartered in Mayo, he'd take young women captive, and when he tired of them, he made them strip naked, and then plunged them down a deep well near Lough Corrib." Aunt Georgina finished her tea and got to her feet. "That's enough of the ancient legends for today. I've got a business to run." She reached across the table, squeezed my shoulder, and said, "I'm glad you're home, Star." With that, she left.

Feeling a lump in my throat, I jumped up and called Ashford from his place under the table for a run. An hour later, dressed and deliberating how I'd get back to Cong, I answered a loud knock on the kitchen door.

Lorcan stood on the doorstep.

"I'm not ready to talk to the police this morning." I didn't want him to know how frightened I'd been. "As far as I'm concerned, they're useless. I spoke with them a few days ago when I found Jane's body. They weren't interested then." I shrugged. "Why would they be now?"

"I'm not here to take you to the police station." Lorcan's smile stretched across his face as he bent to pet Ashford, who had bounded over to him like a long-lost friend. "I'm wondering if you're interested in going flying?"

"Flying?" I shook my head. "I'm too busy. Besides, I have to get back to Cong to retrieve my car and my phone."

"Oh..." He hesitated before continuing. "I didn't think you'd mind, but I called one of my pals in Cong. He drove your car back here this morning. He also found your phone."

I raised my eyebrows in question, but he answered before I could get the words out.

"Your car keys were in the pocket of your sweatshirt. And, I thought you'd want this as soon as possible."

I almost cried with relief when he reached into his jacket pocket and handed the phone to me. Still in its lime green case, it looked none the worse for wear—just a few scratches.

Not knowing what else to say, I holstered it and said, "Thank you."

"And my invitation is about work." Lorcan's smile extended to me as he stood up to explain. "I'm doing a series of aerial photography for Ann Ryan's real estate business in Cong. I thought you'd want to see some of the terrain from the air."

Lorcan's eyes twinkled as he pulled an airfield guide out of his jacket pocket. Like me with my phone, Lorcan always seemed to have a map, guide, or some kind of architectural drawing in his pockets or hands.

"You'll be able to see the Rose Cottage from the air. Maybe someone in town will be able to tell you how to contact whoever's working at the site while I'm busy with Ann."

"Ann Ryan? Is she related to Jake and Luke?"

"Yes, she's Luke's mother but separated from Jake."

"What about Ashford? I can't lock him up here all day," I said.

"Oh, he can come. That's if you don't mind him sitting on your lap."

I grabbed my jacket and Ashford's leash.

Sixty minutes later, Ashford barked as Lorcan shouted, "Clear prop." The Piper's engine roared to life, and the blades cut through the air. As Lorcan maneuvered the controls, we rose. The horizon dipped. The repetitious hum of the engine soon put Ashford to sleep. Lorcan had tied him into a tiny cargo space at the back of the plane. As we gained altitude, I felt the horrors of last night's events fall away. I breathed the crisp air and watched the passing quilts of green fields glide by.

"Will you take the controls for a minute?" Lorcan's voice rumbled in my headset, interrupting my reverie.

"I can't fly an airplane."

"All you have to do is keep it straight and level while I take a few photos." Lorcan glanced over his shoulder at me as he demonstrated how to use the yoke to keep the airplane on course.

"Okay, but don't blame me if we end up in a farmer's field somewhere."

"Well, we'll be landing in a farmer's private airfield." Lorcan's laugh reverberated in the air. "But don't worry, I'll take over that part of the flight."

I kept the plane steady while Lorcan leaned out his window and pointed his camera at the ground.

"Okay, I have the controls again." Lorcan's voice seemed to come from far away. Focusing on the controls had kept me in the present moment. I took a deep breath, realizing how much the search for my mother consumed my past, present, and future. If I knew what had happened to her and who my father was, my life might have been very different.

"We're due to land soon, but I'm going to fly over the airfield toward Rose Cottage," Lorcan said. "You can take a look at it from up here."

The airplane veered to the right of the castle and over a dense forest. I kept my eyes on the ground, looking for the cottage and the nearby mill.

"Over there at the ten o'clock position," Lorcan said.

The airplane's left wing dipped, providing a better view. Like yesterday, the cottage looked dwarfed by all the growth around it, but it was possible to see the dig area. Also, like yesterday, the place was deserted.

"It's a steep descent to Ryan's strip," Lorcan said. "You'll see the horizon rise. It's nothing to worry about." Then, he nosed the plane toward a strip of grass that looked as thin as a pencil from where I sat.

By the time the wheels touched the grass strip, and we'd rolled to a stop, Ashford was barking. Lorcan sprang him from the back while I unfastened my seat belt, removed the headset, and jumped to the well-kept smooth grassy surface. The windsock straightened by the brisk breeze waved over the rooftop of a barn. White lines marked the boundaries of the narrow field. A Welcome to Happy Trails sign hung from a post near a parking lot. A horn tooted, and the car I'd seen at the beach rolled up and edged over one of the boundaries. The signage on the car informed me this was the woman who had commandeered Dan Doherty and son.

"Hello, Lorcan." Ann Ryan emerged from the car, tossed a cigarette onto the hard-packed landscape, and ground it farther into the green carpet with the heel of her muddy shoes without much consideration for the signs warning about littering the runway.

As we approached Ann, Ashford alternated between growls and barks. I tugged on his leash. "Ashford, quiet," I said, wondering what about this woman set him off.

"Oh, dear, not that darned dog again." Ann's laugh echoed

through the trees that surrounded the open field. "I'm afraid dogs don't much like me. This one more than others," she said. She shook Lorcan's hand before she turned to face me. Her eyes narrowed as she looked me up and down. "You were at the beach the other day, weren't you?"

"I was." I kept my answer to a minimum. I agreed with Ashford—I didn't like this woman either. Her obvious lack of consideration for the environment and animals roused my suspicions.

In her car on the way to Cong, she and Lorcan discussed the consulting project for which she'd hired him. I used the time to observe her from the back seat. Strong, muscular hands gripped the steering wheel as she navigated the narrow, winding trail through the Ryan estate out to one of the main roads.

I waited until their conversation reached a natural end before asking questions. "Do you know Evelyn Cosgrove? I understand she's in charge of some kind of dig out at Rose Cottage." I didn't say I'd been at the excavation site.

"Oh, that." Ann shrugged. "A total waste of grant funding. I don't know why Dan hasn't done anything about it. It's impacting his business."

"But it's not on his property. Why would he have anything to say about it?" I asked, thinking about my encounter with him. He struck me as anything but shy about speaking up if he didn't like someone or something.

"But the cottage is on his property. That cottage is his." She seemed to grip the steering wheel tighter before continuing. "A perfect waste of developable land. I've tried convincing him to sell it, but he won't hear of it." Her sigh escaped through pursed lips. "And Evelyn." Another sigh. "That girl is always digging into something. Now, she's got the historical society involved. Or, hysterical society as I call them. Dan will never be able to sell the property." Glancing at me in the rear-view mirror, her eyes held mine. "What's your interest in her?" she asked.

"Oh, I'm trying to locate a missing person that she might have information about."

I don't know why, but my intuition kept me from revealing too much of myself to this woman.

"Star's going to see if she can locate anyone who knows how to get in touch with Evelyn while I'm working with you," Lorcan said.

"You might try Jane's exercise studio. Her business partner is still holding classes despite what's happened. Evelyn's a regular at the place when she's around. In fact, most of us belong to that gym. Jane's aerobic classes were killers."

I winced at her words and caught her narrowed eyes staring at me in the rear-view mirror. "Have the police found anything new?" I asked, watching her response. I wondered again if who'd pushed me into the well had anything to do with Jane's death.

"The inquest was held this morning. Of course, the verdict was: Murder by person or persons unknown. The garda are talking to everyone who knew her. Thank God. I don't know why they'd have suspected Dan to begin with—what he's had to put up with over the years. Some women just don't appreciate what they've got."

The knuckles of her hands whitened as she tightened her grip on the steering wheel.

Why was she so angry with Jane? Could she have murdered Jane? Ann had the muscular strength. The bruises I'd seen on Jane's neck could have been at the hand of male or female. In fact, Ann could have been the one who shoved me into the well. She certainly knew the terrain. But then she wouldn't have known I was in the woods last night. And what would have been her motive? For now, I set the thought aside. I intended to find who had pushed me, but just for today, I needed to shut out the horrors of my entrapment. The search for my mother and whether Evelyn could shed light on it mattered more.

When we reached Cong, Ann parked her car in front of a real estate office with her name over the door. At the same time, Luke, the angry man who'd confronted Pat in the shop where I bought my wellingtons the day before, burst through it.

"What are you doing here?" Ann asked.

Glancing at Lorcan and me, Luke nodded at her and said, "I'll speak with you later." Then he got into his Land Rover and left.

Happy to get away from Ann, I promised to meet Lorcan at 4:00 p.m. for the return trip to the airfield. Ashford followed me.

CHAPTER 11

As I walked along Main Street toward Jane's exercise studio, I looked around for a taxi service. If Lorcan expected me to fly back to Castlebar with him, he'd have to find an alternative means of getting back to the airfield. I had no intention of submitting myself to Ann's toxic personality again.

At that moment, Ashford barked and took off at a run, tail wagging, toward the other end of Main Street. He stopped, perched on his hind legs, and barked up at a bright red door. The sign Jane Doherty's Vitality Fitness Studio hung over the lintel. What would Ashford say about Jane and the other citizens of Cong if he could speak? He'd reacted when we met Ann. Did Ashford know who'd shoved me into the well?

I arrived at the studio to see six or seven women emerge. They wiped sweaty brows with towels and dug for bottles of water in tote bags before climbing into an array of cars parked along the street.

"I wondered where he'd gotten to," said the petite, toned, and muscular woman who remained behind. Then, she turned her attention to me. "Come on inside while I get this vagabond a treat."

I followed her through a narrow hallway to a small desk,

piled high with nutritional pamphlets, protein bars, and appointment books. Beyond the desk, I glimpsed a large exercise room. Its mirrored walls reflected balance bars and Pilates rings.

"If you just wait a moment, I'll get a biscuit for that dog," she said as she rummaged through one of the desk's drawers. "He comes here every day for a treat from my partner. I haven't seen him since Jane..."

She fell silent. Her watery eyes squeezed shut as if to hold back the tears. Finally, she opened her lids and reached for a tissue. "I'm sorry, my partner's dead, murdered actually." She shuddered. "Jane loved that dog."

"Do you know who owns him?" I asked, wondering if Jane had known.

"No. Jane said she knew him from her walks around the castle grounds." The woman's tears began again as she shook her head. "Jane walked through those woods almost every day. It's frightening to think she died in there."

"Here, why don't you let me give this to the dog while you compose yourself? I'll be right back." Reaching for the milk bone, I took it in my hand and retraced my steps back to the sidewalk where Ashford sat. "Here you go. I'll be out soon," I said, wondering when I'd started having discussions with animals.

By the time I returned, the woman had gained control of her emotions. "Are you interested in aerobics or Pilate classes?" she asked.

"Neither," I replied. I explained my interest in finding Evelyn.

"Yes, Evelyn's one of the regulars here—never misses a class when she's around. She's a bit obsessive about it. Thinks her core needs strengthening." The woman shook her head. "But I haven't seen her for some time."

"What about Jane and Evelyn? Were they friends?" I asked.

"No, I don't think they were in the same social circles. But Jane was the one who followed up with people when they missed classes. She was good at that" – the woman paused to catch her breath – "making a call to find out if the person was sick or something."

Her voice faded, her lips quivered, and she sniffed back the tears again.

"I'm sorry," I said. "I don't know your name." I wanted to know but also to give her a chance to regain her composure.

"My name is Sarah."

"Sarah, do you know how long it's been since Evelyn was here? It's important that I find a way to contact her." I eyed the schedule and calendars strewn across the desk. "Do you suppose Jane made notes in her calendars? She might have known why Evelyn missed appointments."

"Why didn't I think of that? Hold on, let me look at Jane's address book. She keeps, I mean she kept her list of clients with contact information along with their program schedule." Sarah quickly pinpointed Evelyn's name. A notation about a standing Friday reservation didn't offer much information.

"I'm sorry. I don't see any reach number here," Sarah said. She glanced up at a wall clock. "I have to get the studio ready for the next class. But if I find anything, I'll surely let you know. Do you have a business card?" She walked over toward a rack containing hand weights.

"Thank you. I'll leave my contact information in case you do hear from her." I placed the business card with my U.S. and Irish phone numbers on the desk.

Rain dampened the sidewalks when I stepped out through the studio's doorway. I looked around for Ashford, but he'd disappeared. Dashing across the road to avoid getting soaked, I turned toward Ben O'Malley's bookstore. I figured, if he were alone, he'd be more willing to discuss Evelyn and how to reach her. I also wanted to show him the letter I'd found. Because of its personal nature, I hadn't shared it with Aunt Georgina or Lorcan yet. I felt I should start with Ben. But when I entered his shop, I could see he was on the phone, head bowed over a stack of papers, which he seemed to refer to as he spoke. I lingered for a few minutes in front of a stack of boxes before clearing my throat in an effort to catch his eye. He looked up at me, then told whoever was on the line that he had to go. He stood and walked over to join me.

"Ms. O'Brien," Ben said. "How do you like the book? I trust you've found some interesting O'Malley history."

I didn't answer. Instead, I extracted the letter I'd found and handed it to him. "Do you know anything about this?"

Ben's eyes narrowed as they moved from the paper to mine. "Where did you get this?" The words escaped his clenched jaw in a whisper.

"It was in the book I purchased here the other day. Were Jane and Jake having an affair? I'm sorry. I have to ask. I just can't ignore the facts. This" – I pointed at the letter – "could be the motive for Jane's death. You've got to give this letter to the police."

Ben handed the letter, folded again, back to me.

"What are you going to do?" I asked.

"Not a thing." Ben shrugged his shoulders. "I deal in old books and old books often have letters and notes in them. I'm sure it's nothing, which is what I intend to do."

Before I could respond, the shop door opened, and the young man I'd seen at the crime scene, Paul, came into view. I placed the creased letter back into my pocket.

Ben nodded his head toward me while addressing his visitor. "Paul, this is Ms. O'Brien. Like you, she's interested in family trees."

Paul turned to extend his hand. "Hi, I'm Paul Doherty. I'm always happy to meet a fellow historian. Although my specialty is in preserving local historical documents." His eyes brightened for a moment. "I was just about to tell Ben here that I've found some old papers and letters of my parents that he might want for the shop." He tried to smile, but it seemed to hurt his face. "So, 'tis the O'Malleys you're interested in? Well, books and articles about the O'Malleys are plentiful. You should have no problem delving into their long and tumultuous history."

"Too much history is part of the problem," I said. "But maybe both of you can help me. I'm looking for a way to contact Evelyn."

Paul and Ben exchanged glances as Ben, back behind his desk, began shuffling papers. He pushed some into folders and others into a few of the books stacked shoulder-high on his desk.

"I haven't seen you in Cong before. Are you visiting or buying land here?" Paul asked.

I considered how to answer. I didn't want to tell him that I recognized him or that I was the one who found his mother's body.

"Visiting. I live in the States and own a small cottage outside of Castlebar. I'm trying to locate Evelyn, but it's been a dead-end thus far. A friend of mine was flying into Cong to do some work today. He invited me along."

"Did you fly in with Lorcan McHale?" Ben asked, studying one of the papers on the desk.

"Yes, do you know Lorcan?"

"I've heard of him," Ben said. "I live at Happy Trails. Anyone who wants to use our landing strip contacts us for permission." Ben lifted the shade covering the window next to his desk. "You'll have to make a run for it if you want to get up before the clouds close in the airfield."

"We're scheduled to meet up again at four o'clock and head for home." For a moment, I thought about what it would be like to be stranded overnight with Lorcan. No, I couldn't let that happen because I wasn't ready for any relationships where vulnerability was expected.

"I don't know how to contact Evelyn, but perhaps Paul does," Ben said. "If you'll both forgive me, I have to run. I have an appointment with Ann Ryan to appraise someone's library. And I need to close up the bookshop."

The three of us exited, and Ben hurried off to his meeting.

"Will you join me for lunch?" Paul asked. "I'm not good company at the moment. My mother was found dead this week and..."

"I know. I found her body," I interrupted him. I hoped to save myself some embarrassment when he discovered that I'd known who he was.

Instead, he took my hands in his and said, "Thank you. If you hadn't come along when you did, who knows how ravaged her body might have been before she was found. Some nasty animals roam the Cong woods."

Maybe I'd been wrong to assume my incarceration in a well had been the result of human hands. But then, I dismissed my doubt because I trusted my intuition. I also felt a rapport with this poor man who'd just lost his mother.

"Yes, I'd love to have lunch with you," I said.

CHAPTER 12

Over bowls of vegetable soup and a basket of brown bread at the Quiet Man Café, we shared our life histories. I also told him why I wanted to talk to Evelyn. "What about Rose Cottage?" I asked, swirling my soup spoon through the thick and creamy liquid. "Do you know anything about the dig? It looks abandoned."

"No, I don't really know what's going on," Paul replied. "I've asked my da about the cottage and the dig a few times, but he puts me off. Says he's got emotional ties to the place—doesn't want to part with it."

"Oh. Is the cottage his family home?" I asked.

"Well, that's the thing." Paul raised his eyes to mine. "It's not. He grew up a few miles from here—a place called the Neale."

I debated whether to tell Paul I'd seen his parents in his father's hometown. I decided I didn't want to upset Paul with a description of the behavior I'd observed. Besides, he probably already knew from the police where his parents were the night his mother was murdered.

"What about the ghost sightings that everyone's been reporting?" I asked.

"Oh, that." He gave a half-hearted chuckle. "This area is full of history, and people like a good scare once in a while. It's probably some local chaps out for a laugh."

I didn't agree. It all just sounded too neat to me, especially since I'd been on the receiving end of the *fun*. But I wasn't ready to tell Paul what had happened.

"Do you think the stories have anything to do with the dig?" I asked.

"I don't know why that would be." He ran a hand through his wavy hair. When he continued, he spoke slowly as if he had to edit his words. "I mean, my da agreed to the government's terms for the dig. No one's lived in the place for years. At least not since Noel Carney's family emigrated to America."

"Does Noel Carney have curly salt-and-pepper hair? About this long?" I used my right hand to demonstrate.

"Well, yeah." Paul nodded. "He does wear it a little shaggy. He works for the national forestry—always looks like a hiker after a long trek in the woods. Do you know him?" Paul asked.

"Maybe." I didn't elaborate. "Would he have anything to do with the dig?"

"No." Paul shook his head. "The only people who're supposed to be on the property are the folks associated with the dig and my da."

"Well, I want to find Evelyn or at least talk to her before I have to leave for the States again."

"Look, I'll contact some of the other historians in the area. They might know more about Evelyn than I do at the moment," Paul promised. Then he signaled the server to bring our check. "Have you spoken to Ben about your mother? You know he has boxes of old ledgers and letters about the O'Malley clan. He might be able to help you find something specific."

"I bought a history of the O'Malleys book from him yesterday. He never mentioned anything else."

"Do you know that biblical saying about the sins of the

fathers and their children?" Paul asked as he cleaned his glasses with the end of the shirt that hung over his jeans.

"What do you mean? That we're flawed because of our parents?" I considered my life and the people I loved as fragile and fleeting but never flawed.

"Well, here we sit. Both of us tangled up in our parents' lives. Parents who are missing, dead, or in the case of my da, so focused on his own life he doesn't know I exist most of the time." Paul's hands shook when he pushed his glasses back on the bridge of his nose. "I mean, what does it take for a parent to let their child know he or she is loved?"

Before I could answer, several people entered the tiny dining room. A middle-aged woman accompanied by a boy approached Paul.

"Paul, I saw the gardai escorting your dad into the station!" the woman said.

Paul rose from the table. His hands grasped the edge as if to steady himself.

"Aye, people are saying he murdered your mom," said the teenaged boy.

"Shush now, Tommy," the woman said to the boy. "That's enough gossip." She glanced at Paul. "It looked like your dad was there willingly. Anyway, I thought you'd want to know." Then, she steered the boy toward an empty table.

"Star, come with me, won't you?" Paul's eyes pleaded behind his glasses.

What else could I do? I threw twenty euros on the table to cover lunch and hurried after him.

"NOW WHAT?" ASKED PAUL, EXITING FROM THE BOWELS OF THE police station. He slumped down onto a wooden bench in the station's foyer where I'd waited for him.

"Did they say whether they're going to arrest him?" I asked.

"No, they mentioned some new evidence has come to light that they want to question him about." Paul ran his trembling hands through his long, curly strands. "When they're finished, he'll be allowed to go home."

"That's good news, Paul," I said. "They aren't holding him. They're just asking questions." But at the same time, I didn't like that the police had new evidence they wanted to talk to Dan about.

"Will you help me?" Paul's eyes pleaded with me. "I know my da is innocent, and if the garda can't see that, then I'll have to help them see it."

"I don't investigate murders," I stated flatly.

"I understand that. But you told me you fight for people who are misjudged. I know my da is innocent. I just have to prove it."

"You seem pretty sure of that. Have you talked to him about what he thinks happened?" I asked.

"No, but I've been sorting through my mother's belongings. You know, getting it all ready for the charity shop. I found a note in one of her anoraks. The note said something about meeting in the woods."

"Did you tell the police?" I asked.

I considered whether or not to show the note I'd found to Paul but decided against it. I didn't have any real proof that Jane was the author. This man had suffered too much loss already. He didn't need to feel pain from my hand, not today anyway.

"I turned the paper over to them, but they didn't seem to care much about it. They explained that the note could have been written at any time, by anyone."

"What do you think? Could it have been from your mother or father?"

"It wasn't. Here, let me show you. I took a photo of it." He scrolled through his cell phone and then handed it over to me. "There. I know that's not their handwriting."

Meet me in Cong woods. We have to talk. The words were written in a loopy, flowering script on a ripped piece of paper. But other than that, there was no date, no signature. How ironic it was that Paul believed in his father's innocence, despite having just a few days ago accused his father of being responsible for his mother's death. But I also knew what it meant to love someone despite how the situation appeared. And I knew the police made mistakes.

"I'll help you," I said, rising from the bench. "Now, I have to meet up with Lorcan at Ann's real estate office. Why don't you walk with me? The fresh air will do you good."

While we made our way to the office, I told Paul I'd follow up with him the next morning. As we approached the office, I spotted Lorcan standing outside on the cement path. Ashford lay at his feet. Where had that dog gotten to this afternoon? And how had he found Lorcan?

"Ashford and I were just about to send out a search party for you," Lorcan said as he glanced at his watch. "Showers are predicted, and I want to get back to Castlebar ahead of them."

Lorcan, turning to Paul, said, "I heard the sad news about your mom. I'm sorry for your loss." As both men exchanged a handshake, I noticed the sign on the office door read Closed. Wasn't Ann supposed to take us to the airfield after her appointment with Ben? I really had no desire to be in her company again. But it seemed the lesser of two evils as I contemplated riding in a small airplane through rain showers.

"Are we waiting for Ann?" I asked, looking around for her car.

"No, she received an emergency call and begged off her commitment," Lorcan said. "I've arranged for a taxi to the farm. Ah, here comes our transportation." Lorcan turned to Paul. "I'm sorry I don't have more time to talk with you now, but I'm sure

I'll see you again soon." Then, Lorcan opened the taxi door and waved Ashford and me into the back seat.

"Not a problem. I have to get back to the garda station anyway," Paul said. He turned to me. "Thank you, I'll call in the morning."

CHAPTER 13

The taxi launched from the shaded confines of Cong toward Ryan's airfield. I glanced back through the rearview window at Paul. My heart went out to him for the inevitable and tragic truth he had to consider—his father might have killed his mother.

"Garda station?" Lorcan's question brought my attention back to my two traveling companions.

"Supposedly, the police found something new they wanted to discuss with Dan Doherty," I said.

"A few people in town are laying odds that the husband, Dan, did the wife in," the taxi driver said. He shifted his eyes from the road to look at Lorcan. "Always cheating on each other. It's a known fact." The driver grunted. "If it wasn't Dan, then it might well have been anyone else around town."

A short time later, we arrived at the airfield. Jumping from the car, Lorcan paid the driver and waved him off. Without delay, Lorcan got Ashford and me on board. After releasing the tie-down ropes, Lorcan climbed in. The sky overhead darkened. Branches rustled in the wind. Lorcan yelled, "Clear prop," and the engine roared to life.

Once we were in the air, the plane followed an invisible path back to Castlebar airport. This time, Lorcan didn't offer the controls. I watched the scenery fly by as I thought about couples. Why did some remain together long after love died?

Lorcan landed the airplane and taxied to its hangar. Luckily, we were in his car before the rain fell in earnest. As he drove toward French Hill, I had to admit to myself how grateful I was that he'd lifted me up and away from the nightmare of having been pushed into a priest's hole cave. The more time I spent with him, the more comfortable I felt. But deep inside, I still carried the fear of losing those I'd come close to in my life.

"You're in deep thought," Lorcan noted, turning his blue eyes from the road to me for a second.

"No," I denied, not wanting him to know what I'd been thinking. "Tired is more the case. But I loved the flight. Thank you. It was just the right thing for me today."

"I thought you'd like it." He smiled. "When I fly, I don't think of anything else but where I am at that moment. It's good therapy. Why don't you rest up for a bit and let me take you to dinner tonight? We can go to the golf course restaurant. It's simple food, sandwiches, burgers, and the like."

I nodded my consent. "Sounds good," I said, covering a yawn.

"Besides, I want to know more about your day, how you came to meet up with Paul."

"It's a deal." I smiled, feeling cheered at the thought of talking over the day's events with Lorcan.

When he parked the car at French Hill Cottage, Ashford bounded through the open passenger door, barking and snarling. With his teeth bared, he disappeared around the back of the cottage. Lorcan gave me a puzzled glance before he leaped out of the car, vanishing after Ashford. *What now?* I dashed after them.

Lorcan stood amidst a pile of shattered glass that once

served as the window to a small room where I'd set up a temporary office with a computer and phone line. His face was a paler and frozen version of its usual self. Lorcan raised a hand to stop me from coming any closer. "There's been a break-in." Then, he pointed to a dangling wire on the side of the cottage. "And it looks like the phone line's been cut."

With a sick feeling in my gut, I thought in horror of being trapped in the priest's hole cave without my cell phone. And now the cottage was without a landline. I tried to answer Lorcan, but the words caught in my throat. Instead, I clutched my phone—for the time being, my only communication link with the world.

"We'd better call the garda before we go inside," Lorcan said. I took some pictures of the damage with my phone before we walked back to the car to wait. Detectives O'Shea and Keenan interviewed us after they surveyed the broken window and my trashed office.

"Are we suspects?" I demanded when they asked us to move to separate rooms. Lorcan flashed a warning look at me. I ignored it. They asked some questions about how long I'd been away from the cottage, locks, and whether I'd seen any strangers in the area.

"Did you get my message about what happened last night to Ms. O'Brien?" Lorcan asked when we'd all reconvened in the living room.

"Oh, right. Yes, I got the message," Keenan said. "Sorry, we've been following up on some major incidents." His eyes avoided the glance O'Shea cast at him. "I didn't have time to discuss it with you," Keenan said to O'Shea. Then, Keenan paged back through his notebook as if looking for the report.

"Being shoved into a hole in the ground and left potentially to freeze to death seems like something you'd consider needing to follow up, especially in light of the recent murder of a Cong resident," I said.

"Description of the perpetrator?" snapped O'Shea.

"It was dark. I was in the woods. The person came from behind," I said. I took care to keep the anger I felt out of my words. Didn't these guys get it? If I knew the answer, I wouldn't be sitting here wasting my time talking to them.

"It's probably a bunch of kids playing pranks," O'Shea said. "So-called ghost sightings have been reported in the area, but we haven't taken the calls seriously."

"Pranks, Detective?" This time, I couldn't keep the anger out of my voice. "First, I'm attacked in the woods. And now, my computer is stolen. I wouldn't describe either of these incidents as innocent fun."

"Of course, you may have just lost your footing and fallen." O'Shea stared at my Rocket Dogs. "The ground is slippery at night. If I were you, I'd stay out of areas that you're not familiar with."

"Tom, you and I have known each other for a long time, and I haven't often disagreed with you. But, this is one of those times," Lorcan said. "Star did not lose her footing. She was pushed."

The anger in Lorcan's voice both surprised and pleased me. He was sticking up for me.

O'Shea acknowledged Lorcan's comment with a nod and then continued questioning me. "I understand you've been asking questions about Evelyn Cosgrove. What's your interest in her?"

How did he know that?

"I'm researching my family's history, and her name came up as someone who might have historical information about the O'Malleys."

"Is that the only reason?" O'Shea asked. "I'm sure I don't have to remind you that Mrs. Doherty was murdered. This is a dangerous situation," he warned.

"What do you intend to do about the break-in here?" Lorcan interrupted O'Shea's lecture.

"Of course, we'll look into it. But I don't hold out much hope we'll find who did this. The town is pestered with burglaries every day. They take any electronics they can get their hands on. They probably saw your computer through the window and considered it easy pickings."

Finally, the detectives left.

"It's too late to get anyone here to fix that window," Lorcan said as he searched through the house, looking for cardboard and tape. "I'll call someone in the morning to get this cleaned up. In the meanwhile, why don't you pack a few things, and I'll take you to Georgina's after we've had a bite to eat."

"I'm not hungry anymore." I felt exhausted and only wanted to get some sleep. "I just want to go to bed if you don't mind."

"Okay, I understand. Just give me a chance to board up this window." Lorcan smiled. "Then, we'll drive over to her place."

While he worked on the temporary repairs, I checked the rest of the cottage. Although nothing else was damaged or missing, I didn't buy the detective's suggestion that this was just one of a rash of break-ins. First, I was attacked, and now this. No, there was more to it. Finally, I tidied up my bedroom and sorted clothes for the laundry. The night before, I'd thrown everything I'd been wearing onto the floor. When I picked up my still-sodden wellingtons and sweatshirt, I found the stone I'd tossed into the pocket as well as a sharp pebble lodged into the tread of one of the boot's soles. Using a nail file, I dislodged the pebble and tossed both rocks, if you could call them that, onto my dresser. With my room straightened up, I returned to the living room, where Ashford and Lorcan waited. At that moment, I felt comforted knowing I didn't have to drive and looked forward to Aunt Georgina's ministrations.

Aunt Georgina lived in a two-hundred-year-old thatched cottage in Turlough Village a few miles outside Castlebar.

Lorcan turned left through a gate in the walled perimeter and coasted along the drive to the front door, which peeked out from behind clusters of ivy hung like ringlets. The door burst open. Georgina ran to throw her arms around me.

"Are you all right? Here, let me look at you! Oh, and you have that dog with you. Come on, all of you, inside right now." She ushered us into the huge combination living room and country kitchen. The air was redolent with the smell of jam. "Sit down." She pointed toward the cozy, comfortable sofas and chairs in the living room half of the cottage. "I'm just finishing up making a brown bread. I'll get it out of the oven, and we'll chat." She moved toward the enormous Aga cooker, which sat on what had been the original open fire hearth, shooing Ashford out of the spot he'd appropriated in front of the oven door, calling over her shoulder to Lorcan to "get yourself a drink out of the cabinet next to the sofa."

"If you don't mind, I'm going to head home," Lorcan answered and turned back across the room to the front door. "I've a morning appointment, and my mother will be wondering what's happened to me. She's not crazy about my flying, and she'll have me lying in every ditch or field between here and Cong if I don't check in with her soon."

"Give her my regards and tell her I'll call her about the annual duck races at the Turlough Museum in a few days," Aunt Georgina said as she took a round brown loaf out of the oven. After setting it on a cutting board to cool, she followed Lorcan to the front door and locked it behind him.

"What a nightmare!" Georgina exclaimed. "First, you're pushed into a hole and left to die. And now this. Did anyone report seeing strangers around French Hill?" she asked, propping her feet up on a tiny, square, embroidered footstool.

"Nothing. But who'd see anything? The closest neighbor is Lorcan, and his place is surrounded by trees and at least a mile away from the road." I let my head drop onto the high back of the Queen Anne chair.

"Do the garda have any ideas?" Georgina asked.

"The police? The only ideas they have are the wrong ones."

"Well, I have some news. Jimmy phoned and wanted to know if you'd had any luck tracking down Evelyn. He was shocked when I told him about your incident in the woods. Said he'd never heard anything like it."

"Is that what you wanted to tell me earlier?" I asked.

"You mean two days ago, don't you?" Georgina reminded me.

"You're right," I shook my head. "So much has happened over the last few hours. The days are merging."

"Jimmy said the pub's been a hotbed of gossip since Jane died. According to him, everyone's sure Dan killed her."

"He seems to be the most likely suspect. You know he met with the police again today. I was at the Quiet Man Café with his son when word roared through town that Dan had been brought in for questioning."

"Paul is such a lovely lad. I don't know what he did to deserve those two parents of his. But he's grown now and out on his own. It shouldn't much matter anymore how much those two fought over the years," Aunt Georgina said as she stood and moved back to the kitchen, where she sliced a piece of the brown bread for herself. "Would you like some, Star?" she asked.

I shook my head in refusal. "No, thank you. I'm beat. I think I'd just like to sleep if you don't mind."

"Get yourself down to bed then. We'll have plenty of time in the morning to catch up on other things."

Too tired to think about what else Georgina wanted to talk about, I said, "Good night," left Ashford sleeping in front of the hearth, and took myself to the tiny guest room. I quickly dropped my clothes onto the floor and nestled under the bed's down comforter. Every ounce of energy seemed to flow out of my body into the mattress beneath me. As I stared up at the low ceiling, I thought about Jimmy's comments and the crowd at the pub the night the Dohertys had their fight. Had Jane's killer been at the bar? Did Evelyn have anything to do with the events in Cong? I knew I'd begin the search for answers tomorrow. For now, I closed my eyes and set my mind on sleeping.

CHAPTER 14

"*I*s anyone there? Do you hear me?" *My words reverberated against the slick, damp, chamber walls. No one answered. Drenched, exhausted, and terrified, I rested my head against the wall of my prison.*

"Are you lost?" the voice whispered.

Someone was there.

"I'm here. Help me!" I stood up, hoping my voice would carry farther into the night air and to my unknown rescuer.

"It's your fault. Your fault..." the whisperer rasped.

"No." My eyes flew open, and I found myself in Aunt Georgina's guest bedroom. Alone. My heart thundered; each beat pounded my brain, but over it all, I could hear Ashford's bark and the clatter of cups and saucers from the kitchen.

What time was it? Sunlight filtered through gauzy lace curtains, and birdsong threatened to drown out the kitchen noises. A male voice mingled with Aunt Georgina's flowing chatter. If she had company, it must be after nine—the Irish rarely called at one's house any earlier.

I jumped out of bed, dressed in the clothes I rescued from the floor and went to the kitchen where Aunt Georgina and Jimmy Mahoney glared at each other across Georgina's farm-house-sized oak table. Ashford's tail wagged a greeting, but he didn't budge from his spot, where he feasted on a large rawhide bone. I poured a mug of hot water from the kettle simmering on the Aga, grabbed a tea bag, and set it to brew before I noticed the long silence.

"What's going on?" I demanded. I'd grown accustomed to Aunt Georgina's energy, and a lull in the conversation wasn't normal.

"Jimmy stopped by with some news." Aunt Georgina's eyes bored into her guest's like a laser cutting into diamonds. "News he should have shared with me months ago." Her index finger beat a steady rhythm on the table as she turned to speak to me. "In addition to his business in the Neale, Jimmy is a silent partner in Jane Doherty's exercise studio."

"Listen here, Georgina, I'm an entrepreneur." The sound of his heightened breathing filled the room. "I make investments. Was I supposed to open my financial books to you?" His eyes focused on the napkin in his hands, folding and refolding it. "You asked about Evelyn Cosgrove. You didn't ask about Jane Doherty. Besides, you broke up with me."

"I've always thought there wasn't enough honesty in our relationship, Jimmy." Georgina pushed her plate away. "I guess that's why we're not an item anymore."

Throwing the napkin on the table, he turned to me and said, "Can you talk to her? I'm trying to help not make things worse. I heard your place was broken into. I came over here to see how you are and tell Georgina I'm sure Dan killed his wife."

"What makes you sure about that?" I asked as I sat down next to Aunt Georgina at the table.

"I saw him the night she was killed. I came into the pub late, after you'd left. He was in a foul mood and drinking like prohibition was about to be enacted the next day. He kept rambling on about killing someone if they didn't get out of his way. I assumed he was talking about Jane because he was always

cheating on her. I figured he'd finally decided to get a divorce."
He glanced over at Georgina. "I never meant to hide anything
from you."

Georgina, her head held high, studied the wall behind him.
"I've been busy with the pub. The entire village is in turmoil
—I just didn't think." Rising from his seat, he carried his cup to
the sink and turned to face both of us. "I'm in the midst of
figuring out the impacts to the studio's ownership. The sooner
the garda find her murderer, the sooner I'll be able to get things
sorted." He wiped his hands on his paint-splattered work pants.
That's when I noticed red paint dried into the edges of his
fingers.

"Maybe your business partnership had something to do
with Jane's murder," Georgina stated.

"You can't mean that!" Jimmy's voice cracked.

"How did you know my cottage was broken into?" I asked in
an effort to defuse the tension between them.

"One of the lads who comes into the pub lives along your
road. He was tending some livestock, and the garda asked him
if he'd seen anything out of the ordinary." Jimmy leaned back
against the sink and crossed his arms. "I heard you agreed to
help Paul. I just thought you might want to hear what I knew
about the situation."

"For someone who keeps his own business to himself, you
don't seem to mind getting into everyone else's," Georgina said.

Before I had a chance to respond to Jimmy, the doorbell
rang. Ashford barked, bounding toward the sound. Jimmy
followed close behind. Georgina and I rose from our seats and
followed him.

"I'm sorry, Georgina," Jimmy said. Then, he exited through
the door, past Lorcan, who looked surprised to see all of us
standing there.

"What's going on?" Lorcan's words echoed my earlier
question.

"I wish I'd never met Jimmy Mahoney; that's what." Georgina's words trailed behind her as she tossed the end of her scarf over her shoulder and walked back to the kitchen table.

Lorcan glanced at me as if he expected me to enlighten him.

"Aunt Georgina can get you caught up," I said. "I need to make a call."

Lorcan followed Georgina into the kitchen, where she placed a mug in front of him. Impatient for action, I pulled my phone out of its holster and called the Consulting Detective. Because of the time, I knew Ellie or Phillie wouldn't be at work, but I wanted them to know that, for now, the iPhone was the only way to reach me. By the time I left my voicemail and hung up, Georgina and Lorcan had grown quiet. Both sets of eyes rested on me. I knew those looks.

"Now what?" I asked.

"I think you should stay with Georgina until whatever is happening in Cong has been settled," Lorcan said. "It probably has nothing to do with you, but we're worried." His eyes sought mine over the rim of his glasses.

"Impossible." The words flew from my mouth. I thought of my promise to Paul. "I'm involved. No one, not even the police, can stop me."

"Then let me help you," Lorcan said.

"He's right, Star. It's too dangerous for you to work on this alone," Aunt Georgina chimed in. "Besides, Lorcan can be a liaison between you and his friends in the garda."

"No," I stated. "My schedule's too busy to manage around someone else's. I also have the resources of the Consulting Detective to help me. And, that reminds me, we'd better get back to French Hill. I need to be there to let the phone company in to repair the cable damage."

"I still need to talk with you, Star," Georgina said.

"Can it wait until later?" I asked. "I really need to get home."

"It can wait but not too long," she replied. Then she turned her back and began rinsing out the dirty cups.

"Right, let's go then." Lorcan pointed toward the door.

I could tell from their reaction that maybe I'd been too sharp in my response. But I just couldn't accept Lorcan's help. I needed to work alone. Although I felt comforted at the thought of spending more time with him, I refused to let him know how much I'd begun to like him.

AFTER LORCAN WALKED THROUGH THE COTTAGE TO SATISFY himself that the place was empty, he left. I made a series of calls to the phone company, a window repair service, and the computer store to order a replacement. The window service team arrived first and quickly installed the new window. Then the phone company techs showed up and began rewiring my broadband connection.

While I waited, I tried to keep myself busy. I glanced through some of the real estate brochures I'd picked up during my last trip. I checked my cell phone several times for a message from Paul, but that too was fruitless. I considered whether whoever had pushed me into the well was the same person who'd broken into the cottage. Were these events connected to Jane? Or Evelyn? Why would anyone care that I was looking for my mother? *So, where do I go from here?* I asked myself. Restless, I walked into the bedroom. The stone I'd thrown onto my dresser twinkled at me. Once more, my thoughts turned to Rose Cottage, where I'd found the unusual-looking rock. Was there a connection with Evelyn?

The techs left after they'd demonstrated connection to several sites on the internet. I logged on to search where I might find someone or someplace to have the rock analyzed. Since I'd found it at a government dig site, I figured there'd be some legal requirement involved in who should assess it. It didn't take long to find an address for the Department of Environmental Studies. It also didn't take long to learn that the archeology branch of the National Museum was in Dublin also. That made sense since all branches of the government originated in Ireland's capital. I figured that, archeologist or not, Evelyn Cosgrove had been required to get a permit from the government. Armed with the addresses, I packed the stones, a map, and a few power bars into my knapsack. Then, I called to Ashford, and we were out the door.

CHAPTER 15

Four hours later, we stood in the foyer of the building in Dublin that housed the Department of Environmental Studies.

"You say you found this?" The security guard's voice and eyebrows simultaneously rose a notch or two higher. Then she added, "You know animals aren't allowed in the building."

"I'd like to have this rock analyzed. How long do you think it will take?" I drummed my fingers on the counter as I looked around for someone to help me.

"I'm sorry, ma'am, but you'll have to make an appointment for an appraisal, and only service dogs are allowed to accompany anyone." Ashford growled when the guard came from around her desk to escort us out the door.

"May I help you?" The tall, gray-suited man strode across the hall as he approached. "What seems to be the problem?"

"I'm sorry about the dog." I directed my answer to the man. "But I couldn't leave him in my car. He's a rescue, and I'm keeping him close until I find his owner."

Ashford edged nearer to me and pushed his head up under my hand to demonstrate how close we were.

"Well, you're fortunate I was passing through the lobby on

my way from dinner," the man said. "I love dogs and have several border collies myself. I know how much attention they need. Now, how can I be of assistance?" he asked. "I thought I heard you say something about a nugget?"

"Yes, I'd like to know what this is." I opened my hand to reveal the rock.

"May I?" he said as he reached forward to take the stone from my hand. "Hmm, interesting." His eyes moved from the stone back to me. "Let's go to my office."

"But the dog..." the guard sputtered.

"Don't worry, Sheila. I'll keep an eye on him." Then, he directed us into an elevator and pressed the button to the top floor. When we exited, he guided us along a corridor toward a large semi-laboratory and office.

"Make yourself at home," he said. He gestured to a sitting area in front of his desk. He plopped his tall frame in a chair and asked, "Where did you find this?"

"In a field in Cong. Is it gold?" I suspected it but was puzzled about why or how it had come to be where I'd found it.

He didn't answer my question. Instead, he offered an introduction.

"I'm Dr. Kenneth Treat, chief scientist here in the department. I'd like to run a few tests on this if you don't mind. Are you willing to leave it with me for a few days?"

I nodded.

"Good," he said. Then he carefully pulled a piece of paper out of his jacket pocket and wrapped it around the stone. "To answer your question, it does look like gold, but that seems impossible. However, stranger things have happened. I'll know for sure in a day or two." He paused and narrowed his eyes. "You understand that if this is gold, you cannot keep it. It would belong to the Irish government."

"I know. I'm merely trying to find out why someone wants

to kill me. And that stone just happened to come under my foot a short while before someone shoved me into a well."

"Kill you?" He shook his head in disbelief. "I doubt anyone would want to kill you for this wee stone." He unwrapped the nugget again and held it in the palm of his hand, where it did look insignificant.

"I agree, but I can't help wanting to know how it's connected to the site of an archeological dig and if it had anything to do with the attack on me."

"Well, we'll let the science tell us what this is, and then you can decide whether it's connected to what's been happening to you. I'm surprised the dog let anyone get close enough to touch you," he said, tilting his head toward Ashford, who'd taken up residence on the rug and lay on his side with his eyes closed.

"I'd probably be dead if it weren't for him. He led my rescuer to me."

I felt horrified when I thought about what might have happened if not for Lorcan and Ashford. Sooner or later, I'd find out who was behind all this. Until then, I'd continue to do what I'd come to Ireland for—to find my mother. Impatient to get to the archeology museum before it closed, I thanked Dr. Treat for his assistance, scribbled out my contact information, and departed with Ashford.

A light drizzle was falling when we emerged from the building; however, by the time we reached the archeology branch of the National Museum of Ireland on Kildaire Street, the rain had stopped.

"Let's see what kind of reception we receive here, boy," I said as I glanced down at Ashford's wet fur. But when we entered the foyer, and I asked for the person in charge of the archeology department, the guard just picked up the phone and announced a visitor to whoever answered.

"Dr. O'Dowd will see you," the guard said, pointing to a

bank of elevators behind him. "Basement level." He turned back to the newspaper he'd been reading when we walked in.

I hurried over to the elevator before someone decided a stranger shouldn't be granted access to the department head. Unlike Dr. Treat's office, the room the elevator opened upon provided little space for movement. You didn't so much as walk into Dr. O'Dowd's museum area as you crept in, keeping arms and legs close so as not to disturb the debris field of bones, metal objects, urns, and other assorted artifacts that lined the walls and floor. The air was cool, laced with a musty smell, and the sunlight filtering in through the soot-smeared, narrow hopper windows shined on a rising column of dust mites.

"Hello?" My words echoed through the corridor. Ashford nudged my knee as if he wanted to get out of this place as soon as possible. Perhaps he was worried he'd end up like one of the animal carcasses that stood on the floor at his eye level.

"Hello?" This time someone else's words circled back to me like a boomerang.

"Dr. O'Dowd?" I still couldn't see anyone or figure out the direction of the voice. "The guard told me to go ahead and come down. Where are you?" I raised my voice and stood on tiptoes to see if I could pinpoint her whereabouts.

"You stay right where you are, dear. I'll find you." Laughter reached my ears. "After all, it's my job to find things."

A few moments later, a tiny woman emerged from behind a pile of mud-stained linens. No higher than my elbow, she had tanned skin and the sort of twinkling blue eyes that always seemed to be laughing at something.

"Oh." She smiled, reaching out her hand to point at Ashford. "I see you've brought along my favorite of the canine species, the Scottish border collie." She narrowed her eyes as she turned from Ashford to me. "But, I haven't ordered any dog specimens in ages."

I tightened my grip on his leash as we both backed away

from her. While I debated with myself whether to flee this labyrinth or not, Dr. O'Dowd chuckled.

"Had you going there for a minute, didn't I?" She laughed as she smoothed down her jet-black hair and turned a serious look at me. "I couldn't resist it. I've watched too many mummy and secrets of the pharaohs films. Come into my office, and you can tell me why you're here."

Photographs of rusted iron, gold necklaces, and broken pottery covered one of the office walls—a glass case holding bits of bones and bleached horse skulls sat against another. The single office window was framed by a palm tree growing out of a barrel on one side, and on the opposite side, old movie posters acted as wallpaper. Unlike the walls and the space outside her office, her desk, devoid of anything, was pristine. A three-piece suite of a loveseat and two armchairs, upholstered in sage green and sprinkled with comfortable-looking pillows, sat in front of her desk.

"Please, take a seat while I ask my secretary to bring us some refreshments." She spoke quietly into the phone on her desk. Then, she turned to me. "Now, tell me why you're here," Dr. O'Dowd said.

A young woman bounded into the room, carrying a tray of mugs, sugar, cream, and Bewley's chocolates, which she left on the oaken coffee table.

Once more, I described the search for my mother and the slim thread to Evelyn, whom I'd traced to the dig in Cong. Perhaps it was the coffee and chocolate or Dr. O'Dowd's sympathetic face, but I found myself telling her all about my mother, the Consulting Detective, and my Irish cottage.

When I'd finished, she put her mug down, reached across the space between us, and took my hands in hers.

"You strike me as a persistent person, Ms. O'Brien. And you may someday learn more about your mother and her family. I hope you do." O'Dowd's blue eyes held mine as her grasp on my hands increased in strength. "But I wouldn't count on Evelyn to help you."

"Why not?" I demanded, tugging my hands away from hers to hide the anger surging through my body. "I'd prefer to determine that for myself. If you know anything about her or how to reach her, it would be helpful."

"I can see your impatience, dear," Dr. O'Dowd said. "But if there's one lesson I've learned in all my years of sifting through dirt and sand, it's that patience is a necessary ingredient in the search for the Holy Grail." She paused, played with a piece of chocolate sitting on her napkin, and then sat back against the sofa cushions. "You may not agree with me, but your search for your mother seems like a similar endeavor. Lots of leads but no treasure." Her eyes sought mine as she continued. "You may find answers, but I wouldn't advise you to depend on Evelyn to provide them."

"What do you mean? Has she been in trouble before?" I asked.

Moving to the edge of the sofa, Dr. O'Dowd responded. "If you call following up on a whim trouble, then she's had issues before. Sometimes, she just picks up and drops whatever she's involved in at a moment's notice." O'Dowd sighed as she finished the chocolate and picked up her coffee mug, holding it between her hands. "She's brilliant and has tremendous potential. I've been her mentor for years, but I've never been able to teach her that most necessary ingredient—patience." She leaned back against the cushions again and eyed me from a distance. "You know...you remind me of her. She has the same quirky movements when you're talking to her."

I relaxed my hands before asking, "Where do you think she is now?"

"I don't know. She's supposed to be at that dig site in Cong and then coming up to Dublin to work with me on a paper we're presenting next summer." She shook her head as she looked around her office. "I'd hoped she could succeed me here as the national director, but if she continues disappearing like this, I'll never be able to name her as my assistant officially."

I wondered if Dr. O'Dowd realized that Evelyn's problems might be greater than following a whim. Did O'Dowd know about the recent murder in Cong?

"Has Evelyn mentioned any strange events at the dig site or in Cong?" I asked.

Dr. O'Dowd shifted her weight forward as she thought about my question. "We haven't spoken recently. I was traveling, and when I called her mobile phone, it went to voicemail. She'll turn up eventually, but until then, if I were you, I wouldn't count on her help with what you're into."

Interesting, I said to myself. She didn't ask about the strange events. "I agree, but if you don't mind, I'd like to try her cell phone number. Perhaps I'll have better luck in reaching her."

Dr. O'Dowd placed the coffee mug back on the tray, rose to her feet, and walked around the table to take my hands again. "I'd love to do that, dear, but you understand I can't provide the personal information of one of my employees to someone I don't know. Now, if you'll excuse me, I must get back to work."

"Will you contact me if you hear from her?" I rummaged one of my business cards out of my backpack.

"Of course." She accepted the card, bent to pat Ashford on the head, and disappeared through her open office door into the jungle beyond.

"Come on, Ashford," I said. We walked on in silence toward the elevator bank. He looked up at me as if to say, "What next?"

"We keep moving forward and never give up, Ashford."

SEVERAL HOURS LATER, WE ARRIVED BACK AT THE COTTAGE. After the long drive, I was relieved to find there weren't any messages from Ellie or Phillie on the office machine. I ate a container of hazelnut yogurt and fixed a bowl of food for Ashford. Finished with our meal, we both made a beeline to the living room, where a small turf fire glowed in the grate. I'd never heard of Irish peat sods, also known as turf until I'd arrived in Ireland. Then I'd learned the Irish dug the irregular-shaped, organic, decayed vegetative material out of what are called bog areas. Aunt Georgina usually left the fire ready to be lit. All I had to do was strike a match.

The real estate brochures on the coffee table caught my eye. Realistically, I knew I'd have to sell the cottage and return to the U.S. full time at some point. But for now, I enjoyed the quiet and seclusion the cottage offered. I reached for the hardcover Mead composition book I kept for research notes and journal entries. While the fire burned down, I wrote. Sometimes all it took was a few words jotted down to focus my thoughts and actions. Tonight, I found myself writing out whole paragraphs that described how I felt about the search for my mother. Some people thought I was obsessed, but I disagreed. I'd rather describe myself as driven and persistent—as someone who was for the dead, the missing, and the lost. My entire purpose, my life, was built upon what had happened. And, that meant action. So, I wrote about what I knew thus far about Evelyn Cosgrove. I wrote about everyone who seemed to know her but didn't know where she was. I kept coming back to Jane, Rose Cottage, and the priest's hole incident. Were any of these related to each other? I didn't really know much about Jane other than no one ever deserved to be murdered. Had I been pushed into the priest's hole cave because I was asking questions about Evelyn or because I'd found Jane's body? All questions I knew I had to investigate. The fire had burned down to a few embers when my cell phone rang.

"Hello," I said.

"Star, this is Paul Doherty."

"Hi, are you okay?" I asked. "I thought I might have heard from you earlier today."

"Sorry about that. I've been somewhat distracted. But I do want your help. Do you think you can meet me at the library in Castlebar tomorrow evening? I'm giving a talk to the historical society there. You wouldn't have to drive all the way to Cong to meet with me."

"That sounds great," I said. "What time?"

"The meeting starts at half five. Can you arrive a few minutes early? You'd have a chance to speak with some of the attendees."

"Yeah, that works." I glanced down at my notebook and asked, "What about your father? Anything new with the police?"

"I'm worried. But we can discuss it when I see you. I've got a few more things to follow up on tonight."

"Sure. I'll see you tomorrow then," I said.

CHAPTER 16

As Paul had suggested, I got to the Castlebar Library before the County Mayo Historical Society meeting started. He guided me around the room, introducing his fellow historians. I used the opportunity to ask people about the dig in Cong and whether they'd spoken with Evelyn lately.

"An American. Well, I suppose you're trying to trace your family tree." The speaker, a petite woman, wore black pants topped with a black knit sweater, cut in a fishnet pattern.

"Unfortunately, I don't have much to go on," I replied. "My mother disappeared when I was six years old. Several months ago, Evelyn posted a message on a missing person's board about a Maggie O'Malley, which was my mother's name. But, it's like Evelyn fell off the face of the earth."

"Have you spoken to our library director, Ivan Hemlock?" The woman looked at the flats I'd worn. "I like your shoes," she said.

Her long string of opera pearls separated her from the rest of the group, all of whom wore jeans and sneakers. I hadn't known what to expect at the meeting, so I'd compromised. Deciding against the red dress I'd worn to a dinner date a few months ago, I'd settled on a sage green linen shirt over a pair of flared palazzo pants. My grey slip-on flats complemented the outfit. Now, I was glad I'd made an effort to dress up.

"Actually, no, I haven't spoken to anyone at the library. I'm just back in Mayo again recently. An acquaintance has arranged a meeting for me with the Director of the National Archives in Dublin. I assume that's the best place to look for records."

The woman waved her hand in dismissal. "That's all well and good. But this building houses many publications about Ireland's past. It's worth looking. Have you tried different variations of her name? That's a big deal in historical research."

She had a point. It's easy for names to be catalogued incorrectly. I'd come across the issue in my own work. But I'd already tried several variations of Margaret—like Margarite or Margie.

The woman finally introduced herself. "I'm Maeve Baldwin, by the way. I'm surprised Paul doesn't know where Evelyn is." She glanced at Paul, who stood at the other side of the room. "Nevertheless, I've seen her several times—around the Augustinian ruins and woods in Cong. She's always got a notebook in her hands."

Before I could thank Maeve for her input, Paul called the meeting to order. I took a seat. Most of the discussion centered around local history workshops and events for children at some of the county's libraries and schools. Paul beamed when he accepted the society's decision to name him the official town historian in Cong. After the meeting ended, Paul and I stood on the sidewalk to say good night to everyone as they filtered out of the building.

"Would you like to get a bite to eat?" he asked. "I know a great café just across the way on Spencer Street. It's a short walk. We can cut across the town green."

The last time I'd walked across Castlebar's Mall, as it's officially called, I'd just come from a meeting with the police, who hadn't listened to me. Suddenly, everything felt like Déjà vu. Here I was again involved in a murder investigation, and the police weren't interested in what I had to say. However, this time, I was determined to tell them what I'd witnessed the night of Jane's murder.

I hadn't expected Paul's question, but I liked the idea of spending more time with him. "Sure, why not?" I replied.

FLOWER POTS FILLED WITH FRAGILE, WHITE ANGELICAS ADORNED Café Rua's windows. Inside, on the ground floor, delicacies and pastries from homemade brown scones to wild Irish salmon kept the wait staff behind the cash register busy. Paul led the way up a staircase to the first floor where an eclectic collection of tables and chairs was available. More cakes, pastries, and pies atop a counter tempted us with their choices. A giant chalkboard with the day's specials covered one of the other walls. We chose one of the tables along the balcony railing, from which we could see the customers coming and going from the shop below. A server appeared with two glasses and a large glass bottle of water. She handed menus to us, which we perused for a few minutes in silence.

"I've had the goat cheese salad with beet greens. It's good. Everything is locally sourced," Paul said.

"I don't think I've ever had beet greens. But I'm willing to try. Provided I can have some brown bread to go along with it," I replied.

Paul laughed. "Oh, to be sure. There's homemade bread here. And you can leave the beet greens off if you don't want them."

"Okay, I'll try the beet greens," I said. The server appeared at the table and disappeared just as quickly after taking our order. Although wine was available, we both decided to stick with water as we'd be driving later in the evening.

"So, you said you had some things to follow up on," I stated. "Anything I should know about?"

"Not really. I just hope you can help me prove my father couldn't possibly have murdered my mother." Paul's eyes avoided mine. I didn't know him well enough yet to determine whether he was hiding something, or he was just shy.

"Have you asked him where he was when your mother was killed?" I'd seen Jane leave the pub, but Dan had remained at the bar. At least that's where he was when I left.

"I don't live at home anymore, so I don't know if either one of them came home before…" Paul's eyes filled with tears. "My father says Noel Carney gave him a ride home from the pub. My father says my mother must have taken the car because it wasn't in the parking lot when he went to leave the pub."

"Where's the car now?" I asked.

"The garda found it in the car park across from the Augustinian abbey's cemetery. They assume my mother drove it there and then got out for some reason."

Jimmy had said that Dan Doherty was pretty hammered and angry after Jane left the pub. And, of course, I'd had an encounter with Noel Carney earlier that evening in the pub. Like it or not, I'd have to talk to him. And why hadn't Jane gone straight home? The only residence near the car park was Evelyn Cosgrove's house.

The food arrived, and we ended our conversation for a few minutes to eat in companionable silence.

"I didn't realize how hungry I was," I said as I buttered a slice of the thick homemade brown bread and smeared on some raspberry jam.

"I'm glad you like it," Paul said quietly.

I knew it was time to resume our discussion when he pushed his plate away. His half-eaten salad remained.

"Paul, I have to ask some sensitive questions. Are you up to it?" I asked.

"Yes," he nodded. The brown eyes behind his glasses met mine directly. "I want to do this. I've already lost one parent. I can't lose another."

"I understand how you feel, but we have to explore any potential motive your father may have had. After all, more often than not, it's the spouse in the end." I paused to let that thought sink in. "I have to know. Were there any issues or tensions between your parents?"

Paul nodded. "Definitely money issues. I don't know all the details, but the mill is involved. The mortgage is in arrears, and the bank is threatening to take the place over. My mother planned to use the fitness studio as collateral. She wanted him to keep the mill. But then they had a major argument after my mother went to the bank. She said she didn't care if he lost everything."

"What happened to change her mind?" I asked.

"I don't know. But she was pretty steamed, whatever it was. When I asked her about it, she refused to say."

I decided then it was time to tell Paul what I'd seen in the pub the night before Jane died.

"I saw your parents in the Neale the night your mother died," I stated.

Paul's eyes opened wide. "I didn't know."

"I haven't made it known. I've tried to speak to the police. Your parents were arguing—about someone. Your father accused your mother of cheating on him. And she accused him likewise. I saw her toss the contents of a beer glass at him before she stormed out of the pub."

Paul's shoulders slumped. "I admit they had their problems. But they still loved each other," he insisted.

"Do you have any idea who they might have been seeing?"

"Not that I can definitely pinpoint. I'm not blind, and I'm not stupid. I know Ann Ryan is attracted to my dad, but whether or not there's any real relationship there, I don't know." Paul's shoulders slumped again.

I didn't want to do it, but I had to show the "Dear Jake" letter to Paul. "Paul, I have to ask you to read this letter." I took the letter from my pants pocket and handed it to him. "I came across that letter in a book I bought at Ben's shop. Ben didn't want anything to do with it. I think you need to show it to the police. They'll probably listen to you before they pay me any heed." I didn't tell him I'd taken a photo of the letter with my phone.

Paul didn't answer immediately. When he raised his eyes to mine, tears ran down his cheeks. Then he said, "Can I keep this? I promise I'll contact the garda."

I trusted Paul's instincts, so I nodded in agreement and said, "I'll try to help you, Paul. But I don't know how much I can do. I'm not a detective. I'll talk to Noel Carney. Maybe I can find out why your mother decided not to help your dad with the mill. But you have to be prepared for the worst. Will you be okay with that?" I asked.

"I suppose I'll have to be," Paul replied.

The server came and cleared away our dishes. "Will that be all?" she asked. "We've got some great upside-down pear cake with fresh whipped cream."

Paul and I both said, "No," at the same time. Somehow our conversation just didn't lend itself to dessert.

The server brought our check. We agreed that Paul would pay the bill and I'd leave the tip. He walked me to my car, which I'd left by the library. He took my hand and squeezed it before saying, "Thank you, Star."

I liked Paul, his calmness and kind eyes. I admired his love for his parents. In some ways, Paul and I were alike. We both shared an interest in research and information. His passion was for local history. I, too, was focused on the past as a way to find my mother. I hoped that one day soon, I'd find an answer.

CHAPTER 17

The knock on the kitchen door was unexpected. The sensor lights illuminated Aunt Georgina's face. I opened the door immediately.

"You're out late. Is everything okay?" I asked, stepping back so she could enter the room.

"No, it's not." She walked through the tiny kitchen into the living room, where she sat on one of the Queen Anne chairs. "I want some answers."

I was used to Georgina's persistence. She never seemed to take "no" for an answer. But she usually persuaded people to see things her way through sustained coaxing. I hadn't anticipated this bundle of anger.

"What is it?" I asked.

"You. This." She swept her hand to take in the walls of the cottage. Her eyes turned to the coffee table. When she raised them to me, they blazed brighter than the embers that burned in the grate. "Those." She pointed to the brochures. "I saw Mary Moran in town this afternoon. She's excited about the prospect of handling the sale of the cottage."

"Aunt Georgina, I..."

"No, don't interrupt. I'm hurt and angry. When were you going to tell me you'd put the cottage up for sale?"

"I—"

She raised her hand to silence me again. "Of course, you can do anything you want. I understand that." She paused. "Have you even considered that you finally have family who cares about you? Isn't that what you've been searching for, Star?" She stopped talking and rose to leave.

"Don't you want to hear what I have to say?" I asked. I couldn't let her leave like this. I felt crushed. I hadn't realized how much my decision to sell the cottage would hurt Georgina.

"I'm listening."

"First of all, I haven't signed a contract with Moran Auctioneers or any other real estate agent. I haven't made a final decision yet. But I've never hidden the fact that I came to Ireland for the opportunity to search for my mother while selling Dylan's assets here."

Georgina sank back down onto the chair. "But I thought, once you'd been here and gotten to know us that you'd want to stay."

I didn't know what to say. I loved my connection to Georgina. I didn't want to hurt her in any way. But I had a business to run and responsibilities in the United States. Finally, I said, "You don't know how much it means to me that I've met you. I never suspected that Dylan had family. I really don't know yet what I'm going to do about this cottage, Georgina. But I do know that I love you." I stood up and walked over to her chair, where I planted a kiss on the top of her head. "Please, don't be angry. I didn't mean to hurt you. I'm deeply sorry."

"I know you're afraid of getting close to people, Star. It's understandable with all you've been through. But you need to begin allowing the people who are in your life now to be a real part of your life. You won't always lose those who love you."

I thought it best to leave it at that.

"I had dinner with Paul Doherty this evening," I said. "He's asked me to find a way to clear his father's reputation. I'm going to need your help."

"What can I do for you, agra?" Georgina's use of the Irish word for "dear" seemed to signal that she'd moved on from her anger, *at least for the moment.*

"Paul's parents may have been having financial issues. And, then there's someone named Noel Carney. I saw him at the pub the night Jane was killed. Dan Doherty claims Noel drove him home from there that night."

"I've heard the Dohertys might have strayed from each other once in a while. And Jimmy mentioned that Dan had money problems. But then who hasn't had them in the current financial crisis." Georgina shook her head. "What do you want me to do?"

"See if you can find out anything about Carney for me. He was pretty sauced when I saw him at the pub. I'm just wondering if he really drove Dan home or is just covering for him."

"Leave it with me. I know just who to talk to about Noel." Aunt Georgina rose and walked into the kitchen. I followed her and watched as she opened the back door and shut it quietly behind her.

I stood there for a long time. I'm not going to pretend I wasn't nervous about getting her involved in my amateur investigation. But I also knew that if I was going to be able to help Paul, I needed Georgina's knowledge of everyone in the county. I also knew that asking her to get involved was my way of telling her that she mattered in my life.

CHAPTER 18

Rudimentary Google searches the next morning turned up the same information *repeatedly*. Dan Doherty was the director of several limited liability companies, all in liquidation.

It was noon when I arrived in Cong. I went straight to Jane's fitness studio. Sarah was just finishing a class when I walked through the front door. I got right to the point.

"Was Jane having financial issues?" I asked.

Sarah's eyes lurched to a pile of papers on the reception desk. "The fitness studio is solvent. We aren't making a lot of profit, but we're able to pay our bills," she said.

"You don't sound overly confident about it, Sarah. What's going on?" I moved closer to the reception desk. I saw a Bank of Ireland letterhead sticking out of the pile. "Sarah, Paul has asked me to help him clear Dan's name. Don't you think Jane would want you to help?"

"I don't know. She still loved him despite..." Sarah stopped and bit her lip.

"If that's the case, then she would want you to tell me what you know. Jane is dead, Sarah. Strangled. Whoever did this probably knows you and knew Jane," I said. "Aren't you worried it could happen again?"

Sarah picked up a pile of towels from the floor and threw them into a laundry basket. She walked over to the desk. "Jane was worried lately. I didn't think anything of it, but then this came from the bank." Sarah pulled the paper with the bank letterhead from the pile and handed it to me. Addressed to Jane Doherty, it summarized the details regarding a new bank account. The account was held in Jane's name and a fictitious business name. "Of course, I asked her about it," Sarah said. "She handled all the finances. But she changed the studio's fictitious business name without even discussing it with me. I've always trusted her, but this just seemed so out of character for her."

"What did she say when you asked her about it?"

"Not too much," Sarah replied. "Only that she'd asked the bank manager to meet with her and Dan. She told me not to worry...that she was doing this for the good of the business." Sarah looked around at the studio walls. "I didn't know what to do. I let it drop. Now, I wish I hadn't. Maybe she'd still be alive."

"Did she meet with the bank manager?" I asked.

Sarah shook her head. "I don't think so. She never mentioned it again."

"Have you spoken with the bank since Jane was murdered?" I asked.

"No, I contacted Jimmy. He said he'd handle it," Sarah replied.

I looked at her in amazement. She'd just told me she was sorry she hadn't pressed Jane further, and now she was letting her other business partner, *the silent one*, take the lead. I refolded the bank letter and handed it back to her. "I know one thing for sure. If it were me, I'd go along with Jimmy when he has that meeting."

With that bit of advice, I left the studio and drove straight to Westport. One of Dan's limited liability companies, called Doherty's Consultants, listed an address in the town center. The office space for Doherty's Consultants turned out to be above a bike rental shop. A For Lease sign was propped in one of the office windows. The bike rental clerk couldn't tell me anything about the office space or how long it had been empty. I'd just stepped back outside when I spotted Noel Carney across the street. He locked the door to what looked like an apartment above a shop, hefted a large messenger bag over his shoulder, and got into a car. I jumped into my Renault and followed him. He drove straight to Cong but didn't stop on Main Street. Instead, he continued through town, onto a forest-lined road for several miles. He finally pulled off onto an unmarked drive that disappeared into the woods. I pulled over to the side of the road and got out of my car. Other than me, the road was deserted. I decided to follow Carney on foot. The driveway wound through the woods for perhaps a quarter of a mile before it opened up to a stone cottage situated on a clearing. The sudden burst of color provided by ivy geraniums brimming from hanging baskets startled me. Carney was at the back of his car, unloading a messenger bag.

"I don't think we've been introduced," I stated.

Carney swung around at the sound of my voice, dropping the bag to the ground, spilling its contents.

"I don't need an introduction. I know who you are." He stooped down to begin scooping what looked like seeds back into the bag.

I moved closer to see what exactly he was so focused on sweeping up with his hands. "What is that?" I asked.

"Seeds," he replied. "Now, if you don't mind, you're on private property. I have work to do."

"Is this your place?" I asked. I looked around at the cottage and neatly groomed landscaping. I could see a path from the backside of the cottage that led into the woods.

"That's none of your business. What do you want here, anyway?" he asked.

"Paul Doherty asked me to talk to some of Dan's friends. Paul's concerned that people may think his father murdered his mother. What do you think?"

Carney rose to his feet. He picked up the messenger bag, swung it over his shoulder, and turned to walk toward the cottage. "I think you should be careful about where you stick your nose. Dan was with me the night Jane was killed. That's all you or the garda, for that matter, need to know."

"What do you know about Doherty's Consulting?" I asked.

When he heard my question, he dropped the messenger bag, spilling the seeds again. He walked toward me, his fists clenched. "I don't know anything more than what I've told the garda and now you. Get out of here before I have you arrested for trespassing." He stood with his arms folded across his chest to watch me as I retraced my tracks to my car.

As soon as I got back to French Hill Cottage, I picked up the phone.

"I suppose you want this information yesterday," Jim Hipple stated.

After retiring from the New York City Police Department, Jim moved to Ridgewood and founded All Towns Investigations, Inc. We were next-door neighbors. Don't get me wrong, I still thought the police were inept, but when Dylan died, Jim had been supportive—not as a cop but as a friend. A licensed private investigator was as close as I'd gotten to making nice with the establishment. Jim had been helpful on more than one occasion. I wasn't going to pretend that asking him to look into the Doherty's bank accounts didn't leave a nasty taste in my mouth. It did. But I had to know what Jane was worried about. And, why Noel Carney reacted the way he did when I asked him about Dan's consulting company. Even as an information broker, there's a limit to how much data I can obtain. Usually, only law enforcement had access to banking information. It was times like this that I had to ask Jim for help. As an ex-cop, he had the contacts I needed.

"Yes, as much as you can learn as quickly as possible, Jim."

CHAPTER 19

The next morning, I was surprised to receive a handwritten note, dropped into the cottage's mail slot. I didn't recognize the ornate penmanship, nor had the sender provided a return address. Upon opening the envelope, I recognized the sender's name, Mrs. Maeve Baldwin. It was a request to meet her for tea at Ashford Castle *that day*. The note didn't indicate what she wanted to speak about with me. And, how had she gotten my address?

Several hours later, I was back in Cong. This time, instead of parking in town, I drove past Evelyn's cottage to the castle's visitor parking lot. Two young ladies greeted me inside the front door. When I told them I was meeting Mrs. Maeve Baldwin, they smiled, and one of them led me to a small sitting room on the main floor. There, I found Maeve. Today, her opera pearls were twisted into a double knot, close to her neck like a tie.

"I'm so glad you were able to join me," she said, indicating that I should sit on the sofa next to her.

"How did you know I'd show up?" I replied.

"Oh," – she waved her hand in dismissal – "I'm here for

lunch most days, so it didn't matter to me much if you showed up today or not."

"Well, I'm here. What did you want to talk to me about?" I asked.

"I want to know more about you, Star O'Brien," Maeve replied.

"Why is that?" I asked. Her words startled and put me on edge. A woman had been brutally murdered. I'd been attacked. Now, this stranger wanted to *know more about me.*

"Oh, please, just humor an old woman." She waved her hand again. "I spent several years in New York City in my younger days. My time in the Big Apple was wonderfully exhilarating. And, when I heard you're from the States, I wanted to know more about you. I don't often get to meet with people from across the pond, especially women who have a certain air."

"I don't know what you mean by that," I said. "But since I'm here, maybe you can answer some questions for me."

"It's a deal." She laughed. "I'll go first, of course."

"Go ahead," I said. She had a steeliness and, I must admit, pushiness that I admired. I wondered if she knew Aunt Georgina.

When she finally admitted she'd exhausted her questions, most of which focused on my adoptive parents, where I went to school, and my life as an information broker, I asked her again about Paul, Dan, Jane, Noel Carney, and why it seemed that Evelyn Cosgrove had abandoned the dig she started.

"I don't know anything about the Cosgrove girl, other than what I told you before," she stated. "As for the others, Paul is a lovely lad. He's done a wonderful job with getting the young school children involved in local history." She reached forward to take a sip of tea from the tray someone had brought in while we were talking.

"He's asked me to speak to people about what happened to

his mother. He's worried his father is getting blamed for Jane's murder."

"Dan's got a reputation for the women, all right. But I don't think he'd kill anyone over it." She brushed a scone crumb from her lap.

"Was he involved with anyone in particular?" I asked.

"I don't know the details of his personal life. But, going down that route with your investigation seems to be a waste of time. He has an alibi for the night Jane was murdered. Noel Carney was with him."

"How do you know that?" I asked.

"I know Noel. And if he said he was with Dan, then he was with him."

"Really, you know Noel that well?" I said.

"Yes, since he was a wee lad. He's a good egg."

Somehow, this statement didn't align with the image I had of a threatening guy with bags of seed. "What's he doing with the satchels of seeds?" I asked.

"He's restoring the native woodlands!" Maeve's eyes widened as she explained further. "He works for the forestry, and one of his duties involves reforestation. I suppose, coming from the States, you think more of land development rather than restoration."

I ignored her last comment, choosing to remain focused on Noel Carney and Dan Doherty. "It's surprising that a man who restores the land is a drinking partner with someone who owns a sawmill," I commented.

Maeve didn't respond. Instead, she picked up her napkin, wiped her lips, and said, "When Lady Marcella described you as independent and feisty, she wasn't far from it."

I shook my head. Did she just refer to Lorcan's mother? "You know Marcella McHale?" I asked.

"Well, of course, I do. That's how I knew where you live, my dear."

Boy! I guess I'd assumed a little too quickly that she'd gotten my address from one of my cards.

"Now," Maeve said, "I must go, but I've enjoyed our chat. Perhaps we'll be able to do it again sometime."

I'd been dismissed.

I headed straight to The Davitt Restaurant in Castlebar, where I sequestered myself in one of the velvet-lined booths at the back. It didn't take long for Aunt Georgina to show up after I phoned her.

"Do you know a Maeve Baldwin?" I asked as soon as Georgina sat down.

"No" – she shook her head – "should I?"

"She knows Lorcan's mother. And she seems to want to know a lot about me." I dropped my iPhone onto the table when I realized I'd been clenching it.

"Could it be this Maeve person is just curious about you? Villages like Cong notice when an American comes around asking questions about the residents. I can ask Marcella about her if you like."

"That's a good idea." Maybe Maeve was naturally inquisitive. But I wasn't so sure her questions were mere nosiness. "With everything that's happened, it won't hurt to verify her story."

Georgina leaned in over the table. "I have something to tell you." The server arrived, and we placed our order before Georgina spoke again. "Noel Carney's family used to own Rose Cottage."

"Yes" – I nodded – "Paul told me the family immigrated years ago."

"But did he tell you why?" Georgina asked. "It's an awful story. Noel Carney's father had an alcohol problem. One night, when he was drinking heavily in a pub, he lost a bet to Dan Doherty. He lost the cottage!" Georgina shook her head. "The entire family left Cong. Some went to the United States; some went to England. Noel's parents are dead now, but he's since come back to Cong on assignment from the Department of Agriculture." Georgina leaned back from the table.

I considered what she'd just told me. Why in heaven's name would Noel give Dan Doherty an alibi? Or was it the other way around? Why hadn't Paul told me the details? Before I had a chance to say anything more, my cell phone rang.

"This Doherty character is in debt up to his eyeballs." Jim Hipple's voice sounded like the cop he used to be.

"How much?" I asked.

"He cleaned out a joint account, and he's taken out high-interest loans. My contact didn't give me figures but said it could be a motive in the wife's death. Oh, and one of his limited liability companies is some kind of land development venture."

"Thanks, Jim." I hung up in a hurry.

"Who was that?" Georgina asked.

"It was the office." I didn't say anymore because I didn't want to get her more involved than she already was. "Thanks for finding out about Noel Carney, Georgina. The information is very helpful. I'll have to ask Paul about it." I dropped a few euros on the table to cover the check for our tea. "I'm heading back to the cottage to follow up on some emails. And, Ashford's home alone. Hopefully, he hasn't remodeled the place."

We left the restaurant together. Georgina headed up Main Street, and I ran to my car. I had to talk to the police!

CHAPTER 20

I almost collided with Noel Carney outside the door of the Castlebar Police Station. In his haste, he bumped against me and continued toward the curb. I followed him.

"Just a minute," I stated.

He kept walking, but I wasn't giving up. When I grabbed his elbow, he finally stopped. "What do you want?" he asked through compressed lips.

"I know your history with Rose Cottage."

"Didn't I tell you to mind your own business?" He nervously glanced at the door to the police station, when a few officers walked through to a police car parked at the curb. "Get out of my life, woman, or you'll regret it."

"Do the police know about Rose Cottage?" I asked. "I think they'd find it interesting in the investigation of Jane Doherty's murder."

"You've got this all wrong. I don't give a damn about what my father did. That's old history. But I do care about protecting the environment. And I don't need some nosy Yank stirring up dirt that could get me pulled from this assignment."

"Yes, Maeve told me about the reforestation work, which

seems very noble of you. But if that's the case, why are you palling around with Dan Doherty?"

"Haven't you ever heard of keeping your enemies close, Ms. O'Brien?" Noel asked.

The police had driven off, but Carney continued to shift his gaze from me to the street between the police station and library.

"Is that what you were doing the night I saw you at the pub?" I asked.

"Oh, yeah, I remember you. I wasn't that drunk. And, yes, I keep an eye on Dan from time to time. But not for the reason you think. I moved on from my father's losses long ago." Carney paused to exhale slowly. "Rose Cottage isn't anything more than a pile of stones to me. Now, you'll have to excuse me. My ride is here."

Carney turned and strode toward the Toyota Prius, which had quietly appeared at the curb. As soon as he got into the car, it accelerated. But not before my eyes caught a glimpse of the back of the driver's cropped gray hair and a strand of pearls. Could it be Maeve Baldwin? In the dim twilight, it was difficult to be sure. I leaned forward in an effort to get a closer look, but by then, the car and its occupants were too far away.

The thought of Maeve Baldwin brought back our recent conversation. I was still puzzled as to why she'd taken such an interest in me. But if it were her whom I'd just seen, maybe Aunt Georgina was correct in thinking Mauve's questions were motivated by events in Cong.

Determined to confront the police, I turned my attention back to the building behind me. After I stated the purpose of my visit, the policewoman on duty made a call, and within a few minutes, guided me to a conference room. Detectives O'Shea and Keenan sat at a desk with a pile of papers in front of them.

"Miss O'Brien, what can we do for you this evening? You

haven't been on any walks recently, have you?" O'Shea might have been trying to be funny, but I noted a certain tiredness in his voice.

"It's more like what I can do for you," I stated. "I want you to know what I overheard the night Jane Doherty was murdered."

O'Shea sighed. "Believe me, Miss O'Brien, we are working this case. You don't need to be involved."

I didn't care whether they wanted to listen. I was going to have my say.

"I heard an argument between Jane and Dan Doherty at the pub in the Neale. Are you aware of that? She threw the contents of a beer glass in his face before she stormed out of the pub. Have you looked at their bank records? Dan's been siphoning money from their joint accounts." I stopped speaking to gauge whether they were surprised by what I'd said.

Keenan stood and picked up the papers from the table. Before he left the room, he nodded to O'Shea and said, "I'll see you in the morning."

O'Shea invited me to sit down. I remained standing.

"I saw Noel Carney leaving the station just now. Was he here to talk to you about Dan?"

O'Shea sighed. "No, Miss O'Brien; he was here to make a report for another reason. You may not believe this, but some citizens are on good terms with the garda."

"Is that so?" I didn't wait for his reply, continuing instead. "Paul told me Noel Carney drove Dan home the night Jane was killed. I'd think you'd want to talk to Carney."

"That's correct, Miss O'Brien. We have confirmed Mr. Carney's view of what happened that evening. He's in the clear." The scar over O'Shea's eye seemed to deepen when he continued. "Miss O'Brien, we're not big fans of amateur detectives, especially in cases where a murder's been committed. I appreciate you wanting to share what you observed; however, we are overworked. We don't have the time or resources to pursue all angles of a case. But I can assure you we are focused on finding this killer." O'Shea's eyes drilled into mine. "I can't say this any more strongly, Miss O'Brien. Don't get involved. Now, I'd like to finish up on some paperwork in my office." He stood and opened the room door. "I'll walk you out *now*."

Darkness had settled in since I'd entered the police station. The evening's commuting traffic had dwindled. Streetlamps cast murky silhouettes on the wet macadam. From where I stood, I could see the library's lights. Thinking again of Maeve Baldwin, I headed toward the building's glass doors. When I inquired at the front desk, I was surprised to learn I was speaking to the director, Ivan Hemlock.

"Oh, I take over in the evenings. The staff gets to go home, and I get to talk to some of our patrons. Something I love to do." Ivan smiled. "Now. You say Maeve Baldwin referred you to me?" His voice held a question.

"Yes, I'm researching a woman named Maggie O'Malley. I believe she was born on Achill Island around the nineteen sixties. Maeve thought the library's archives might hold old records like marriage or birth certificates."

Ivan's cheeks billowed while he contemplated my request. "Well, we don't have any information like that here. I know Maeve. She's a respected historian. I just can't imagine why she'd point you here, though. I mean, the best place for the research you're doing is the National Archives."

"So, you don't have local parish records here?"

He shook his head. "No, and I'm sorry you had to come out on this damp evening for nothing."

"Thank you," I said.

A pouring, bone-chilling rain fell as I departed the building. My heart and soul felt as bleak as the weather. I ran to my car and escaped to French Hill. Ashford's joyous bark when I came through the door shook me out of my melancholy. After a meal of scrambled eggs and an herbal tea, he and I sat in the living room. A blazing turf fire burned in the grate. When I reached for my notebook, I ended up drawing mind maps. With Jane as the centerpiece, the spokes and circles emanating outward contained the names and possible motivations of everyone I'd met who knew Jane. Dan Doherty's name was the first on my list. He was with her at the pub the night before she was killed, and they were arguing. But was that motive enough for murder? No, lots of couples argue. But financial shenanigans most definitely could be. I immediately eliminated Paul; my intuition told me he just couldn't hurt anyone. Jane's partners in the fitness center, Sarah and Jimmy, would have had a motive if Jane were about to mortgage the place in order to bail out Dan's debt. Ann Ryan, from what I'd observed, had plenty of motive. She wanted Dan and, most likely, the sale of his cottage. I put her second on my list, right after Dan. Then I considered Luke Ryan and his obvious anger issues. Was it all because of a will? Which led me to Pat O'Malley. She seemed caught up in her farm and fighting Luke's attempts to overturn Jake Ryan's will. Did she know about Jake's supposed affair with Jane? I put her at the top of my list, along with Dan and Ann. Ben O'Malley, although unfriendly, didn't seem that interested in anything or anybody but his books. I kept him on the list because I felt sure he knew how to reach Evelyn Cosgrove but wasn't telling me. And, although I had no idea whether she was tied into Jane's murder, I included the mysterious Evelyn on my list.

Now, I added Maeve Baldwin. She'd sent me on a wild goose chase to the library. Why was she so interested in me? And, so protective of Noel Carney? Which brought me to Noel Carney. The police seemed to have eliminated him as a suspect. If so, what had he been doing at the police station? I put him at the bottom of my list. Then, I looked at the map I'd just drawn. Like most family members, Paul didn't want to accept what the police might find. He wanted an outside party to find the *real culprit.* I didn't know if I'd be able to do that for Paul; Dan just looked guilty to me. When the piles of turf finally burned down to glowing red embers mixed with gray ash, I headed to bed, exhausted and more than a little uncomfortable that I'd have to tell Paul about his father's financial infidelity—the perfect motivation to commit murder. But then I would soon learn that things never turn out as expected.

CHAPTER 21

T he next morning, the lightly frosted grass sparkled under the sun's rays. Without a breath of wind, the cloudless blue sky seemed like it could become a permanent fixture. I tidied up the cottage and put my office back together now that my new computer had been delivered. After checking my inbox, I made a list of action items for Ellie and Phillie. Satisfied that my emails were in the sent queue, I made a note to phone Phillie later in the day. Maybe she'd be able to unearth Evelyn's cell phone number and have an answer about the questions I'd emailed the night before.

I shook my head, thinking about all the cases the Consulting Detective handled in a year. From experience, I knew the only way to get information about Evelyn's whereabouts would be from someone who knew her or from public records if they existed. Both of these avenues could be untrustworthy and difficult to access. I'd have to provide lawful reasons why I wanted personal information to anyone I asked.

Ashford's barks beckoned me to the back door where I'd left him on the cement patio, basking in the warm sunshine. Now he stood on his hind legs, tail wagging, front paws planted on Lorcan's chest. I paused and watched the two of them playing.

Lorcan's eyes met mine, and for an instant, I relished the domestic scene.

"I didn't expect to see you," I said after I opened the back door.

Lorcan gave Ashford a final pat on the head and brushed the dog hair from his shirt. "I'm on my way to Dublin for a meeting myself, but thought I'd stop by to see how you made out with the repairs." He looked over my shoulder into the kitchen. "I see the window was replaced. Are the phone lines working?"

"Yes, as a matter of fact, since last night," I said. I stepped back into the kitchen and waved him inside.

"No." He shook his head. "I can't stay, but I'll call you later." He glanced at his watch, adding, "I'm already behind schedule." His blue eyes smiled at me over his pewter-rimmed glasses. "How about meeting up with me this evening for supper at Johnny McHale's pub?"

"Okay," I replied, feeling cheered at the thought of having company. Besides, his knowledge of some of the people in Cong would be useful as I tried to help Paul. If he still wanted my help, that is. He hadn't called as promised. I was sure of that —I'd checked my cell and landline a million times.

"I'll pick you up at 8:00 p.m.," Lorcan said. Then he disappeared around the gable of the house.

A short time later, I packed up my knapsack, and with Ashford along for the ride, we set out for Cong. I intended to keep asking questions. I left my car in the parking lot across from the Augustinian cemetery, headed toward the woods, and found the sign pointing the way to Happy Trails. As for Ashford, I had no idea where he had bolted to after I opened the car door. Wider, muddy, and rutted from horse traffic, this branch of the path seemed to drive deeper into the woods. Pulling my iPhone from its holster, I checked the time. It was getting late. I needed to check in with Ellie, but the time difference worked in my favor. Weighing my options, I turned onto the path leading to Jake Ryan's and Pat O'Malley's stud farm.

As I walked, I recalled the times Dylan and I meandered around the duck pond in Ridgewood with Skipper at our side —a simple pleasure but one we treasured. One which often ended in a stop for a scoop of Van Dyk's German Chocolate Crunch ice cream. I missed Dylan and wished he'd told me about French Hill. I understood why he hadn't. But still.

When I reached the gate to Happy Trails, I saw a solitary white stallion munching a patch of grass with unbridled focus in one of the fenced fields. I gazed at nature's simplicity with eyes that never ceased to be amazed at this island's beauty. Happy Trails seemed to blend into the landscape. Solid, practical, and unpretentious came to mind as I stepped up to the intercom system and asked to speak to Pat O'Malley. The gate swung open.

I found Pat in one of the stalls, smoothing the coat of a horse whose chestnut hair glistened in the waning afternoon light. Pat's hair was tucked up into a baseball cap; the Happy Trails logo emblazoned across the front. She wore a red plaid work shirt held in place by faded jeans. Carhartt boots completed her ensemble. If I hadn't met her previously, I'd have mistaken her slender profile for one of the male horse groomers.

"Mrs. O'Malley. We met before in Ben's shop."

Pat gave a final stroke with the brush she held in her hand. Then she left the stall, dropped her gloves onto a workbench, and gripped my hand in greeting. Her hand transmitted a force in contrast to her diminutive stature.

"Yes, I remember you. I guess you want to know about the O'Malleys," she replied. My face must have communicated my surprise because she went on to explain. "My son, Ben, told me about your interest in the O'Malley family. How can I help you?"

I hadn't expected her question. Stepping back for a moment, I considered her request. "Yes, my mother's disappearance. Unfortunately, Ireland is dense with O'Malleys. I know she came from the Achill area. But beyond that, I haven't been successful in finding a trace of her or any relatives."

Taking in my flats, capris, and pink sweater, Pat smiled. "You're not dressed for a stable yard. Come on, let's go up to the house and have a hot cup of tea."

I followed her along a mulched path that opened up to a circular drive. The stone-faced house, perched on a rise, overlooked beds of heather. After a short climb around chunks of boulders lining the stone steps, we walked around to the back of the house and entered the kitchen through a wooden door. It didn't take Pat long to decorate the center of an immense planked table with mugs, a hot water filled carafe, tea bags, and raisin scones.

"So," she said, plunking herself onto one of the four chairs surrounding the nicked and stained furniture, "you're interested in the O'Malleys."

For now, I decided not to reveal the real reason I sought her out.

"Yes. I'm interested in anything or anyone who might be helpful in my search for my mother. I think I mentioned when I met you in Ben's shop that I'm looking for Evelyn Cosgrove. I believe she may have information about my mother."

"Of course, I know Evelyn. I'm not sure, but Ben might have dated her." Crumbling a bit of scone onto her plate, she laughed. "As much as he dates anyone these days. He's preoccupied with the bookstore. He never has time to develop any lasting relationships." She paused, tilting her head at me as she smiled again. "In fact, the way he spoke about you, I thought he might have asked you out, Miss O'Brien."

I nodded. "I haven't met Evelyn, but she's been posting questions on an ancestry thread about a Maggie O'Malley. My mom is Maggie O'Malley. I've been trying to contact Evelyn, but no one seems to know where she is."

In between bites of scone, Pat responded. "Yes, that sounds like Evelyn. She hasn't lived in Cong for too long. She keeps to herself and disappears for weeks at a time. Acts very mysterious. Although I think it's just a pose." She paused as if considering what she'd just said. "I think she might be trying to protect herself."

"Self-defense? From what?"

Remembering Sarah's mention of Evelyn's concern with strength, I wondered whether physical or emotional fears motivated her need for shielding.

"Being misjudged. People thinking because you're a woman, you won't or can't handle the job." Pat laughed. "She's in a tough field. Competition and politics are rampant in these government positions. Which historically, I might add, have been weighted too much to the opposite gender." She offered me another scone before helping herself to a second. "Look at me. People thought I wouldn't be able to take care of Happy Trails after Jake died. But they're coming to realize how capable and strong I am, Miss O'Brien."

"You and Jake were together for a long time," I said.

Her gaze shifted to several jackets and sweaters tossed on top of brown cardboard boxes.

Her eyes turned to me. "As you can see, I'm in the process of gathering up Jake's belongings for the charity shop." She paused to take a deep breath. "Jake asked me to join him when Sean, my husband, died. Sean was a schoolteacher. I was working here as a part-time stable hand at the time. Jake and Ann were in the process of splitting up." She stopped twisting the paper napkin she'd picked up after finishing the scone. "I didn't initiate it, but Jake and I...well, it just seemed right. Ben and I moved in. I missed Sean. Ben was just beginning secondary school. Jake was wonderful with Ben. And Ben adored him. We never married, but we felt like family." Dropping the shredded remnants of the napkin on the table, she sighed. "Here I am again. Alone. But I'm grateful to have known the love of two men in my life. And Ben's been so supportive since Jake died." Shifting in her seat, she shook her head and focused her eyes on me. "But I digress. You wanted to speak to me about the O'Malleys. I'm afraid I'm not going to be much help. Sean wasn't from the Achill area, and I lost touch with his siblings over the years."

"What about Evelyn? Any idea where she might be?" I asked.

"If Ben or Paul don't know, I don't think you'll find anyone else who would."

"I suppose you're right," I replied. At that point in the conversation, I knew I had to get to digging into what Pat might know about Jane. "Were you and Jane friends?" I asked.

Pat glanced at the cardboard boxes and Jake's clothing again before she replied, "I just don't understand what happened to Jane. This village used to be a quiet place. Everyone got along. But since Jake died." She shook her head in denial. "I just don't know. Everything's crazy. Even Luke. He's threatening to break Jake's will." She looked around the kitchen, her eyes taking in the trophies that lined the shelves over the fireplace, the baseball hats hanging on pegs inside the kitchen door, the horse breeder magazines scattered on a small table between the lounge chairs. "I've worked hard. I'm stronger than they think. That will can't be broken. They won't displace me."

I reached for two tea bags and plunked one into each of our mugs, taking my time to pour the hot water from the carafe. Then I brought up the letter I'd given to Paul. "Mrs. O'Malley, I found a letter. And, it seems to indicate that Jake had an affair with Jane."

"A letter? Where is it? I want to see it," she demanded. Her spine seemed to have stiffened as much as the oak chair she sat on.

"I don't have it. I gave it to Paul."

"I don't understand. Where did you get a letter like that?"

"I found it in a book I bought the day I saw you and Ben in the bookshop."

She shook her head. "You want me to believe you found a letter about Jane and Jake that you can't even show to me."

"Because of the personal nature of the letter, I thought it best to return it to Ben. But he didn't want it. In fact, he refused to take it. Instead, I gave it to Paul. I recommended he show it to the police."

"Ben knows?" Her blue eyes widened. This time, the tears rolled down her face. "I didn't want him to know."

"I'm sorry, but I couldn't just destroy the letter. I thought it best to return it to Ben." I didn't say anymore because I just couldn't fix what I hadn't broken. The truth had to come out.

Pat's shoulders slumped, and her body seemed to shrink several sizes as she wiped tears from her face with the backs of her calloused hands. "Yes, Jake and Jane were having...had a relationship. Jake played around. I've known for years. I overlooked it. But Ben. He loved Jake...loves this place. I didn't want Ben to know. I just wanted things to be like they used to be."

"Do you think the affair with Jake had anything to do with Jane's murder?" I asked.

Her knuckles paled from the grip she tightened around the tea mug. "Jane and I were best friends since we were young girls at the secondary school. We knew each other's secrets. I wasn't happy about what went on between her and Jake. But she was lonely and insecure. And Jake. Well, I'd accepted his infidelities long ago." She shifted her body in the chair, sat up straighter, and wiped away the flow of tears. "If anyone had any reason to kill Jane, it was Dan. He always wants to be the center of attention. His ego wouldn't have been able to take Jane's interest in another man."

My iPhone pierced the tension in the air with sounds of Presto—Phillie's ring tone. Rescuing the phone from its holster, I rose from the table, apologized to Pat, and said I had to take the call. Like a coiled spring released from its tension, she sprang from her chair and strode to the door with me.

"I have to get back to the horses. I hope you find your mother. I really do."

As the door closed behind me, I heard her take a deep breath that ended in a sob. I turned my attention to Phillie. "Phillie, hold on a few minutes. I want to move away from where I am right now."

"Okay, boss," she replied. When I'd walked well out of earshot of Pat's house, I asked, "Did you get the info I wanted?"

"Yes, and I can tell you the inheritance laws in Ireland are way different than the States."

"Phillie, just give me the explanation."

"Okay, boss. In Ireland, if you die without a will, your assets go to the spouse, who inherits two-thirds of the estate, and the remaining third is divided equally between your children."

"What if the person has a will?" I asked.

"Yeah, it gets even more complicated. If you're not married, you only inherit if you are left a bequest, but the spouse is entitled to what is called a legal right share. And, oh, the kids are affected as well."

I'd been walking along the path back toward Ashford Castle while Phillie spoke but stopped when the gravity of Pat O'Malley's situation sank in. No wonder she was worried. Luke Ryan might have a chance of overturning his father's will. "Okay, Phillie. Thanks for the update. I'll talk to you later."

I reemerged from the castle's driveway into Cong just before the start of the 1:00 p.m. lunch hour. Looking around, I realized I was the sole occupant of the street. Shaking away the feeling that I was being watched, I walked into the café and scanned the bustling room for a seat.

The same person who'd served me the last time guided me to a table where one of four chairs stood empty and planted a steaming mug of tea in front of me. I nodded a greeting to the other three occupants of the table, recognizing one of them as Luke Ryan.

I still hadn't gotten used to the Irish custom of strangers sharing tables in crowded restaurants. But with just about everyone in the village choosing the Quiet Man Café as their favorite eating place, I didn't have much choice. Besides, I couldn't have done better at getting everyone together than if I'd sent out party invitations.

"Now, what can I get ya? We've vegetable soup, sandwiches, and" – she paused to look over at the blackboard with its list of specials – "there's still some lamb stew left in the pot."

As I poured milk into the tea mug, I glanced up at her. "Brown bread and vegetable soup will do it. And I'm wondering if Dan Doherty's been here today?"

"He should be here soon. He and Ann meet up every day. Discussing real estate issues." She laughed as the bell over the café's door heralded more arrivals. "Well, now, speak of the devil." Winking, she turned to seat Dan and Ann at a table for two.

Not far behind them trailed Pat and Ben O'Malley. That was a surprise. I guess she'd finished up quickly in the barn. Next came a group of people wearing postal uniforms—one of whom was Tom.

It didn't take long for the server to clear the debris left by customers who'd finished up their meals, seat the new arrivals, and deposit my food order in front of me. While I waited for the vegetable soup to cool, I concentrated on studying the people around me, including Luke, who seemed rooted in place as he too stared at the occupants of the café.

"Is the restaurant always this crowded?" I asked him.

"What?" His eyes turned to me for a moment before moving back to survey the room. The hands at the end of his muscular arms clenched the knife and fork he'd used to finish the lamb stew he was eating when I sat down.

"The café seems like a popular place," I said, adding, "especially for businesspeople." I nodded toward the other tables.

His eyes narrowed as they moved to scrutinize me. "I've seen you around town in the last few days. Are you on holiday?"

"No, I'm looking for someone named Evelyn Cosgrove. She lives on Abbey Street, but it appears she's the one on vacation. Do you know her?" I said as I poured more tea from the pot on the table into my mug.

"She's the one who's involved with that archeological site out at Rose Cottage, right?" His eyes opened wider as he took a closer look at me. "Do you have anything to do with the dig? Are you an inspector?" He fired his questions across the table at me.

"No, and I'm not an inspector," I shot back. "Why would that matter?"

"Humph," he grunted. "Everything that touches or comes near Happy Trails stud farm is my business." He raised his voice, glaring across the room at Pat.

"Why is that?" I asked.

"It should be mine. By rights, it should be mine. And by God, it will be." His words ricocheted throughout the dining area. Then, throwing his tableware to the ground, he stomped out, jostling Jimmy Mahoney on his way into the café. The momentary silence ended—pierced by the clatter of utensils against plates and the chatter as people leaned toward each other to talk.

Seeing me, Jimmy slid into Luke's seat. "I want to explain," he said.

I nodded in agreement and waited.

"I didn't mean to shut Georgina out or hide anything." Rubbing his hands on the pressed pants that hung over the paint-stained boots he'd been wearing at Aunt Georgina's, he continued. "I didn't think it was that important. I'm just a businessman."

"Georgina's a successful entrepreneur too. She understands how business works. But she's hurt that you didn't think to tell her."

"Aye, you're probably right." Slumping down in his chair, he looked directly at me before adding, "Do you think she'll ever talk to me again?"

"Aunt Georgina? Of course, she will" – I laughed – "provided you tell me whatever you know about Evelyn and Jane."

"I've already told anything I have to tell." His shrug punctuated his point. "Jane approached me several years ago for capital to put into renovating the exercise studio. She had a good business head, that one. I agreed. That's all there is to the story." Glancing over at Dan and Ann, he leaned forward and said, "It's too bad the husband didn't realize just how smart she was."

Before I could ask another question, my phone rang. Hoping it was Paul, I answered by the second ring.

"This is Star."

"Miss O'Brien, it's Dr. Treat."

"I thought it would take more time to do the analysis."

"I had the lab rush the tests. Your instincts were correct. The nugget contains gold."

"Okay. What's going to happen now?" I asked.

"Do you remember where you found the specimen?" Dr. Treat asked. "I'd like to send an engineer to examine the area."

"Yes, I found it on the grounds of an abandoned house," I replied. "Specifically, the house is called Rose Cottage, located near the village of Cong."

"Do you think you can meet the engineer there and show him the cottage? It could save a lot of time."

"Sure, as a matter of fact, I'm in Cong now," I replied, glancing at the time on my phone. "Do you think someone can get here later today before it gets too dark?"

"That's wonderful news. Let me go call the engineer now."

"Dr. Treat, before you rush off the phone, I have another question."

"Go ahead, Ms. O'Brien."

"The site's archeological dig is being led by someone named Evelyn Cosgrove. Do you think you need to contact her before the engineer disturbs her work?" I held my breath as I waited for his answer. This might be a way to reach her. "She works for Dr. O'Dowd in the archeological branch of the national museum. She might be able to help you."

"O'Dowd." Dr. Treat chuckled. "We go way back, Ms. O'Brien. If experience is any indication, she won't want to agree, but I don't need to contact her or ask for permission. My department has jurisdiction now."

"You're sure? I wouldn't want to ruin any historical artifacts." I tried to keep the disappointment out of my voice.

"Not to worry, Ms. O'Brien. Now, I'll go and get this project started."

The call ended.

CHAPTER 22

Even though I felt crushed that my question didn't get me anywhere near getting a contact number for Evelyn, I knew I had to act. First, I needed to talk to Paul. He should know about the gold nugget. I also wanted to ask him again if he'd had any luck tracking down a cell phone number for Evelyn. I apologized to Jimmy for leaving, rose, and walked to the cash register to pay my bill just as Dan and Ann finished up at their table.

I was outside, standing on the sidewalk when Dan called after me. "I overheard you mention Rose Cottage." Then he raised a fist to me before shouting, "Stay away from that place, or else."

Before I could respond, my phone rang again. This time it was Phillie. I turned my back on Dan and walked farther away from the café.

"Hi, boss, I've got some news." The excitement in her voice vibrated across the connection.

"Go ahead. I'm ready."

"Evelyn's maiden name is O'Malley. Cosgrove is her married name." There was a pause on both sides of the connection as Phillie waited for me to respond. Hearing that

Evelyn bore the ubiquitous O'Malley name was like a punch to the gut. She was the one slim thread that might lead to finding my mother. Maybe I'd be able to find Evelyn Cosgrove. Finding Evelyn *O'Malley* was probably quite another story.

"Boss, did you hear me?" Phillie asked.

"Yes. Where did you unearth this? Is she still married? Does she have children?" Perhaps I could contact her husband. Was he an archeologist? Was she visiting him somewhere? The possibilities were endless.

"Her husband disappeared not long after they married." Phillie rattled through the information quickly. "No children. Lived in London before moving to Cong."

"London?"

"Yes, I combed through Ireland's museum office of publications to look for her name. I found a research paper authored by an Evelyn O'Malley about an exhibition at the Museum of London. I searched for the article and found the author's biography. She attended Trinity College" – Phillie paused to take a breath – "all I had to do then was look up the exhibition information, and the rest followed."

"What happened to her husband?" I asked.

"Don't know. Newspaper accounts just note that a young archeological student reported her husband missing when she went to meet him at a local pub after work."

"Send it all to me, Phillie. Whatever you found. The paper, the newspaper accounts, any pictures. I want it all."

"Sure thing, boss." The line went dead.

Impatient for action and knowing it would be hours before Dr. Treat's engineer would arrive, I tried phoning Paul again. This time, he answered.

"Is everything okay?" I asked. "I've tried calling several times."

"Sorry, Star, but I" – he hesitated before continuing – "I

meant to call you, but I just had to have it out with my father first."

"You did? When? I just saw him in the café with Ann. He seemed angry. Told me to stay away from Rose Cottage."

"That cottage! I wish he'd gotten rid of the thing years ago."

"Paul, someone from Dublin's environmental studies group is on the way here to look at the area around the cottage."

"What? Why?" The sound of his voice rose with each question.

"Do you remember when I was pushed into the well? Earlier that evening, I picked up a stone near the cottage. It looked unusual, so I took it to Dublin to be analyzed."

"No." Paul's terse response sounded desperate. "You've got to call them. You've got to stop them. My father...he didn't kill my mother. I... He's innocent... My mother..."

"Paul, slow down," I said. "What about your mother?"

"You've got to help him. He's innocent. I can't say anything more. My mother...argument near the priest's hole...woods. I'll call you later."

"Wait. Where are you? I'll come meet you."

The only response I got to my question was dial tone. He may have ended the call, but my concern for him was far from over. He sounded terrified. He must have learned something about his mother's murder since the last time I'd spoken to him. And what did it have to do with the visit from the engineer? *So, where do I go from here*? I had to do something. I couldn't stand around, waiting for the engineer to arrive. I had to get to Paul. I rang his number again, but he didn't pick up.

After placing my phone back into its holster, I drove over to the Neale to continue my interrupted conversation with Jimmy. I found him in the bar area, organizing bottles and glasses for the evening.

"What happened to you?" he asked as he polished a wine glass with a white towel.

"I'm sorry, but I had to make an important call."

"Can I get you anything?" he asked.

"No, but I'm still wondering if you know anything else about Jane or Evelyn that might be helpful." I twirled one of the bar coasters as I continued. "It just seems they're connected in some way, but I can't figure it out."

"I don't know anything more than what I already told you and Georgina. The studio was going well; otherwise, I wouldn't have gone into partnership with Jane. But she had issues at home. This time, it was more than relationship troubles. Dan likes to spend money. It turns out he was cheating on Jane in more ways than one."

"She told you about the bank statements, didn't she?" I asked.

"Yes, she did. But she didn't want my help. She planned to meet with the bank manager and Dan. But conveniently, she was murdered before any of that happened." Jimmy swiped the counter with the towel he held. "Pretty solid motive for murder, if you ask me."

"Were you the only other partner in the studio?" I asked. If Jane had money troubles, she might have looked for additional investors.

"I wouldn't have gotten involved if other people were in on the deal. Too complicated to manage those types of relationships," Jimmy said. "I already have enough headaches managing the pub's suppliers. Just the other day, some distributor thought he could pressure me concerning a particular brand." Jimmy laughed. "I told him to take a hike. In fact, I think you caught me in the middle of it when you rang."

"What about Evelyn? She attended Jane's exercise studio. Was she ever mentioned? Did you ever meet her?"

"No, lass. I don't know her." He studied me from across the bar that separated us. "I'm sorry, but I can't help you with the search for your mother," he stated flatly.

I didn't want to admit it to myself, but searching for my mother was the least of my worries at the moment. *That* would have to take a back seat until I tracked down Paul. Was this why Paul wanted to keep the engineer away? Had Paul convinced his father to sell the place because they needed the money? Maybe Paul thought more excavating would delay the sale. Thanking Jimmy, I rose from the barstool, walked to the car, and started the drive back to Cong. Glancing at the dashboard clock, I sped up, hoping the engineer might be there by now. If not, I'd return to Rose Cottage alone.

CHAPTER 23

Back on Main Street in Cong, I parked the car, put on the wellingtons, and turned to cross over the street toward the woods. My phone rang. I grabbed it from its holster—hoping it was Paul.

"Paul…"

"Paul?" Lorcan's voice interrupted me.

"Paul said he'd call. I thought you were him."

"Is everything okay?" Lorcan asked. "Where are you?"

"I'm standing on Main Street in Cong. I'm supposed to meet an engineer from Dublin. But I'm about to go looking for Paul Doherty."

"Star, what's going on?" Lorcan didn't waste words on lengthy questions.

"I spoke with Paul earlier. He sounded distraught. He hasn't answered my calls, and I don't know where he is."

"Stay where you are. I'll meet you there." I could hear the worry in Lorcan's voice.

"No. I can't wait. And, obviously, I won't be able to go to dinner with you this evening." I paced while I thought about what to do next. "Call Georgina for me and tell her I'm okay."

"Star, you shouldn't go back into the woods alone. Not after what's happened in the last week."

"Sorry, Lorcan. I have to go."

The lights were on in Ben's Rarities as I walked past. Thinking about my calls with Paul and Phillie, I turned on a dime and strode through the door—Ben was alone in the shop. It was time to demand answers.

"Ms. O'Brien, I've already told you that I don't know Evie's phone number..."

"Did you know she was married? That her maiden name was O'Malley?" I interrupted.

"No. I've only known her as Cosgrove." He moved from behind his desk and began tidying a jumble of books that lay on the floor.

"When Paul and I had lunch the other day, he suggested I ask you about the O'Malley collection of letters and documents you've compiled in your library. Why didn't you offer to help when I first told you about my search for my mother?"

Dust motes floated through the air. He picked up a book and looked at its title before placing it on the shelf.

"Do you think you're the first person, the first Yank, to come in here asking questions about their ancestors?" He grunted, turning now to face me. "Time-wasters, that's all ye are." Pausing to read the title of the next book he lifted from the floor, he continued. "Time and money. Ye all want to reminisce and romanticize the past. I'll bet you haven't even read the book you bought the other day."

"I haven't had time..."

Not letting me finish, he interrupted. "There you go. Now stop wasting *my time*. I've other things to attend to here."

"Have you seen Paul today?" I asked.

Ben looked surprised at the sudden change in conversation. "And what does he have to do with Evelyn or your mother?"

"I didn't say he had anything to do with them. He was supposed to call me. He's not answering his phone."

"Ah, that's Paul—the egghead historian. Get used to it, Ms. O'Brien. When he gets going on one of his research projects, it's difficult to tear him away."

"You didn't answer my question. Have you spoken to him today?" I asked.

"No, I haven't."

Impatient for action, frustrated that I'd squandered daylight talking to him, I left the shop. I dialed Paul again, in vain. I'd have to return to Rose Cottage alone. But just then, as the sun began to sink into the horizon, a jeep, labeled with the words Environmental Studies, pulled up in front of the café. I crossed the street to the vehicle.

"I'm Star O'Brien. I take it you're the engineer Dr. Treat told me about," I said as I extended my hand.

"Yes, Edward Rogers, but people call me Ted." He pointed to the photo ID badge he wore clipped to his shirt pocket. "I take it you're the one who found the nugget."

"Yes. And if you don't mind, I want to get going now."

"Right. Just let me get my tools and lock up the vehicle." The tools clanged as he swung the knapsack's strap over his shoulder.

Before long, we headed into the darkness. As we neared the end of the path that opened upon the cottage grounds, Ashford, whom I hadn't seen since he ran off earlier, appeared, barking and pacing back and forth in front of me. I wondered where he'd come from.

"Not now, Ashford," I said.

Chuckling, the engineer said, "It's best you do what he wants. I've got one of those fellas at home, and they're relentless when they want your attention."

Not knowing what to expect, I followed Ashford, who was alternately running in circles and then charging ahead. I didn't recognize where he was leading us. Of course, the entire area was heavily wooded, but we soon found ourselves on a dirt track surrounded by woods on all sides. The track, about as wide as the tires on a bicycle, seemed to run parallel to the tourist walking path alongside Lough Corrib. I couldn't see where the path led. In the already faded day, all I could see was a tiny beam of flickering light at the farthest point of the horizon. Finally, Ashford stopped, barked, and looked at me.

"Wait, stop here." Ted touched my arm. "See where the dog is standing?" He raised his hand to point at a spot beyond Ashford. "See that change in terrain? The round depression—it may be a well." Taking a flashlight from his knapsack, he turned the beam toward where Ashford stood. "Better let me look first."

As Ted stepped forward, Ashford came to rest at my side.

"Hello. Are you okay?" Ted yelled.

"Is someone down there?" My heart beat against my breast as I recalled what had happened to me a few days ago.

"Call for an ambulance," Ted ordered. "I cannot see any movement. The person may be unconscious."

I grabbed my phone and dialed emergency services. Just as I ended the call, a slip of paper held in place by a rock fluttered, catching my eye. Moving closer, I picked it up. The handwritten words jumped at me...taunted me...

I'm no longer able to live with this guilt. I'm sorry.

"No..." The cry escaped from my lips. I raced forward, peered down into the cavity, and followed the beam of light to the bottom—recognizing the long curly hair fanned out onto the jumble of rocks below.

CHAPTER 24

Paul lay in the darkness below while Ted and I waited for the ambulance. Ashford sat at my feet. His head rested on my boots as if to keep me stationary. For once, I didn't want action. Instead, I stood in the damp, chill air that settled upon us as we kept guard—not as protectors but as silent witnesses to loss.

After what seemed to be an interminable amount of time listening to the leaves rustling in the drafts that came and went, several emergency services technicians arrived. Ted waved them toward the well, their hands and arms laden with ropes, flashlights, and tactical medical kits. With few words spoken, they assessed the situation, set up a rappel, and descended the long, steep space to Paul. After confirming that this was a recovery effort, they asked us to step back while we all waited for the police to arrive.

Before long, the scene mirrored the sequence of events when Ashford and I found Jane with one exception—this time, Paul was dead. While the police conferred with the technicians and floodlights were set up, I perused the faces of the gathered crowd. Snippets of conversation reached my ears as I watched for familiar faces.

"Potholing. Who does that at night?" a middle-aged man, standing at the front of the spectators, said.

"Whomever that body turns out to be, they must be daft," the man next to him replied. "Sure, I'd wager the poor soul's some visitor, didn't know the dangers." He shook his head. "Especially after heavy rain."

"Maybe the fool or fools who's been ghosting Rose Cottage," the middle-aged man answered.

"I heard it's Paul Doherty," a third person added to the conversation.

Once again, Detectives Thomas O'Shea and James Keenan arrived, took charge of the scene, and began the interview process with Ted. I overheard the words—loss of blood, gash on back of head—amidst glances in my direction. After what seemed like an eternity, they walked over to where I stood.

"Miss O'Brien. You seem to have a propensity for this." O'Shea tilted his head, studying my face.

"It's Paul Doherty, isn't it?" I ignored his comment.

"Aye, yes." For a moment, O'Shea's face softened as he glanced over at the place where the forensics team and EMTs discussed how Paul's body would be lifted to the surface. Then it was back to business. "What were you doing out here?"

I handed the note I'd found to him. A painful shadow passed over his face when he read it. Then I said, "I have a right to be here. I have a right to ask questions, especially when the police don't want to listen." I couldn't help it—I didn't like their attitude. I had to remind them that I'd tried to share information with them when I found Jane.

"And, as I've explained before, these are garda matters." The scar on O'Shea's face deepened with each spoken word. "Your role is to answer our questions. Now, what were you doing out here?"

Keenan stepped forward with his notepad while I explained how I'd contacted the Department of Environmental Studies, agreed to meet Ted, and show him the area where I'd found the gold ore. Before I could finish filling in the details, Dan crashed out of the woods from the direction of Rose Cottage.

"You. I told you to stop your meddling." His words echoed throughout the clearing, and the crowd shuddered, all eyes following the direction of the finger pointed at me. "This is your fault. I told you to stay away. Paul..." His voice, lowered to a whimper, cracked as he collapsed to the ground.

The crowd hushed as Paul's name passed among them. I clenched my iPhone, wishing I could do something, anything, instead of standing still. I was telling myself everything that had happened was related—Jane's death, being pushed into the well, the missing Evelyn, the break-in at my cottage, and now Paul's death. Believing that someone here was responsible, I perused the crowd to discern familiar faces and gauge their reactions to Paul's death and Dan's breakdown.

"Out of my way. Out of my way," said Ann.

She elbowed through the crowd and ran to Dan's side. Then she stroked his arms, all the while trying to get him to stand up. I noticed the rips in her nylons and wondered if they were the result of walking through the woods in her work attire or from something else. Like the first time we met at Happy Trails airstrip, mud dotted the length of her spike heels.

Abandoning his conversation with me, Keenan followed his boss over to Dan.

"Mr. Doherty. I'm sorry, sir, but when the body is raised, we'll need you to make an official identification." The scar over O'Shea's eye throbbed as if in pain. "In the meanwhile, is this Paul's handwriting?" The note I'd found earlier looked minuscule in O'Shea's hand. How could one's life be boiled down to a few words and sentences on a scrap of paper?

"Don't you see? He's in no condition to speak with you." Ann's eyes glared at the detectives as she continued to stroke Dan's arms.

"I'm sorry, but I have to ask you to step back from the area. I need to speak with Mr. Doherty now," O'Shea said while Keenan offered his hand in assistance to Ann.

She gestured him away. Then, she squeezed Dan's hand, rose, and walked to the edge of the clearing where Luke hovered, fists resting on his hips. His direct stare swept over the crowd, settling on Pat and Ben, who stood off to the side. Ben's arms were wrapped around his mother's shoulders. Tom, the postal worker, seemed to scan the crowd, his eyes darting and shifting among the onlookers. Then he slouched his shoulders and tried to melt away into the woods. Jane's partners in her fitness studio, Jimmy and Sarah, huddled on the periphery, edging closer to each other as if seeking security or protection.

What were they all thinking? What were they hiding? How many secrets did they have? Some secrets, I have learned, live parallel and undiscovered lives—destroying all around them.

After the police and EMTs finished closing off the area from any spectator's view, O'Shea and Keenan informed Ted and me that we'd need to be available for more questions if they arose. Then, O'Shea directed two of the police officers to disperse the crowd to wherever they'd come from—houses, cars, the castle, or the village. Ashford and I joined the throng, but not before I overheard O'Shea say to Keenan, "She's just too smart for her own good, isn't she?"

∼

FEELING DEFEATED, TIRED, AND HUNGRY, I HAD MY HANDS ON A container of yogurt when Ashford nudged the back of my knee, shouldered me aside, and peered into the refrigerator.

"I know," I said, ruffling his mane. I reminded myself that when I'd brought this dog home, I'd accepted responsibility for him. I put the yogurt back on the shelf and took out the ingredients for a two-egg omelet. When the food was cooked, I shared half with Ashford. After I demolished my portion, I felt more like myself. I rinsed off the dishes, turned off all the lights, and headed to the bedroom. Ashford followed behind and settled himself on the floor at the foot of the bed. Before long, his snores filled the room. I gazed at the ceiling, rerunning my recent conversations with Paul in my mind. What hadn't he told me? What secret was he keeping?

THE PERSISTENT RINGING OF THE PHONE WOKE ME.

"Miss O'Brien, this is Detective O'Shea. We have a few questions for you. Are you able to come to the station this morning?"

"What is this about?" I asked. I was a little annoyed with the directive tone of his voice. I could hardly believe he'd finally decided to listen to anything I had to say about Jane and Dan Doherty.

"I just need to go over some details with you concerning Paul Doherty."

"I'll be there," I said.

Later that morning, I was ushered into O'Shea's office. Detective Keenan was with him.

"Please, have a seat, Miss O'Brien. This won't take too long." O'Shea indicated the only empty seat in his office. "Now, I understand you knew Paul Doherty. Is that correct?"

I nodded. "I've spoken with him several times. We shared some of the same interests."

"Would you say the relationship between the two of you was romantic?" Keenan asked.

"Why are you wasting my time with these questions?" I shouted. "Two people, a mother and her son are dead—and you're asking me about my relationships." I think I might have gone mad at that moment.

O'Shea shot a look at Keenan and said, "I'm sorry, but we have to follow up on some things."

I didn't want to, but I responded to their question. "No, we did not have a *romantic relationship*," I emphasized the last two words. "We were friends, and because of that and my work as an information broker, Paul asked me to help him prove that his father isn't a murderer." I stopped talking then, waiting to see their reaction to my statement.

"I've warned you before to stay out of garda investigations, Miss O'Brien. Now, I want to know immediately whom you've been speaking with on behalf of Paul?"

"I have a suspect list if you'd like to see who I think might have the most motive to kill Jane. We could compare notes."

"No need to see your list, Miss O'Brien. I can't tell you what we're pursuing, but we do have some leads and persons of interest," O'Shea stated.

I couldn't help myself. "Have you spoken with Ann Ryan? And what about Dan? Have you eliminated him as the number one suspect?"

The uncomfortable silence that followed told me all I needed to know.

CHAPTER 25

I didn't sleep much that night; I kept thinking of Paul. When I couldn't bear it any longer, I threw back the covers, donned my sneakers, and went for a long run with Ashford nipping at my heels. The run didn't do much for my state of mind as I debated whether the police would accept the suicide note at face value.

When we arrived back at the cottage, I found a voicemail from the director of the Hall of Records in Dublin. His crisp voice noted that he could see me that day and only that day at 2:00 p.m. That left me two hours before I'd have to get into the car and begin driving—enough time to check in with Ted Rogers about the excavation at Rose Cottage.

Ted answered on the first ring. "Edward Rogers."

"Ted, it's Star O'Brien. I thought I'd call and see how you are."

"Yes, yes. I'm fine. No problem with me at all. I slept like a baby. And, how are you, young lady? I understand this isn't the first time you've found a body in Cong. You must be cursed." He laughed.

I responded to his flippant remarks with raised eyebrows. Maybe he perceived my astonishment because when he continued, he said, "Sorry. You'll think I'm insensitive. It's just my way of dealing with nasty events. I'm usually long on analysis and short on empathy in tough situations. I guess it's the engineering part of my brain."

"I understand what you mean," I said in response to his apology. "Emotional wounds hurt. Sometimes, we raise a psychological wall to protect ourselves. Well, I'm glad you're okay. What are your plans regarding Rose Cottage? Have the police said anything about preserving the area as part of a crime scene?"

"No, I've heard nothing from the garda since last evening. I don't expect to at this point. It looked pretty much like an accident to me. And I've been in touch with the Dublin office. I'm instructed to continue with my evaluation."

"Accident?" I asked.

"Aye, I'd say so. The country is full of local wells. Too bad it hadn't been covered to protect people from falling in."

I felt a chill. In my mind's eye, this was no accident. But I didn't waste time trying to convince him otherwise.

"I'm on my way to Dublin this morning," I said. "I'll check in with you later. Thank you."

Hanging up the phone, I wondered what he'd find. Well, it wouldn't be too long before I knew. Reminding myself that I still had to change out of my running clothes before leaving for Dublin, I headed into the shower. As I sat in the living room, towel drying my hair, the creak of the gate and the glimpse of a scarf billowing past the window alerted me to Aunt Georgina's arrival.

She closed the kitchen door before she began. "Why didn't you ring me last night? I saw the news this morning." Before I could answer, she continued. "It's terrible. First Jane and now Paul." Shaking her head, she turned on the electric tea kettle and reached for two large mugs.

"I know." At a loss for words, that's all I said. I kept my hands busy with rubbing Ashford's ears.

"Sit down there and have some tea," Georgina directed.

"I don't have much time. Dr. Steven Shannon, the Director of the Hall of Records, contacted me. He's going to see me today at two o'clock."

"Maybe you shouldn't go alone." Georgina glanced out the kitchen window before adding, "The temps are supposed to drop. There's a chance of freezing rain."

"I have to keep this appointment."

"I know, Star. I know how important this is to you. But I don't want you to get hurt." She reached across to stop my hands from fidgeting with the teaspoon that lay on the table between us. "I'm not just talking about the roads. I don't want you to be disappointed."

At that moment, I almost broke down and cried, but instead, I took a deep breath and nodded in agreement. "I understand. I've been in the information brokerage business long enough to know how it might end. But I still have to do this." Smiling, I squeezed her hand. "Besides, what would Lorcan say if he knew I reneged on this meeting when he's used his relationship with the director to set it up?"

Before Aunt Georgina could reply, Ashford moved from his place under the table with a short bark and bounded over to the door. Lorcan stood outside, hand raised as if to tap his arrival on the glass. Aunt Georgina waved him in while rising to pull another mug out of the cupboard.

"No tea for me, Georgina." Then he turned to face me. "Are you okay?" he asked. "I heard about Paul. Were you with him when he fell?"

"Fell?" I asked.

"That's what I heard from Ann Ryan this morning," Lorcan stated.

Fell and accident weren't the words that came to my mind.

What was Ann up to? Was she covering for murder, or *if* the note I'd found near where Paul died were valid, was she covering up the suicide to save the family embarrassment?

"She called me about the aerial photos I took. She wants a rush on their delivery and told me about Paul's unfortunate accident. She mentioned seeing you where Paul's body was found." Lorcan said.

"I heard she's supporting Luke's case contesting his father's will," Aunt Georgina added to the conversation. "I don't know how in heaven's name he expects to win. Pat and Jake were together for many years. You'd think Ann would talk some sense into her son."

Pushing his glasses further up the bridge of his nose, Lorcan said, "Yeah, but changing the mind of someone with the drive and determination such as what Luke's got is difficult. He wants that stud farm."

"Do you know him well?" I asked.

"Not too. We were in some of the same classes back in the university days. I see him sometimes at planning committee meetings I've been asked to attend. He's one of the most vocal members of the audience."

"That's interesting. What about?" I asked.

"In the last few months, it's been about his stud farm, Dan Doherty's property, and Happy Trails. Something to do with boundaries. But that's neither here nor there. You must be shaken up. Are you okay?"

"Star is on her way to Dublin to meet with Dr. Shannon. I think someone should go with her." Georgina stared at Lorcan as she continued. "I can't go, but since you know him, I was wondering..."

"No." I rose from the table, placed my mug into the sink, and holstered my iPhone. "I'm going alone." Ashford rose from where he'd been sleeping at Lorcan's feet to stand by my side. "No, Ashford. You need to stay here."

"I'll take him with me for the day," Lorcan volunteered. "I have some appointments at a couple of farms in the Bofeenaun area. He can keep me company."

"Well, okay. But be careful. He has a habit of running off," I cautioned.

"Well, at least that's settled," Aunt Georgina said. She pushed back her chair and placed the remaining mugs into the sink. "I'll clean up here, Star. You'd better get going while the temperature is still above freezing."

I could tell from the frown on her face that she disapproved of my decision. But this was my journey and one I had to take alone. Without delay, I packed a knapsack with snacks, threw a heavier jacket into the car, and began the drive to Ireland's capital.

CHAPTER 26

By the time I reached Dublin, my upper thighs felt frozen after driving the four-hour journey straight through. That, combined with the threat of being late for my appointment, convinced me to skip idling in the city's typical snarl of traffic. Instead, I decided to pay the parking fees that proved the colloquialism "highway robbery" true and headed to a car park as near to the city center as I could get. With time to spare before my meeting, I made my way toward Grafton Street and Bewley's for tea and to call Ellie and Phillie.

Grafton Street, the heart of Dublin's central shopping area, throbbed with the zigging and zagging of moving bodies— tourists gazing into the windows of the trendy boutiques, earnest-looking students crossing the pavement toward Trinity College, employees rushing back to work from lunch or on their way to the bus or train station.

If Grafton Street was the heart of Dublin's consumerism, then Bewley's Oriental Café was the main aorta—supplying tea, coffee, pastries, cakes, hot food, and sandwiches in its dark, cavernous chambers along with stained-glass windows and cozy open fireplaces.

After paying for a brown scone and tea for one, I settled

into an empty corner booth where I could keep an eye on the crowd of people coming and going into the café while I dialed Ellie.

"I was hoping you'd call." Ellie's clipped style of speaking sent her words dancing across the line.

"Oh, is something wrong?" I pressed the iPhone to my ear. "Are you and Phillie okay? Is Skipper?"

"We're all fine. Especially that spoiled Schipperke of yours." Ellie's chortle lasted longer than usual. Then she added, "You wouldn't recognize him. He's gained a few pounds. Everyone is giving him treats. Even the mail carrier."

I pictured him standing up on his hind legs and fanning his front paws in his patty cake begging routine.

"Yeah, I'm sure he's doing a great job. Now, what's wrong there?" I asked.

"It's the new Southern contract. They want to meet with you. They're persistent."

"Hmm. Any idea why?"

"No," Ellie replied. "I asked them that, but they said for your ears only."

"Call and offer to have Jim Hipple talk to them if that would help until I get back."

"Okay, will do," Ellie responded. "It just might be they don't want to share sensitive information with the office staff."

Although Ellie and Phillie were more than office staff in my eyes, that wasn't always a client's perspective. They were used to it and didn't let it affect their professionalism and dedication to the Consulting Detective or me.

"I agree," I responded. "Let them know that Jim has a signed non-disclosure with the Consulting Detective. His credentials are solid."

"Any luck getting in touch with Evelyn Cosgrove?"

"Not yet," I said. I crumbled a piece of scone onto my plate.

"Oh. Then will you be returning home soon? Should I look into flights? We really miss you."

"Right now, I'm in Dublin to meet the director of the Hall of Records. I'm not sure when I'll be back." I hesitated to tell her about Paul. I didn't want to alarm her and Phillie.

"Oh, Star. That's wonderful. I hope you find a thread that gets you closer to finding your mother."

At that moment, I spotted Dr. Treat walking past, carrying a tray of tea and sandwiches toward one of the fireside tables.

"Ellie, I've got to go. Email the details of the Southern call to me. Say hello to Phillie and kiss that dog of mine."

Zigzagging my way through the crowded café, I caught up with Dr. Treat just as he tucked his napkin into his shirt collar.

"Dr. Treat," I said.

"Ms. O'Brien. It's nice to see you." He patted the chair cushion next to him. "Please, join me."

Glancing at my watch, I confirmed twenty-five minutes remained before my meeting.

"Thank you, but I can't stay long," I said as I chose to remain standing. "I'm wondering if you've heard anything more about Rose Cottage?"

"As a matter of fact, Ted called earlier. He's found more evidence of gold ore at the cottage this morning."

Raking his gaze across the floor around me, he asked, "Where's your companion, the border collie?"

"Ashford is with an acquaintance for the day. But what about the excavation work at the cottage?" I wasn't about to change the subject, no matter how much I sensed that Dr. Treat might want to shift the conversation.

"Hmm, that." Drumming his long fingers on the table beside his teacup, he continued. "I just left a meeting with my colleague, Dr. O'Dowd. The dig will cease today."

The drumming stopped as he raised his hand to stir his tea and then take a bite of his sandwich before saying, "She's a tough cookie, that one. We've had several" – he cleared his throat and took another sip of tea – "challenges working together over the years. And I've heard the assistant she's grooming as her protégé is even more persistent. But in the end, this find takes precedence over some ancient artifacts." His tea sloshed over the sides of the cup as it landed with a bang into its saucer. His blue eyes looked up at me over the rim of his glasses as if assessing my response to what he was about to say. "That's if there even are any. She wouldn't admit it, but I don't think they've found anything of value."

"Did you speak to her assistant?" I asked, hoping Evelyn was in Dublin.

"No sign of her at the meeting, my dear. And what are you doing here?"

"Dr. Treat. What a coincidence that I'd bump into you," a booming voice came from behind me. It could have been heard several city blocks away. Dr. Treat squeezed his eyes shut and almost knocked over his cup of tea when the speaker continued. "May I join you?"

Not waiting for an answer, the voice's owner slid his tray onto the table and took possession of the chair that Dr. Treat had offered to me.

"Leonard." The name escaped from Dr. Treat's narrowed lips. Gone was the friendly, collegial professor. Instead, he appeared to stiffen in place when he said to the newcomer, "I was just leaving."

"I heard about the find," Leonard said. "It's wonderful news for you and the department."

"What are you talking about?" Dr. Treat asked.

"Why, Cong, of course. Come on, don't tell me you're going to hold out on me?" Leonard looked up at me as he explained. "I was visiting my sister in the area over the weekend, and I heard all about what's been going on in the village." He paused to shove a large hunk of raisin scone into his mouth. In between chews, he said to me, "You look familiar. I saw you in Cong over the weekend."

Dr. Treat's shoulders slumped, and his fingers drummed the table again. "Yes, Leonard. There may be ore, but, and I stress the *but*, testing and analysis haven't been completed. I'd appreciate it if you kept this low-key for the time being."

"Indeed. Of course. I'm the soul of discretion when it comes to these matters," Leonard said.

He looked far from discreet to me. The fact that he'd rudely interrupted and pushed himself into my conversation with Dr. Treat spoke volumes about his lack of tact. Neither did he seem to care who heard what he had to say, as evidenced by his shouted words. But his abrupt intrusion reminded me I had an appointment that I couldn't miss—I may never get this chance again. After checking the wall clock across the room, I excused myself, explaining that I had a meeting with Dr. Steven Shannon.

Looking relieved at the chance to redirect his attention to me, Dr. Treat said, "Still looking for your mother, I see. I wish you luck, my dear. Steven's a good egg. He should be able to help. Anyway, we'll talk again soon."

Nodding in silent agreement, I turned to go. Just as I walked through the exit, I glanced back to see Dr. Treat and Leonard leaning toward each other, engaged in what looked like a heated discussion. I made a note to myself to find out more about Leonard—I didn't believe in coincidences.

CHAPTER 27

The National Archives of Ireland was located on Bishop Street, a five-minute walk from the café. The modern, innovative building that housed the government archives belied the fact that more than eighty years ago, the records of Ireland's administration and demographic history went up in ashes and bits of paper when an explosion of munitions almost totally destroyed five hundred years of history. Looking up at the vertical hanging banners that identified the building, I couldn't help but think Ireland's quest for its identity and the lost demographic history of pre-famine Ireland—names and family structures—paralleled my search for my mother and whatever my own unique family ancestry might be.

The security guard stationed inside the front door directed me toward an open-architecture, gray steel staircase up to the second-floor landing. There, I found the director's receptionist looking as polished as the solid mahogany desk where she sat.

"May I help you?"

"I have an appointment with Director Shannon at two o'clock."

"Your name, please."

"Star O'Brien." I handed one of my official Consulting Detective cards to her.

Taking the card, she reviewed it, checked something on her computer screen, and pointed to an oversized, prim-and-proper-looking, Queen-Anne-style chair.

"He's running a bit late. Please, take a seat. Would you like some tea?"

"No, thank you."

I sat down—happy to have time to collect my thoughts about how this meeting might go. Closing my eyes, I imagined for the millionth time what my mother would look like now. What changes had fate and time made to her face? It had been almost twenty-two years since I'd last seen her. Uncertain whether it would match my memory of her and the worn and crinkled snapshot taken in the arcade at Coney Island, I extracted the black and white photo from my wallet, fingering its border, and gazed at her smiling face framed with short, wavy, thick, black hair. I remembered how black her hair was and knew that at least that part of me must have come from her. Her dark eyes had crinkle lines around the edges as if she'd spent her life laughing and didn't have a care in the world. Why had she disappeared? Had she left me alone to fend for myself? No. Never.

Just then, a buzzer rang at the receptionist's desk, prompting her to rise and walk over to me. "This way, Miss O'Brien, to the director's office."

Taking one last look at my mother, I placed the photograph back into my wallet and followed the receptionist through a door behind her desk, down a long corridor whose walls were lined with pictures of various administrators and historical figures to another set of double doors. She stopped, knocked, and turned to me.

"The director will see you now." With that, she retraced her steps in the direction from which we'd come.

"Well, hello, Miss O'Brien. Welcome. Come on in," said Dr. Shannon.

The three-piece, light gray suit he wore looked like it might be a couple of sizes too small. His unbuttoned jacket revealed a wrinkled white shirt. My first reaction was to wonder if I was wasting my time. He just didn't carry the gravitas I'd come to expect from government officials.

"Sorry for the delay. I'm running late," Shannon said. He paused to smooth his trouser pants with his hands and then straightened his tie. "First day back and all that." He grinned down at me from his over-six-feet height. The grin accentuated a set of dimples and laughing blue eyes. "Please, sit down." He pointed to one of two visitor chairs. Then, to my surprise, instead of moving around to the other side of the desk, he chose the chair next to mine.

I moved quickly to sit down and get over the introductions. "Thank you for taking the time to meet with me. I understand Lorcan McHale has spoken to you about my interest in the archives." I placed one of my Consulting Detective cards on the table in front of him.

"And how is Lorcan? I haven't seen him in ages. Wonderful fellow." There was that grin again.

"Lorcan is fine." I kept my answer short. Why did everyone gush over him? *Well, everyone except me,* I told myself.

"Okay, let's get to your reason for being here. Your mother, right?" His tone softened with the question.

"Yes, my mother. Margaret O'Malley is her given name, but she went by Maggie O'Malley."

"I see," he said. Then he reached forward to turn over my card. He took a few moments to read the information about the Consulting Detective. "Your name is O'Brien. Your father?"

"No. My adoptive parents were O'Brien. I don't know who my father is."

"Have they been able to shed any light on the matter?" he asked.

"They're deceased. They died when I was eighteen." My hand moved to touch my cell phone in its holster. "My adoption was never a topic of discussion."

"I'm sorry to hear that." The tone of his words was gentle. "What about their legal papers? Anything from your days as a child? A Bible, perhaps?"

I shook my head back and forth with such force that, as short as my hair was, I felt each individual strand move. I searched for the right words to express my frustration.

"No. Nothing."

I'd been over it all many times. The O'Brien's—I loved them. I knew they loved me. Had they known anything about my mother—they would have told me. My mother's Bible was another story. Why was the page that recorded births and marriages ripped out?

"I see." He shifted in his chair before continuing. "Well, the hardest people to find are women. Many change their names when they marry."

"No. My mother didn't change her name. She wouldn't," I insisted.

I've had a hole in my heart for a long time. And it wouldn't be fixed until I knew what happened to her, one way or another. But being placed in foster care and then adopted had done nothing to destroy what she'd instilled in me—we were connected by love. I was confident she wasn't some fallen angel who'd left me behind while she went on to live another life—a life without me. Nothing could have broken our mother-daughter bond.

"But..." He tilted his head and leaned forward in his seat before saying, "Twenty-two years is a long time to be missing. I want to caution you that anyone who hasn't been located in that length of time, and with a name like O'Malley—well, there just may be too many possibilities to sort through."

"What about the census data?" I asked, not giving up.

"I've arranged for you to access our archives this afternoon. But I'm warning you—it's a slog that may not net anything to help you, Miss O'Brien."

"I understand, but I'm determined to keep looking. Something happened to my mother—foul play, kidnapping. For all I know, she's being kept hidden somewhere because someone doesn't want her to be found. Maybe she was hit by a car the morning she went missing. She could have amnesia and is homeless." I clutched my phone, which I'd pulled from its holster in an effort to hold back the tears that threatened to erupt. "I just know she wouldn't abandon me like the police said."

Shannon looked at my card again. "It says here that you're an information broker. What is it that you do?"

"Yes, I find information that a private investigator may not have access to, or the police have failed to find. Mostly regarding birth certificates, marriage licenses, that sort of thing."

"Well, then, have you checked the U.S. Social Security Death Index?" His face looked like it hurt to ask the question.

"All of that. I've done it all. I haven't found any records. But that doesn't mean she's dead. If my mother was the victim of a hit-and-run and no witnesses came forward, and she was identified as a Jane Doe...well, then, she'll never be found."

Upon hearing my words, I saw empathy and kindness in his eyes. At that moment, my earlier assessment of his seriousness changed.

"This must be difficult for you," he consoled. "Having access to data that other people normally don't have and still not able to find your mother—finding others instead."

"Abandoned—that's what the police said. It's what a private

investigator would think and say. I've been disappointed by the police. And too many people have been misjudged by them. That's why I became an information broker—to help people who are disillusioned by a private investigator or the police—I am a voice for the dead, the missing, and the lost."

"I admire you, Miss O'Brien. I can see why Lorcan wants to help you." He stood up with a take-charge attitude, saying, "Right. Let's get you situated in the archive room. Follow me, if you please."

We made our way back out to the receptionist's desk, where he shook my hand. "I'll check in with you before you leave today."

CHAPTER 28

The silence struck me—solemn, soft, deathlike quiet. For a moment, I paused at the reference room's entrance. My stomach ached with dread while my mind raced with anticipation. Would the records vault hold its tongue or speak? Would my decades-long search be ended—for better or worse—or was it just beginning?

As I moved across the threshold farther into the room, my eyes read the plaques identifying benefactors who expressed gratitude and support for preserving lineage and facts by funding the furnishings and equipment—the room was a living memorial. The two reference staff persons, seated at a work-table, looked up as I approached the desk. One of them rose to greet me before I could introduce myself.

"Miss O'Brien, Director Shannon instructed us to provide access to one of the vault rooms." Then she gave me what sounded like a speech she'd delivered many times before. "After the eighteen-nineties, parish priests were required to register births, deaths, and marriages with the government. Scanning and digitization are in progress, but not, I'm sorry to say, for the years you're interested in." Picking up a set of keys, she motioned me to follow her to a door along the back wall of the room. After opening the fire-resistant entry, she continued with her speech. "This particular chamber holds records from County Mayo between the years 1960 to 1970. Each aisle is dedicated to one of the years in that decade. Each container is marked with the year and the name of a parish." She nodded toward the photocopier and microfilm/microfiche equipment. "You may copy any records you'd like. But you may not remove any of the original documents. Good luck, Miss O'Brien."

With that, she turned and exited.

I moved quickly and got to work. First, I carried one of the five boxes labeled 1962—the year of my mother's birth—and Achill Island over to a worktable. I detected a faint odor, like that of an old house on a hot and humid day, emanating from the jumble of papers stuffed into the long and narrow coffin-like containers. Glancing at my watch, I realized I had little more than two hours to comb through what these cherished documents had to offer.

WHEN I FINALLY DROPPED MY PENCIL ONTO THE PAD OF PAPER, I had a list of five Margarite O'Malleys, *none by the name of Margaret*, registered by the Dooega parish priest. Most of the certificates and licenses were difficult to read. Some had been written in crabbed letters or watercolor-like fountain pen ink that had disappeared with the passage of time—making the small, jammed-together letters and words indecipherable. Some documents were missing entire sections of information such as the parents' forenames or their residences. I knew that names on birth records were often misspelled or changed completely. I hoped this was the case with the names I'd found. Nevertheless, I had five potential leads—any one of which might be my mother—I had a place to start.

The sound of a soft click and a shift in air temperature

broke into my optimistic musing. Thinking one of the staff members had entered the room, I called out to say I was almost finished. Instead of an answer, I heard another soft click. I called out again. Silence. The air seemed warmer than it had before, allowing the musty smell of the room's contents to take precedence. Knowing now that I had to investigate the noise, I rose from the worktable.

With my recent mishaps in mind, I cautiously moved along the aisle of shelving back to the room's only access point. No one was there. Shrugging my shoulders, I returned to the work-table. The last box I'd been working on wasn't quite in the same place on the table where I'd left it. I looked around. I was sure I'd left the box to the left of chair I'd occupied. I shivered. The room was cold again. Maybe one of the staff had stuck her head into the room to see how I was doing but had decided not to interrupt me. Sitting back down at the table, I took a picture of my list with my phone and sent it to Ellie and Phillie immediately. Then, as a backup strategy, I wrote out several copies, placing one in my knapsack, another in my wallet, the last one, I tucked into the holster with my iPhone. Taking one last look around the room, I stepped out and walked over to the reference desk, where the librarians were packing up for the day.

"Thank you for letting me use the archive." I shifted the knapsack on my shoulder, still wondering about the feeling that someone had been in the room with me. "I guess you have to make quite a few trips back and forth into the vaults during the day," I commented.

Looking at each other before responding to me, the librarian who'd delivered the speech earlier, glanced down at a slip of paper with what looked like the letters *l-e-o* scribbled on it. Crunching the paper into the palm of her hand, she shook her head back and forth before saying, "No, we take care to enter the room no more than once a day, usually in the morning. It's our job to be mindful of the delicate nature of the documents."

"Really? Neither one of you came in or out of the vault while I was in there?" I asked incredulously.

Maybe it was politeness, or they didn't want to linger any longer at the end of the workday, or perhaps they'd seen too many people leave the archives in disappointment, but they didn't ask me if my search had been successful. And they didn't answer my question. Instead, one of them picked up a phone to call the receptionist, who escorted me back to the welcome area. Director Shannon was waiting for me there.

"Ah, Miss O'Brien. I trust your visit to the archive was helpful," he said.

"Thank you for letting me look at the original documents. I have a list of names. There are lots of gaps and no exact name match, but I have something to go on."

"I do hope it turns out well for you, Miss O'Brien. Now, let me see you to the door. The security personnel are getting ready to lock up for the day."

When we arrived on the ground floor, he shook my hand and grinned, reminding me again to give his regards to Lorcan. I nodded my agreement to do so.

Once outside, my eyes blinked at the steady flow of headlights lining the streets of Dublin. Realizing how hungry I was, I decided to stop back into Bewley's before retrieving my car. I ordered a hot chocolate and a slice of The Mary Cake. I needed an indulgence—and not the religious kind, but then maybe a special dispensation would be required after devouring the chocolate mousse, apricot jam, and almond and hazelnut sponge cake. While I waited for the hot chocolate to cool, I extracted the slip of paper from my iPhone case and looked at the list of names again. When I tasted the first sip of the chocolate beverage, I thought of my mother—she always had a Hershey bar in her purse, which she'd share with me.

"Just a bite, Star. We'll save some for later."

Feelings of anger and disappointment surged like lightning deep in my bones. My heart ached for her. What if this list led nowhere? Would I *ever* accept that I'd never learn what happened to her? At a rational level, I knew I hadn't, but I felt like I'd failed her in some way. What if she'd actually abandoned me and was living another life somewhere? How would she receive me if I found her? I didn't have any answers, just silence—a silence that deafened the noise of the nearby café's patrons laughing, reading books, and seeming to find joy in each other's company.

No! She had not abandoned me. Never! Leaving the hot chocolate half-finished, I shook myself, folded the list, and went to find my car to begin the long journey back to French Hill Cottage.

"EXCUSE ME."

My hand froze on the car door as I looked around for the source of the voice. I hadn't seen anyone other than the lot attendant when I'd settled up the parking fee.

"Excuse me."

This time louder. Most of the lot was empty now—rush hour was over. Not seeing anyone, I shrugged, thinking someone's voice had carried over the walls that created a boundary between the car park and one of the apartment buildings.

"Excuse me."

This time closer. Suddenly glad I'd changed from my Rocket Dogs to my Brooks Ghosts when I'd parked the car, I prepared to run.

"We met earlier today. With Dr. Treat?"

"Leonard?" I asked, startled.

He stood just on the other side of the car. Remembering the

feeling that someone was with me in the vault room, I began moving away from the car, all the while clutching my phone, ready to hit the speed dial for 999—glad now that Aunt Georgina had made me add it after ending up in the cave.

"Please, don't be afraid," he said quietly. "I was hoping to catch you before you left the city. I just want to know more about the dig in Cong."

Where was the booming voice from earlier in the day? I asked myself.

"Get away from my car now, or I'll call the police," I demanded. "How did you know where my car was parked? Have you been following me?"

"No, no. I saw you earlier, leaving Bewley's. I've been trying to get your attention, but I don't think you heard me."

By this time, I'd reached the sidewalk with Leonard close behind me. I saw a few passing pedestrians glance our way, but they continued on their journey.

"Give me one good reason why I shouldn't call the police." I held the cell in my right hand, ready to press the emergency number or clobber him with the phone. I wasn't sure yet which.

"It's not what you think. I work in the department with Dr. O'Dowd and Cosgrove," he said in a whining voice.

"Really?" I asked. "Then, why do you need to speak with Dr. Treat or with me? I imagine you know all there is to know about the dig in Cong. Didn't you say you were there over the weekend? Visiting your sister?"

"Yes, I was. You know when they found that poor fellow's body at the bottom of a hole. I just spend a lot of time in Cong, visiting family. And it would be great if I were assigned to lead the dig. But—"

"That's what this is about?" I interrupted. "A work assignment?" I shook my head in amazement. Something wasn't adding up. "Who's your sister?"

"My work is important to me. But that Evelyn Cosgrove, she

won't share any information. I don't know why. After all, we're colleagues. Of course, I've been in the department longer than she has. And my requests should be considered a priority. But she and Dr. O'Dowd just don't include me." His words exited his mouth in a long, high-pitched plaintive voice that grated on my ears and my patience.

"Have you ever considered that popping up on someone just as you did this morning with Dr. Treat and now me, might make them wary, even afraid of you?" I asked.

"I'm just a colleague."

"You didn't answer my question. Who's your sister?" Something about him gave me the creeps. I couldn't help but remember the feeling that someone had been in the vault room with me earlier.

"Ann has nothing to do with this." He spoke the words in rapid succession.

"Ann? Your sister's name is Ann? What's her last name?" Impatient now for answers, I moved closer to him. I raised my iPhone high over his head. He backed away from me.

"Why, Ann Ryan. She's an auctioneer there," he replied.

Ann Ryan. This was interesting. Relaxing the hand that held my iPhone so that it hung by my side, I dismissed Leonard. "Colleagues or not, you just don't approach people this way. Now, if you'll excuse me" – I couldn't help it, I emphasized the phrase he'd used earlier – "I have a long drive in front of me. Just know that if I see you around me again, I will call the police."

I continued to clutch my phone until I drove through the parking lot exit. At that point, I glanced in the rear-view mirror. Leonard still stood where I'd left him.

CHAPTER 29

I returned to Castlebar after 11:00 p.m.—too late to call Lorcan and ask him to drop Ashford back to me. Instead, as soon as I got inside the cottage, I kicked off my sneakers, dropped my clothes onto the bedroom floor, and climbed into bed. Exhausted and lonely, especially without Ashford, I sank deep under the covers and surrendered myself to sleep.

The soft tones of the phone broke through my slumber, and I dragged myself up far enough in the bed to glance at the clock: 6:00 a.m. Geez, who was calling at this hour?

"Good morning. Did I wake you?" Lorcan asked.

"No. Not at all. Is something wrong?"

"No, nothing like that," he replied. "I just wanted to ask if I can keep Ashford with me a little longer. I'm driving to Sligo for a consultation with an organic herb farm. They're considering one of my wind energy patents."

"Well," I hesitated.

Before I could say another word, he continued. "I don't know if you've heard, but the garda have determined that Paul committed suicide."

"Suicide." I vaulted out of bed, shocked awake. "No way!"

"They believe he felt responsible for his mother's death and couldn't live with the guilt."

"There's just no way he killed himself." I shook my head in anger while I attempted, with the phone pressed between my shoulder and ear, to pull on the clothes I'd dropped to the floor last night. "Lorcan, I saw Jane's body, and Paul couldn't have been capable of violence like that. Ineptitude. That's what I think. As usual, the police just want to close out their case as soon as possible. I'll bet they didn't look much further than the note I found at the scene."

"They're seasoned investigators. I've known them all my life," Lorcan stated.

"That doesn't make them right. I know better than anyone how often the police let evidence slip by or something doesn't get followed up. I'd bet this is one of those times."

"I don't think so. The findings will be released to the public this morning. According to Thomas O'Shea, someone came forward with information about Paul that strengthens their conclusion of suicide."

"What kind of information? How did you find out? It hasn't even been more than forty-eight hours since..." I stopped. The police were wrong. I was sure of it.

For what seemed like an eternity, there was silence on the other end of the phone, then Lorcan explained, "O'Shea called me. Said he'd tried to phone you. He wanted to make sure you weren't trying to solve the case on your own."

"I didn't get any call," I said through gritted teeth.

"Star, look, I have to go. I can't cancel my appointments, but O'Shea mentioned that Ann Ryan shed light on the investigation—enough that he and Keenan are satisfied with their conclusions." Lorcan paused. "Maybe I should bring Ashford to you..."

"No," I interrupted. "I'll be fine. I'm just a little tired this morning. I got in late last night. He'd be bored with me here all day."

"I know you don't always agree with law enforcement, but I've known these two since school days, and they're thorough," Lorcan said.

Yeah, like they'd been when Matthew Sumner died. My current state of shock and fatigue kept me from reminding Lorcan how that had turned out. When I didn't answer, he asked again, "Are you sure you're okay? Steven rang me. He said you were optimistic about your visit to the archives." The pace of his words slowed as he made this last statement.

"Give Ashford a big hug for me. Thanks, Lorcan." I hung up the phone.

Ann. It was all too coincidental. Leonard—her brother—approaching me in Dublin. She, providing condemning information about Paul to the police, which led to the closure of the investigation into his death. No. As much as I wanted to, I wouldn't be driving out to Achill today. Instead, I'd go to Cong to confront Ann. I swung my knapsack over my shoulder and walked down to the barn where my car was parked. As soon as I started the engine, I realized my trip to Cong would be delayed. The dashboard's gasoline indicator registered near empty.

The smell of bacon and the long line of people waiting to purchase fried egg breakfast sandwiches when I went into Mulroy's shop to pay for the gas I'd pumped into my Renault, set my stomach rumbling. In my haste to get to Cong, I'd rushed out of the cottage without eating breakfast. Deciding I didn't want to stand on Mulroy's breakfast line, I moved my car to a parking space a few streets away and walked the rest of the way to the Davitt Restaurant. Once settled into one of the booths, I ordered peppermint tea, brown bread, and scrambled eggs. I was standing at the register, paying for breakfast, when a voice hissed my name.

"Miss O'Brien."

I turned to find Ann Ryan. Surprised and yet not, I nodded my head in greeting.

"We need to talk." The words flowed from her lips in a staccato rhythm.

I didn't tell her about my intention to drive to Cong. I invited her to join me at one of the restaurant's empty tables.

Her stiletto heels hammered the linoleum floor as she followed me to a four-seater at the back of the restaurant. She looked the same as the last time I'd seen her—pressed and starched. Her salt-and-pepper hair was styled in a short bob, and her rimless eyeglasses highlighted smoky shadow and winged eyeliner. The only difference today was the addition of a smile that didn't reach her eyes. The overall effect was a face that was oddly off—-beauty that didn't seem to mask the hardness under the surface.

She ordered a pot of tea for two and waved off the server when she asked if she wanted anything to eat.

"I'm glad I ran into you. I've been meaning to call you for a chat," Ann said.

I waited for her to continue, noting how she glanced around the room, taking in its occupants.

"How is Lorcan?" she asked. "I've seen you two together. He's quite the catch, you know."

Lorcan? Was this going to be one of those keep your hands off the guy I'm interested in warnings? No. She wasn't interested in Lorcan. Her question was a diversion—the warm-up exercise before she pitched whatever garbage she'd peddled to the police. I wasn't gullible enough to think she happened to bump into me here in Castlebar. Nor was I about to engage in idle chit-chat with her over tea.

"Lorcan? There's nothing going on there. But how is Leonard?" I asked.

"Leonard?" For a moment, she sat back in her chair, eyes turned down to the table.

"Yes, your *brother,* Leonard."

"Oh." She laughed. "He's fine. He works in Dublin, so I don't get to see him often. Something in archeology."

Before I could call her out on her lie, she got to what appeared to be the real reason for wanting to talk.

"I suppose you've heard that the garda have closed the investigation into Paul's suicide." As she spoke, she picked at the cuffs of her blouse with her manicured fingers. "I knew you were helping Paul with what happened to his mother, so I thought I'd explain. You know, put your mind at ease."

"Yes, I heard something to that effect. But I don't understand what led the police to that conclusion."

"I can help you with that. You see, Paul confided in me that he thought his father was guilty."

"Guilty?" My face didn't move a muscle as I listened.

"Guilty of killing Jane." For a nanosecond, her smile seemed to reach her eyes.

"I don't understand," I said, shaking my head. "Paul asked me to help him prove his father's innocence. Paul would have told me if he was suspicious of his father."

"No," she hissed. "He thought his father was innocent in the beginning. That's why he asked for your help. But then he changed his mind about it all."

"He didn't tell me that," I stated.

"He told me," she insisted. "You see, he remembered something that happened not long before Jane died."

"And that was?"

"He heard his mother arguing with someone in the woods at Cong. Paul forgot all about it until recently." Ann paused for a moment before continuing. "Now that I think of it, the place where the argument occurred is close to where Paul was found."

"Hmm," I said, allowing my voice to sound doubtful. "When did Paul tell you that?"

"Oh, please, don't try to interrogate me, Miss O'Brien."

She had to be lying. Right up until the last time I'd spoken to Paul, he'd told me his father was innocent. I kept asking questions. "So, he heard two adults having a discussion. That doesn't add up to committing suicide. Who was the other person? What was the argument about?"

My words prompted a half-smile that, once again, barely reached her hazel cat eyes.

"I'm sure the person was male. Someone who lives, or should I say, lived in the area. Jane had affairs with just about everyone in town, including my husband, Jake. He never admitted it, but I suspected. I even think she tried to come on to Luke a few times." When Ann glanced down at her hands, I could see the winged eyeliner that underscored her dramatic statements. "Of course," she continued. "Paul didn't hear what his mother and the man were saying, but Paul recalled shouting. At first, he assumed the two people were his parents. They were never a compatible couple, always bickering. Poor Paul. He was always a sensitive kid. The guilt of not having confronted his mother about the argument was probably just too much for him to bear."

I wouldn't fault her about the bickering. I remembered the scene I'd witnessed in Gibbons' Pub.

"You still haven't told me when Paul told you all this—or why he would he confide in you," I said.

"Oh, he's confided in me since he was a toddler. All our kids, Pat's Ben, Jane's Paul, and my Luke grew up together. I was the mother who took charge of getting everyone together for holidays, running the kids around to games, listening to their stories, and putting bandages on their cuts and bruises." Shrugging her shoulders, she fixed her eyes on me before continuing. "Pat had her hands full after her husband died and Jane...well, what can I say? I was always the organized one in the group. I guess that's why I'm a successful real estate auctioneer."

"And you sought me out to tell me all this because?" I asked.

"I've heard you're persistent and don't take no for an answer. I've also heard you don't think much of the garda." She paused, wrapped both hands around her teacup, and took a sip. "I admire that trait in a person, but I know Dan better than anyone else. He's depending on me now. And, it's better if he just leaves all this behind. I'm sure the garda will find who killed Jane. Believe me; this is what's best for Dan."

I could see from the set of her mouth and the cold darkness that emanated from her eyes—she thought she'd accomplished her mission. I didn't believe for one minute that Paul killed himself, but I wasn't about to argue with her on that point. I decided to change the topic.

"What about Rose Cottage and the mill? Dan owns those, right? How is he dealing with an archeological dig at the cottage?"

"Oh, yeah, you haven't been very successful in finding the so-called missing Evelyn. I've been looking for her too." Placing the teacup back on the saucer, she rested her manicured hands on the table before making her accusation. "She tricked Dan into getting that dig started at the cottage. Now, he's stuck with it until the government says the project is completed. I wouldn't be surprised if she's the one who started the rumors about the ghost. Too bad. If he sold it, he'd get a nice pile of euros for it."

"Dan doesn't seem like the type of person who can be tricked." I sat back in my chair, thinking about being shoved into the priest's hole cave and Paul...lying at the bottom of a well. No, the cottage wasn't haunted. This was the work of someone trying to keep people away from the dig. Had Jane and then Paul happened upon the gold? Had that made them targets? Paul had panicked when I told him about the engineer from Dublin. Who else knew about the gold? What about

Evelyn Cosgrove? Her husband disappeared while she was working on a dig in England. Another case the police hadn't solved. Were all these events connected?

"Dan never met a woman he didn't think he could charm." Each word dripped through Ann's lips. "Evelyn was no different. Except this time, the roles were reversed."

"What do you mean by tricked Dan? He must have known what he was getting into when he agreed to the dig."

"Why, government compensation, of course. She told him he'd be reimbursed for the value of the property. He thought he could put the money into the mill. But then, she disappeared, and the whole project ground to a halt. Now, it's all just sitting there."

If this were the case, then it seemed like the only avenue left to Dan was for Jane to bail him out of his debt.

"You said you've been there for everyone's kids when they were growing up. Was Evelyn one of the kids?" I asked. I didn't think so. But I hoped Ann might know more about Evelyn than she was saying.

"No." Ann's lips looked almost frozen shut as she shook her head in denial. "She's only lived here for a few years. I was her realtor when she purchased her house. Who knew she'd cause all this commotion? She was awfully keen on digging up that site." Finishing her tea, Ann rummaged through her bag before withdrawing a few euros, which she tossed onto the table. "Now, if you'll excuse me. I have to go. I have a meeting with a client here in town. Anyway, thank you for all you did for Paul. I'm sure he appreciated it. But when it comes to Dan, I'll take it from here."

Her heels dug into the floor as she rose from the table and stalked through the exit. She was done with me. She didn't have to say it; the erect way she carried her body said it for her. But her sophisticated aggressiveness was hiding something. I wondered if Dan knew how deeply Ann cared for him. Or was he oblivious? Or was she a pawn—lying for him in her desire to win his love—providing him with the perfect fall guy for Jane's murder. His own son. Could Ann be that callous? Maybe—unrequited love can be quite the psychological trigger for all kinds of behavior.

I sat at the table, mulling over Ann's story when loud voices from outside flowed into the restaurant. I glanced toward where the din was coming from and glimpsed Leonard waving sheets of paper at Ann. She yanked them from his hand and shoved them into her handbag. Then, she spun on her heels away from him. I sprang from my seat, intent on confronting him, but he spotted me and ran after Ann. When I got to the sidewalk, I was too late; they were nowhere in sight.

CHAPTER 30

I considered how to spend the rest of the day. I decided not to begin the drive to Achill Island along the narrow, deserted, and sometimes winding roads through the coastal town of Mulranny to the bridge over Achill Sound—this time of year, the sun sank into the horizon by mid-afternoon. Pulling my iPhone from its holster, I checked for messages. Nothing. When it came to Paul, my mother, and even Evelyn, I had nothing to go on but my gut. I just knew the police were wrong about Paul. I decided to pay Pat O'Malley another visit.

When I reached Happy Trails, the farm's gate was open, and unlike the scene I'd come upon during my last visit, the fields were empty, almost as if the place was abandoned. Pat O'Malley answered my first knock on the door.

"You again?" She stood to block my entrance into the house. The laugh lines I'd noticed the previous times I'd seen her seemed to have become permanently etched as wrinkles. She didn't look happy.

I didn't waste time getting to the point. "I came to talk about Paul. The last time I was here, I told you about a letter I found and gave to Paul. Do you think that's why Paul was killed?" I asked.

"But I thought he jumped into that well." The shadows under her eyes sank deeper into her skin. "That's what the garda said."

"You don't believe that, do you? You knew Paul since he was a child. Do you really think he'd kill himself?"

She stepped out onto the driveway, pulling her front door shut behind her. I wondered if someone was inside, whom she didn't want to hear her answer. "Paul was sensitive. I don't know. It's possible—especially with that cad of a father. Until Paul died, I suspected Dan might have killed Jane. But his own son? He's up to something, but I don't think any parent could kill their child. Now, if you don't mind, Miss O'Brien, I have business to get back to. You know the way out."

I drove back to Castlebar and went to find Aunt Georgina in her shop. She was in the midst of explaining to a young woman what colors and dress styles suited her frame, eyes, and hairstyle.

"Georgina, you're the best." The young woman's head nodded up and down in vigorous agreement to everything Georgina said. After she wrapped up her customer's purchases, the young woman embraced Georgina in a hug and left.

"Star, how was the trip to Dublin?" Georgina asked. "I'm sorry I didn't ring this morning, but I was swamped with calls and customers. And then Lorcan called to say he'd spoken with you, so I didn't worry. That lad, he's a godsend."

I threw my hands up in the air and said, "Okay, okay. No need to beatify him yet."

"Come on, sit down here and tell me everything about Dublin," Georgina said, patting the cushioned window seat. For once, the shop was empty.

"I don't know what to say about Dublin. On the one hand, I have a list of five names—none of which is a Margaret O'Malley. On the other, much of the information is sketchy. I can't rely on a database. If it were that easy, I'd have done that already. I'll have to knock on doors and ask questions myself." While I was talking, I extracted the paper from my iPhone case and handed the list to her. Pursing her lips, she moved her reading glasses from where they hung around her neck to the edge of her nose.

"Hmm, I can tell you right now that most of the people listed as birth parents are probably dead or in the old-age home. I know you've spoken to the parish priest before, but I'd try him again. With a specific set of names, he might be able to tell you the whereabouts of some of the younger relatives of these people." Refolding the list, she placed it back in the palm of my hand. "Don't be discouraged, Star. Births were often registered long after the event and many times by a relative. It could be a case where someone got the name wrong. The story isn't over yet."

"I'm not. Someday, someway I will know what happened to my mother. It's just" – I squeezed the slip of paper when I felt the tears threaten to gush – "it's just hard sometimes."

"You're not alone anymore. You know that, don't you? You have me, and" – she paused as her eyes lit up in a smile – "you have Lorcan, and there's his mother, Lady Marcella. You have family and friends on this side of the Atlantic, girleen. So, chin up."

The mention of Lorcan's name stiffened my spine. My tears dried up.

"Lorcan, again? Don't get me wrong; I appreciate what he did, getting me into the National Archives. But does everyone report to him? He already knew this morning about my list and then..." I stopped, realizing Aunt Georgina may not know about Paul and the police's determination of his death. "Did Lorcan tell you about Paul?"

"No, Paul wasn't mentioned. Lorcan was in a hurry. Just said he wanted me to know that he was taking Ashford for the day, and you were probably heading to Achill." She looked at me again. "By the way, why are you here? Why aren't you in Achill?"

"The police decided to close Paul's case. Ann Ryan claims that Paul suspected his father, and out of guilt for not intervening in his parents' nasty relationship, Paul killed himself."

"What?" Georgina exclaimed.

I shook my head in total agreement with the look on her face.

"Ann Ryan is peddling misinformation," I replied. "Why, I don't know. I didn't tell Lorcan, but I decided to drive to Cong this morning instead of Achill. Before I could get there, though, Ann cornered me while I was getting a bite to eat at the Davitt. Apparently, she's intent on weaving this fairy tale about Paul."

"Hmm," Georgina mused. "You don't usually eat breakfast in town. How did she know where to find you?"

"Well, that's just it. She admitted she wanted to talk to me, and she had a meeting in town this morning. But then, when she left the restaurant, she and her brother were outside having some kind of discussion—what looked to me like a heated argument."

"I didn't know she had a brother. How did you figure that out?"

"That's part of my Dublin trip story. I was in Bewley's speaking with Dr. Treat when this man, Leonard, comes up and wants to know about the dig. Says he works in the archeology department and is in Cong a lot visiting his sister."

"If he works for the archeology department, he should know what's going on, shouldn't he?"

"I would think that's the case, but he claims he's frozen out by Dr. O'Dowd and Evelyn Cosgrove. He's creepy. Later in the day, after I'd been to the archives and was getting my car from the car park, he showed up."

"What? Did you call the garda?"

"No, I handled the situation. He told me that Ann is his sister. I'm sure he must have followed me from Bewley's, and seeing him here in town this morning makes me think he followed me from Dublin and told Ann where to find me. That and the whole Paul committed suicide story are bizarre." I sprang up from the window seat, pacing back and forth in frustration. "And, of course, the police aren't doing anything about Paul."

"And, neither should you, Star. This is getting crazier by the day. You might be in danger." She sighed, pursed her lips, and tilted her head up at me before continuing. "I wish you'd told all this to Lorcan. You might not want to talk to the garda, but he knows all of them. They'll listen to him."

"Sure, I'm the persistent Yank that the police would love to see go back to the States, but I won't do that. Not yet, anyway." I stopped pacing, too tired to even talk anymore; then I sat back onto the window seat. The shop's phone rang. Georgina disappeared into her office to answer it. When she reemerged, she placed a mug of hot peppermint tea on the seat beside me.

"Drink this," she ordered. "I need to follow up on this phone call."

While she was gone, I sipped the tea, watching cars drive by, and pedestrians meander up Main Street. Because of his height, Ted stood out from the crowd—that and the cell phone he had glued to his ear. He shook his head up and down as if in violent agreement with whatever was being said on the other end of the line. Just as he moved past the shop window, I jumped up, knocked on the glass, and waved to catch his eye. Seeing me, he ended the call, placed the phone into his jacket pocket, and stood looking through the glass as if he were surprised to see me. In two strides, I reached the door, opened it, and invited him in. Still looking puzzled, he stepped inside.

"Miss O'Brien. I didn't expect to see you here," he said, looking around at the shop's merchandise.

"Yes, I guess it does seem out of context, doesn't it?" I replied, glancing down at my flats and capris.

"Oh, no. It's not that I meant anything by it," he said, as his face reddened and his voice quieted.

"Don't worry about it. I'm not insulted," I laughed. "This is what I call my work and play uniform." Still seeing the confused look on his face, I explained about Georgina and my relationship with her. Looking relieved, he nodded. "Actually, I'm surprised to see you here in Castlebar. I thought you'd still be in Cong," I said.

"Aye, I was there but drove over here to file a report with the garda. Someone's still digging at the site. I thought the garda should know."

"More digging? Since last night?"

"Yes, someone is up to no good. The site is well posted now, with warnings that the government is in charge. No one should be on the property." He pulled his phone out of his pocket, waving it at me. "I called Dr. Treat to update him. He's going to meet with Dr. O'Dowd just in case someone from her department has been around again."

I doubted it. Whoever was digging up the site was from the area. *Or maybe was related to someone from the area*, I thought, thinking of Leonard. "The property belongs to Dan Doherty. Have you spoken with him?" I asked.

"Arrah, I well have. He's not happy. He even threatened me when I approached him." Shaking his head, Ted continued. "I run into it all the time when I have to complete an engineer's report. Property owners don't take to government regulations and interference."

"Did the tea help?" Aunt Georgina's voice broke into our conversation as she bustled from the back of the shop toward where we were standing. Stopping short, she looked at me and then up at Ted. "Oh, I'm sorry. I didn't know you were talking to someone."

"Ted, I'd like you to meet Georgina Hill, owner of the Golden Thread."

Ted smiled, extended his hand in greeting, and then turned toward the door. "I have to be off. Take care, Miss O'Brien. Pleased to have met you, Miss Hill."

"Who was that?" Aunt Georgina asked, watching Ted as he continued walking along the sidewalk.

"He's the engineer who was sent to Cong to analyze the origins of the nugget."

"Well, I hope he doesn't find much."

"What do you mean?" I asked.

"Every time someone finds a gold hotspot somewhere in the country, people go a little crazy. Cong is just too pretty of a place to have to put up with strangers traipsing through in search of gold."

"You seem pretty opinionated about it."

"I guess I am," she replied. "I'd just rather see salmon anglers and nature enthusiasts enjoying Ireland's rivers than gold mining fanatics. Anyway," – Georgina smiled, changing the subject – "I talked to Marcella about Maeve Baldwin."

"Does she know her?"

"Yes," Georgina replied, "Marcella says they go back to their school days. They went to boarding school together. Marcella says Maeve's harmless enough. And, Star, Marcella told me Maeve is Noel Carney's godmother. It seems she's always looking out for him, especially since he has no other family."

"Hmm, that's interesting. Maeve did say she knew him since he was a child. And, when I spoke to Detective O'Shea at the police station, he more or less said Noel Carney wasn't a suspect. I guess I was wrong about her and Carney as well. But I just think it's funny she's so interested in me."

"Well, based on what Marcella said, it's probably a case of Maeve feeling she has a stake in Noel's welfare. And here you are with your American accent coming into the area, finding a dead body and asking lots of questions. I'd imagine a lot of people would want to know more about you."

"I hope you're right," I said, handing her the mug. I touched her arm, thanked her, and headed back to French Hill, where I changed into my running clothes. I ran the entire length of Barney Road and back. With five miles racked up, I tossed my sweaty clothes onto the bathroom floor and stood under the hot water streaming from the showerhead until my fingers began to shrivel. Wrapped in an oversized L.L. Bean red plaid nightshirt that had belonged to Dylan, I made a steaming cup of peppermint tea and settled into one of the living room's deep, oversized Queen Anne chairs.

I reached for my Mead composition book and began writing. As the grate filled with the ashes of turf sods burning down, I committed my thoughts to paper as I'd been doing since I was a child. The writing process, like a magnifying glass, clarifies my intuitive notions and bits of information. I didn't edit my thoughts as I wrote about what I'd seen and whom I had spoken with regarding Paul, my impressions of the mysterious Evelyn, and my heartfelt gratitude for this place and the people I'd come to know here on this island. No wonder my mother had cried when she'd receive a letter from Ireland.

As I continued to write, a mind map formed of potential motives for Paul's murder. Ann Ryan and Leonard were at the top of my list. What did they have to do with Paul? Was Leonard the man whom he'd heard in the wood's arguing with Jane? Why hadn't Paul told me about the argument he overheard? Was Ann's story about the argument even true? She hated Jane; that much was obvious. Ann seemed to love Dan in a weird, possessive way. Enough to kill Jane and then Paul, eliminating all competition for Dan's affections? What would Paul tell me if we'd had a chance to talk? Who would Paul want me to talk to? Where did Evelyn belong in this tangled web, and *where was she*?

I finished the tea and closed the notebook, resting my head against the back of the chair. The phone rang. By the time I reached the kitchen to pick up the landline, the ringing had stopped. Moving from there to the guest bedroom where I'd set up my office, I pressed the blinking message button.

"Miss O'Brien, this is Dan Doherty. I know you befriended Paul. I'd like to talk to you. Please, ring me."

I raised my eyes in surprise. What could he want with me? I called the number he'd rattled off, but the line went straight to voicemail.

"Mr. Doherty, this is Star O'Brien returning your call. I'll be in Cong tomorrow morning. I'll let you know when I get there."

The scratching and barking announced Ashford's arrival. I ran to open the back door. He burst in, ran a few circles around me, and then zoomed to his bowls, where he alternated between wolfing down food and lapping up water. Lorcan stood in the doorway, his face lit by a smile.

"He looks like he had a good time," I said and gestured for Lorcan to come in. But he remained standing.

"I enjoyed having him with me. He's got lots of energy. Almost..." He paused for a second before continuing. "He's very much like my Ace."

"You have a dog?" I asked.

"I lost Ace a year ago. He was a collie, much like Ashford."

"I'm sorry. I didn't know," I said quietly.

The smile he gave me crinkled the lines around his blue eyes.

"It's fine. I miss him. That's all. Being with Ashford today reminds me that it's time to make room for another puppy in my life."

I didn't know what to say. I wanted to console him. I understood loss. But I just couldn't do it.

"Well," he said, "I've got an early morning tomorrow. I'll be going. Thanks for letting me take him today. Good night, Star."

"Good night, and thanks, Lorcan."

With that, he was gone.

CHAPTER 31

I jumped out of bed the next morning, intending to take a long run before leaving for Cong. Ashford took several spins around the garden, ran back into the house, and curled up on the love seat in the living room. By 10:30 a.m., I was showered, dressed, and on my way. Ashford drowsed beside me on the passenger seat. Funny, no one had claimed him yet. I'd checked with the vet but still no luck in identifying an owner. I decided to ask at The Quiet Man Café. Farmers invested time and money into border collies, and someone must be looking for him.

I parked my car in the lot across from the church. Ashford jumped out as soon as the car door cracked wide enough for him to squeeze through. Then he was gone over the bridge in the direction of the castle. As I headed toward the café to ask about any missing dog reports, I caught sight of Dan coming out of the fitness center with Sarah and Jimmy Mahoney. I pulled my iPhone from my holster and dialed Dan's number. Identifying myself, I told him I'd meet him at the café in five minutes. I didn't tell him I had him in my sights and with whom.

I'd already checked with the café owner and scanned the

bulletin board about missing border collies—all to no avail—
and ordered a pot of peppermint tea when Dan entered the
café. I sat at the farthermost back-corner table, facing the room,
which provided me with an opportunity to observe him. As he
approached the table, I was struck by how much he and Paul
looked alike.

"Miss O'Brien," he said, depositing his lean body in the seat
opposite me, "thank you for seeing me."

"I'm only doing this for Paul."

"Should we order some lunch first?" He didn't wait for my
answer. Instead, he turned to wave to the server.

"Your usual salad, Dan?" she asked.

"Yes, please put the dressing on the side, love." Patting his
stomach, he explained, "It's all about keeping the weight under
control."

"Nothing for me," I told the server.

Giggling at him, she wove her way around the tables toward
the kitchen door.

"Now" – sitting back in his chair, he observed me – "I know
Paul asked you to help him prove my innocence. I didn't
approve."

"Why not?" I asked.

He studied the plastic checked cloth covering the table
while he considered his answer.

"I'm well-liked and well known in this area. I'm not worried
about the garda. Everyone knows I didn't kill my wife."

"Any idea who might have wanted to?" I asked.

"No idea. I just know I didn't. Or Paul, for that matter."

"Paul? Why would anyone think he killed his mother?"

Dan barked a laugh. "Well, now, isn't that the rumor circu-
lating around town? Disparaging me and my family. I can't have
it. Paul adored his mother. Besides, I can think of many a man
who might have had it in for her."

I remained silent.

"She played around. I didn't like it. I didn't like what it did to my reputation. But I put up with it."

At that moment, the server arrived with his salad and dressing. His lips curled into a broad smile. "You're a great lass. Thank you."

Another giggle and a slight bow.

Even if I were hungry, I don't think my stomach could have taken his narcissistic personality. "So...what do you want from me?" I asked.

"I want you to talk to Paul's friends and some of the young people around town. Paul's contemporaries. Luke, Ben. He didn't commit suicide, and he didn't kill his mother. I'm sure of it."

Interesting. Did he know about the theory Ann Ryan was fomenting about Paul?

"What's your relationship with Ann Ryan?" I bluntly asked.

Almost choking on his lettuce leaves, he placed his fork on the table. "How do you know about that?" A slight red tinge rose across his cheekbones, confirming my guess about an affair.

"I understand that Jane was involved with Jake Ryan. I just wondered what had driven her into the arms of another man?"

Reaching for a glass of water, Dan laughed. "I'm not a believer in what's good for the goose is good for the gander. She shouldn't have strayed." His drinking water sloshed over the rim of the glass as he brought it to his mouth. He took a few sips before returning it to the table. "Especially with Jake Ryan." He pounded the table in emphasis.

I couldn't believe his ego. I wanted to throw the pitcher of water at him. But I remembered Paul's belief in his father's innocence. Dan was right about one thing—Paul hadn't committed suicide. "Why should I help you?"

Leaning forward in his chair, his eyes caught mine.

"I can see you don't like me, Miss O'Brien. But I'm not a

murderer. I loved Paul. Losing him, these rumors—my reputation is ruined. I need to put an end to it." Shrugging his shoulders, he toyed with the remainder of his salad. "I don't know what went wrong between Jane and me. But it was between us. We had no idea how it affected Paul."

"What about Jake Ryan? I know he's dead, but if he and Jane had an affair, could that have something to do with her death and with Paul's? Ann claims Paul remembered hearing an argument between Jane and another man in the woods. Could it have been Jake?"

"I don't know if t'were him or not."

"Did Ann know about the affair?"

He hesitated before responding. "If she didn't know about it then, she knows now. I told her. And I told Pat about it. Jake had no right to meddle in my marriage."

If it weren't for Paul, I'd have cut the conversation right then, but I couldn't let my suspicion of Dan keep me from finding out what happened to Paul. "Did Paul know?" I asked.

"I didn't tell him." He shrugged his shoulders. "Someone else might have. Anyway, that's neither here nor there. Will you help me? Will you help Paul?"

I didn't trust Dan. Even if he hadn't killed his wife or son, he was up to something. Whatever it was, it wasn't good.

"I'm not a detective," I stated.

"I know, but I've heard that you often assist people in situations where the garda have given up. I'd appreciate it if you would just ask around. Someone killed my Paul." He didn't wait for a reply. Instead, he threw euros onto the table and left the café.

I remained seated, thinking about what he'd said and hadn't said. I knew where I needed to go next.

Ben's shop was open. He stood before one of the shelves, rearranging books.

"Ah, Miss O'Brien. What brings you to me this morning?"

I didn't waste time on pleasantries. "You knew Jane Doherty was having an affair with Jake Ryan when I showed you that note."

"You've been talking with Luke, haven't you?"

"What does Luke have to do with this?" I asked.

Ben's hands stopped in midair as he turned to face me instead of the bookshelves.

"You've got to be kidding, Ms. O'Brien. You do know he's contesting his father's estate."

I recalled my angry interchange with Luke in the café and Aunt Georgina telling me something about Jake Ryan's will and Luke. I shrugged. "That doesn't mean I heard about an affair from him," I stated. "Besides, what would a relationship between two consenting adults have to do with Luke?"

Ben walked back to his desk, sat behind it, and beckoned me into the opposite chair.

"Well, first, very few people knew about Jane and Jake. Dan came around here after he'd talked to Ann and my mother. He seemed roiled up by the whole thing." Ben snorted a laugh. "I don't know what he expected me to do. After my father died, Jake opened his home to my mother and me. He was the only father I ever knew. If Dan thought telling me about the affair would tarnish Jake's reputation in my eyes, well, he was wrong." His lips tightened. Then, he picked up a paper clip from the desk. "I'm sure Luke's mother told him. She's been pining after Dan for years. She'd only be too happy to let everyone know that Jane and Dan weren't a loving couple." He paused for a moment. "I know she told Paul."

"Why would she do that?" I asked.

With each passing moment, I grew more suspicious of Ann's motives. For someone so starched and wrapped up in business deals, she seemed to enjoy creating emotional wounds with everyone in her circle—contemporaries and children.

"I don't know why she told Paul. He talked to me about it. And, he was angry—especially at his mother."

Another person was claiming Paul confided in them. Why hadn't he told me any of this?

Ben dropped the twisted and broken paper clip onto the desk. Turning his green eyes toward me, he swept his wavy locks away from his forehead. "As to telling Luke, maybe her motherly instincts kicked in. If she suspected a relationship between Jane and Luke..." Picking up what remained of the paper clip again, Ben tapped the desk as if to underline what he said next. "Well, Ann'd do anything to drive the knife deeper into Jane." He settled back into the chair, keeping his gaze on me. "Talk to Luke. He's crazy mad to get his father's stud farm. If he knew something that would help him win his case, he'd pursue it to the ends of the earth."

"It doesn't make sense. What could Jane's and Paul's deaths have to with Luke's case for his father's estate?"

Ben laughed. "You don't know the half of it. Rose Cottage and Doherty's mill sit between Happy Trails and Luke's stud farm. He wants the land. He won't be satisfied until he has it all. And I think he'll do anything to get it."

I wasn't buying it. Could an affair between Jake and Jane be used as fodder in a court of law to overturn a will? Had Luke been the man Paul heard arguing with Jane in the woods? Possibly. Had Luke used an affair with Jane as leverage to get Dan to sell the property? Had Paul learned something that would have made whatever claim Luke had on Jake's will null and void? I didn't have the answers to these questions. But I did know that Rose Cottage happened to be at the nexus of it all. The abandoned—or so it seemed—excavation site, the gold ore, and the desire of people like Ann to see it sold, were all bound together in some way and connected to Paul's murder. What that connection was, I didn't know yet.

Deciding to change direction, I asked, "Do you think Paul was capable of harming himself?"

"Anything is possible, Miss O'Brien. There are old hurts here that go back years. I don't know what motivated Paul. He wanted his father to sell Rose Cottage. Maybe that's why Ann told Paul about the affair." He gazed toward the books that lined the shelves behind me and shrugged his shoulders. "But Luke. Although he won't admit it, he's like his mother. It's all about the business and jealousy of his father's success. If I were you, I'd look there for the answer to my question."

The landline's jarring ring ruptured the conversation. Shifting in his seat to lift the receiver, Ben listened to whatever the person on the other end had to say before covering the mouthpiece with his hand.

"Please, excuse me, Ms. O'Brien."

Knowing when I'd been dismissed, I rose to my feet and headed toward the exit. Looking back as I closed the door, I caught him—still listening to whoever was on the other end— slamming his fist onto the desk after he tossed the paper clip onto the floor.

Outside the shop, a flurry of activity at the other end of the street garnered my attention. Ashford lay on his back while Luke Ryan bent over him, rubbing and fluffing the hair on the dog's belly. This wasn't a picture I'd ever have imagined. Yeah, sure, Ashford seemed to love making new acquaintances. But Luke? Where was the anger I'd witnessed and experienced on several occasions? Maybe Ben was right about an affair between Jane and Luke. Could he have been the man in the woods arguing with Jane? At that moment, Ashford saw me, barked, and ran toward me. At the same time, I headed toward Luke with the intention of getting answers to some direct questions.

CHAPTER 32

L uke Ryan uncoiled from his crouched position. His broad, muscular shoulders overshadowed a lean torso that twisted itself toward me.

"I have to go, Miss O'Brien. One of my mares has a foal on the way."

The words hung in the air as he turned to open the door to his Land Rover. Whenever I'd seen Luke, he'd been stomping around, creating scenes to display his anger. Today was different. His anger seemed cold, remote—held in check.

"You love animals, don't you?" I asked.

For a moment, he froze in place before dropping his hand to his side and turning to face me.

"Sometimes, animals are more compassionate than people, Miss O'Brien. I learned that years ago."

Nodding in agreement, I lowered my hand to rub Ashford's head, recognizing that Luke's anger masked some deep hurt and disappointment.

"Luke, were you having an affair with Jane Doherty before she died?" I asked.

His blue eyes widened. His head recoiled. "I'm sorry, Miss

O'Brien. I made a mistake about you. I thought you wanted to talk about Paul's unfortunate accident."

"I don't believe Paul committed suicide. Do you?"

Luke hesitated before answering, his shoulders broadening again. "I don't know what happened to Paul. Our last conversation was about Rose Cottage. I wanted to buy the place, and he wanted his father to sell the cottage. Beyond that, Paul and I didn't have much of a relationship."

"Did he ask you about his father's relationship with your mother? Paul didn't believe the police's theory that his father might have murdered his mother."

A harsh laugh escaped from Luke's narrowed lips.

"Ah, yes, the parents. They have a way of messing up our lives, don't they? Paul's parents enjoyed spending time with other people's spouses. It's anybody's guess, Miss O'Brien, who might have had it in for Jane and why."

"What about your parents? Do you think they messed up your life?" I asked.

"My parents never knew I existed." The words erupted through his lips like a growl. "Now, I really have to leave."

"Did you have an affair with Jane Doherty?" I asked again.

"That, Miss O'Brien, is my secret. Please, don't bother me anymore. My stud farm may be small, but it's successful. I don't have time to atone for the missteps of my parents or anyone else's, for that matter."

Twisting his body toward his Land Rover, he gripped the door handle, hopped in, and gunned the engine, stoking a cloud of stones, debris, and bits of notepaper to rise above the pavement. When the dust settled, one of the scraps landed with the scribbled words facing up. Reaching down to pick it up, I read the words *in trust for*. The uneven edge did not reveal any name. The other pieces were blank. Had this been here when I approached Luke, or had he dropped it?

Nudging his nose into the backs of my knees, Ashford

moved me in the direction of the road leading up to the castle. Dusting off my hands, I took in the name plastered across the building where Luke had been parked—Blake and Kenny Solicitors. So...he was meeting with lawyers.

"Let's go for a walk," I said to Ashford.

For once, Ashford stayed at my side as we sauntered along the castle's driveway. Once in a while, cars passed us on their way either to or from the castle grounds. It didn't make sense to me that an affair was the motivating factor here. If I believed Dan, Ann, and Luke, affairs were normal operating procedure. When Ashford and I left the wooded path behind us, the castle loomed ahead. I glanced back at the ancient trees, wondering what secrets they held. I stopped to look at Ashford.

"What secrets do you know, boy?" I asked.

In response, he barked and leaped toward the castle, leaving me standing with my hands on my hips, wondering why in the world someone wasn't looking for him.

I continued walking, intending to check on any reports of a lost dog at the castle's reception area. My feet froze in place midway up the wide stone steps to the impressive lobby doors. Detectives Tom O'Shea and James Keenan exited. Keenan, seeing me, tapped his partner's arm. As he looked down at me and then back to the papers in his hand, the scar on O'Shea's face seemed to throb. He folded the papers in half before placing them into his pocket. Both men continued their descent, brushing by me on their way to a car parked just to the side of the castle.

"You're wrong," I stated. I couldn't help myself. I had to say something.

O'Shea turned back. "Wrong? What is it now, Miss O'Brien?" he asked.

"Paul Doherty didn't commit suicide."

"This is a constant refrain with you, isn't it? We're wrong. We're always wrong." Throwing his hands up in the air, he continued. "Do you think we're involved in some kind of conspiracy?" Keenan moved closer to O'Shea, tapping him on the arm again. O'Shea shrugged him off and kept on with his questions. "Do you want to be responsible for shifting our attention from real crimes? Because that's what happens when civilians waste our time."

"Paul didn't kill himself. I'll prove it."

"I'm sorry, Miss O'Brien, but we've confirmed Paul Doherty's handwriting on that note you found. Now, stay out of garda business." O'Shea nodded to Keenan. They turned to walk toward their car. Looking back at me, O'Shea opened the driver door, and his voice rose to deliver one last bit of advice across the macadam. "This time, it's a warning. Next time, you may find yourself brought up on charges for interfering in an active investigation."

I stood on the castle steps, thinking about his words. Interestingly, he used the phrase *active investigation*. Was he referring to Jane? Or to something else? The only way I'd find out was to keep asking questions, which is what I intended to do.

A short time later, after the lobby staff assured me that no one had reported a missing dog, I stood in the castle's shadow, wondering if I'd lost Ashford. As usual, he'd disappeared.

I left the manicured castle grounds, headed back into the woods toward Cong. I hurtled along the path, taking care as I went not to stumble on dead branches or get caught up in thorny bushes. Worried now that I wouldn't be able to find Ashford in time to get home and call my office, I thought about whom I might enlist to help me find him. That was the trouble with being left alone as a child or abandoned as Ashford seemed to have been—sometimes, we slip away from others before they have a chance to leave us. The sun had settled into the horizon when I traversed the bridge into the Abbey's cemetery. A movement at the base of one of the obelisks flickered across my peripheral vision. I stopped moving. The monument's shadow hid whomever, or whatever was there. I could hear cars moving along the street at the far side of the grounds. I wasn't going to be frightened. Neither was I going to end up in a well or a hole in the ground. Grabbing my iPhone, I turned on its flashlight and marched in the direction of the towering stone. Then I saw Ashford. His bark bounced off the headstones, reverberating around me as if to contradict my thoughts. In seconds, he reached me, running circles around me. He proceeded to follow me from the cemetery to my parked car. But before we got in, I hugged his sturdy, furry body to mine.

CHAPTER 33

I kept to the speed limits through the villages and towns of the Neale, Ballinrobe, Partry, Balintubber, and Castlebar while in my mind's eye, I turned over the conversations I'd had with Pat. Seeing her in the stable, handling the horses, I'd describe her as nurturing and supportive. The invitation into her home for sustenance reminded me of Aunt Georgina. But unlike Georgina, Pat seemed like she kept to herself most of the time. Private. Now, I realized these personality traits might have been fostered by the emotional wounds she suffered when she learned her partner had cheated with a close friend. How many times had she accepted his behavior just to keep their relationship intact? Despite it all, she'd kept her home together, building a legacy with Jake in the form of Happy Trails. She may have been able to accept his infidelities, but would she be able to accept losing what she'd spent her life building?

Back in French Hill, I poured food and water into Ashford's dishes. He ate like he hadn't seen food in days. Wherever he'd wandered this afternoon, it hadn't been to someone's kitchen. Satisfied that he was taken care of, I picked up the landline and dialed Phillie. She answered on the first ring.

"I can't find any sign of this Cosgrove woman, boss."

"What about other excavation sites in England and Ireland?" I asked. "Have you checked to see if she's back at the dig in London where her husband disappeared?"

"I've looked into everything. And I can't find anything. There's nothing." Her voice rose as she spoke, punctuated with a sigh of frustration.

On my end, I stared at the computer screen as if it contained the answer. I hid my disappointment from Phillie, asking her about the Women in Technology group, where she served on one of the committees. "How's the conference planning going?" I asked.

"I'm working like the Energizer Bunny to get more women involved in our mission." Her clipped words transmitted their energy from the other side of the Atlantic.

"You're making a difference, Phillie. Let me know how I can help."

"Well, yes. Already done, boss." There was a slight delay during which I heard her clicking away at her keyboard. "Sorry, one of my alerts just pinged."

"Anything I should know about?" I asked.

"Not yet. Oh, so, yes, you are helping, boss. I volunteered the Consulting Detective's resources to identify potential companies who might want to serve as a sponsor."

"That's—"

Before I could say anything more, Phillie interrupted. "I'll keep looking for info on the Cosgrove woman and the dig in London where her husband disappeared. In the meanwhile, I've got to go. The meeting conference call is starting. Here's Ellie."

Ellie's voice came on the line. "When are you coming home? Sheila Bixler wants to know when she can speak with you."

Sheila Bixler and my adoptive parents had been friends. When I'd lost the O'Briens to a small plane crash, she'd stepped in, giving moral support that got me through their funeral. Now CEO of Southern Aircraft, her schedule kept her busy. If Sheila herself had contacted Ellie, the issue must be serious.

"Did you talk to Jim Hipple?" I asked.

"Yes, but based on what I told him, he said it sounds like you need to speak with Sheila first. Besides, he's involved in several projects right now. He couldn't give it the attention it might require."

"Okay, contact her assistant and arrange a time that suits Sheila's schedule. Anything else?"

"Yes, the Schipperke Rescue network called. They'd like you to sponsor another Schipperke. They've just rescued more than a dozen Schipps from a puppy mill."

I kicked the leg of the computer table, wishing I could direct pain on the lowlifes who ran these mills. "I don't know how I can do that, Ellie. I'm fostering a dog here until his owners turn up."

Ashford, who'd situated himself at my feet after he'd eaten, lifted his head. I ruffled his hair. "And, then, with being away, it's not fair to you, Phillie, or Skipper. If I could bring Skipper with me to Ireland, it might work."

"We researched the quarantine rules. Hold on a minute; let me check the details." I could hear papers rustling in the background. Then, Ellie was back. "It doesn't look like quarantine is an option. The compliance rules require something like six months of isolation once he gets to Ireland."

"Well, then, I'll have to travel between home and the cottage here for brief stays at a time." I couldn't imagine being away from the Consulting Detective for long periods of time. And, since I didn't plan to remain in Ireland permanently, I didn't want to put Skipper through an extensive quarantine just to have him with me.

"Don't worry, Star. He's doing fine here with us." Ellie

laughed. "I'll admit he looks for you all through the house, but then he gets involved with visitors and neighbors."

"Yeah, I know Skipper is quite the extrovert." I smiled, picturing him doing his patty cake begging routine. "Especially when he's on the receiving end of the treats people bring to him."

"That reminds me. Joanne sends her regards."

"Don't tell me. She's been baking puppy cookies for Skipper again."

Ellie's giggle was all the answer I needed. I knew I shouldn't do it, but I couldn't help myself. A rescue is a rescue. "Go ahead and let Sue know that we'll take one of the Schipps. We'll foster until we find a compatible owner."

Ellie's laugh reverberated through the phone line. "Good, I was hoping you'd say yes. Our treehouse family needs growing."

"I don't know what I'd do without you and Phillie," I said and ended the call.

Then, my phone rang again. I picked it up quickly, thinking Ellie was calling back but was surprised instead to hear Dr. O'Dowd's voice on the other end.

"Miss O'Brien, I'm glad I caught you at home," she said.

"How are you, Dr. O'Dowd?" I asked.

"I'm fine. I hope you don't mind me ringing you, but you did give me your card. I've heard from Evelyn."

My hand clutched the phone. Finally, I was about to get a contact number.

Dr. O'Dowd continued. "She asked me to tell you she's sorry for being so unreachable. And, she does want to talk to you at some point. But she hopes you'll understand that she cannot do so at this time."

What! I almost pulled the phone line from the wall, but I managed instead to ask, "What's going on?"

"When you and I met in my office, I chose not to tell you about Evelyn's history..."

I interrupted her immediately. "If you mean about her husband's murder in England, I already know all that."

"Well, then you'll understand that Evelyn gets very nervous. She's always felt what happened to Donal had something to do with her."

"I agree a murder or disappearance in someone's life changes how safe one feels. But I can assure you; I'm not a threat. And, I'll remind you she initiated the questions about someone with my mother's name."

"Yes, yes, I know all that. But I have to respect her wishes."

"Did she tell you why she's not at the dig in Cong?" I asked.

"She thought someone was watching her when she was at the dig site. A few times, she was sure someone followed her home. So, she decided to get out of Dodge, as you Yanks would say."

"But her recorded message on her phone said she'd be back by the tenth of September."

"I told you that Evelyn's flighty. Things like voicemail greetings and messages aren't usually up-to-date. I'm sorry, Miss O'Brien, but Evelyn did say she'd get in touch with you when she's ready. That will have to suffice. Now, good night."

And with that, the call ended. I headed toward the bedroom to change into a pair of sweatpants. Ashford abandoned me in the living room, plopping himself in front of the fireplace. Then, the phone rang again.

"Hello," I said.

"Good. You are home," Aunt Georgina stated.

"Where else would I be?"

"Don't get testy with me, girl. I worry about you."

"Okay, okay. I'm fine. How was your day?" I didn't know why, but I just couldn't bring myself to tell her about Dr. O'Dowd's call.

"I'm exhausted and thought I'd have an early evening of it. Otherwise, I'd have stopped to see you."

"I'm okay, really."

"I happened to see Pat O'Malley this evening in town. She said you were at Happy Trails today."

"Yes, I was hoping she'd shed some light on what happened to Paul. But she wasn't much help. She seems troubled."

"You mean because of Luke contesting the will."

"No, I mean because she's put up with Jake's infidelities—including with her best friend—for years."

"Mother of God. What kind of carry on is that? No wonder Luke thinks he might be able to contest the will."

"Even so, I don't think he'd stand a chance."

"You'd be surprised what happens in these cases. Especially if he's got proof of the affair with Jane."

Just as I began to tell her about my meeting with Luke, I heard her doorbell ring.

"Star, I've got to go. Someone's at the door. I'll see you in the morning."

Not long after, I joined Ashford in the living room, nestling myself into one of the chairs. An hour passed as I wrote up my notes. I'd just finished when my iPhone rang. Realizing it was almost midnight, I rushed to pull the phone out of its case.

"Ms. O'Brien?"

"Yes." The voice sounded familiar.

"Bridgett Sumner. I've been meaning to ring you."

Another unexpected call. I'd helped Bridgett clear her brother's reputation last summer but hadn't ever expected to hear from her again.

"How are you? Is everything okay?" I asked.

"I'm fine. I'm calling about you."

"Oh?"

"Yes, Matthew's work on Clare Island won posthumous recognition last month."

"I read something about that in the *Connacht Telegraph* newspaper."

"Well, during the ceremony on Clare Island, I happened to get talking to some of the residents about the O'Malley name."

"Yes." My empty hand reached for my phone case, holding it close to my side.

"Someone mentioned O'Malleys on Achill Island." She hesitated before continuing. "I don't know if what the person told me is relevant, but I decided you'd want to know."

"Of course, I do."

When she spoke again, her voice was stronger. I remembered how she'd raise her left arm into the air when she wanted to emphasize her point of view. "A family of O'Malleys all died in a house fire with the exception of one daughter. She went to America. It happened ages ago, but people still talk about it. House fires were prevalent at one time, and people don't forget it when family members perish."

"I'd like to talk with the person who told you the story," I said.

"I thought you might. I have her name and mobile number here."

I wrote the information into my notebook and thanked her.

"I don't know if it will lead anywhere. But it's worth a try. I haven't forgotten all you did for my parents and me. I hope it works out for you, Star."

I thanked her again, pressed end on my iPhone, and stared at the words I'd written. Maggie O'Malley Hanlon. Maybe it was the name. Maybe I was tired. Maybe it was the call from Dr. O'Dowd. But I just couldn't think anymore. Maybe I should just put these thin threads, Hanlon and Evelyn, aside. Maybe it was time to just go to sleep. Ashford followed me into the bedroom, where I turned out the light and pulled the covers over my head.

At two in the morning, Ashford's deep-throated barks woke

me. Realizing he was standing at the bedroom door, back arched, I sat up and grabbed my iPhone from under the pillow. The sensor lights over the front door of the cottage were on. Moonlight filtered through the gauzy curtains. If anyone was outside, they had a good view of me. I slipped from the bed onto the floor, where I would be out of sight. My hands felt for the pants and T-shirt I'd thrown onto the floor before dropping into bed. I pulled them and my Rocket Dogs on. Crawling across the rug to Ashford, I tried to quiet him unsuccessfully. He was keyed into something, ready to pounce on whatever or whoever was on the other side.

Getting to my feet, I swung the door open, ready for a confrontation. Ashford bolted toward the kitchen and the back door, his barks louder, each one separated from the other in a staccato beat. Following behind him, I arrived in the kitchen in time to hear a car door slam and an engine start. I opened the door in the hope of getting a glimpse of the car model or its owner. Ashford took off after it, barking each step of the way. The driver didn't turn on the headlights. Whoever was out there, stealth was an objective. After Ashford was sure the car was well on its way, he returned, stopping to give one last bark before nosing me back into the house. Once inside, I dialed the police. The dispatcher said he'd make a note of it, but since no apparent break-in occurred, nothing could be done.

After checking all the windows and doors for a second time, I abandoned the bedroom, lying instead on the living room floor, nestled up against Ashford. The desk dispatcher had suggested maybe some teenagers had found a deserted nook to smoke and drink away from their parents' eyes. He was probably right. I'd noticed cigarette butts strewn around near the barn. I'd also noticed the sensor light in that area of the property wasn't working. First thing in the morning, I'd call a local electrician to check all the lights around the cottage.

I dragged myself into the kitchen at 5:00 a.m. I hadn't slept at all. I wanted to go for a run but knew I had other priorities. I called Aunt Georgina.

"Well, this is early," she answered.

"Sorry, I hope I didn't wake you."

"No, I'm up. Just packing up some food to bring over to you later this morning."

"That sounds wonderful. Do you think you could come over now?"

"What happened?"

"I've been up most of the night. Ashford heard something, and then there was a car…"

"I'm on my way." She didn't wait to hear the rest of what I had to say.

A short time later, she arrived, her arms wrapped around two full grocery bags. After she placed the packages on the table, she threw her arms around me.

"Are you okay?" she asked when she stepped back.

"Yes, I'm just exhausted."

"Well, girleen, you sit right down there while I make breakfast. I want to hear all about what happened last night."

CHAPTER 34

While Aunt Georgina basted eggs with butter, fresh chives, and lemon juice, I explained, in between bites of her homemade brown bread, about Ashford sounding the alarm, the car, and the sensor lights.

"Hmm, I'm glad to see you still have your appetite," she said as she ladled the eggs onto our plates and sat down at the table. "Did you call the garda, Star?"

"I did. But they couldn't do anything. Or didn't want to!" My frustration with them showed as I dug my fork into the soft egg yolk.

"Well, it's a farming area, after all. The garda travel through the community as best they can. I'm sure if they see anything suspicious, they'll investigate."

"Hmm. Well, I'll call an electrician this morning." I said, finishing the last of the food on my plate. "I'm just glad Ashford was here."

"I've got to get the shop open," Georgina said, rising from the table. "Why don't you go shower while I keep an eye on Ashford and tidy up here."

Shortly after, I walked back into the kitchen, feeling refreshed and ready to begin a new day. Aunt Georgina sat at the kitchen table, writing in a pocket-sized, green-covered diary.

"I didn't know you kept a diary."

"Oh, just something I do once in a while to sort through decisions and such."

Now it was my turn to worry about Georgina. She never seemed to have to *sort through decisions*.

"Is everything okay?" I asked.

"Yes." She shut the book, placing it into her voluminous messenger bag and turned toward the door. "I'll see you later."

"I'll call. I have some things to follow up on here, including a nine o'clock phone appointment."

As soon as Georgina left, I went into my office space to wait for the call from Sheila Bixler. As usual, she was punctual despite the fact that it was 4:00 a.m. on her side of the Atlantic. I answered on the first ring.

"Sheila, it's been too long since we've spoken."

"I'm well. But the company has a problem," she replied.

"Yes, Ellie said you only wanted to speak with me," I said. "I'm sorry I'm not there to meet in person, but if you agree, I can have Jim Hipple do some work for us until I get back."

When she didn't respond, I said, "What's going on?"

"It's a patent issue. A distant, very *distant*, relative of the original Southern founders is claiming we don't own the patent for one of our engines."

"Don't you have the patent paperwork?" I asked.

"That's the problem, Star. It's missing. Whether it's misplaced or stolen, I don't know. I have several private investigators looking into it. But...I'd feel better if you were doing some of the information gathering and hunting down of documents."

"I'll do everything I can to help you," I said. "I've signed the contract. Ellie has it. And, I expect she's returned it to your lawyers by now. Do I have your permission to have Jim get started? I'll be in Ireland for a few more days."

"Yes, I'll speak with the legal department and have Jim identified as one of your consultants... Hurry back, Star. I need you."

~

THE ELECTRICIAN QUICKLY FIXED THE SENSOR LIGHT, REPLACING the bulb. He promised to return later in the day to install a second light at the other corner of the barn, telling me I didn't have to be home. Instead, he'd place his bill for the work through the mail slot in the front door. Satisfied that everything was under control, I took Ashford and left for Cong.

When we arrived, rather than park in the village and walk through the woods to Rose Cottage, I opted to drive along the road that wound past the mill and the cottage. Just as I came abreast of the mill's driveway, I spotted Dan's Prius backed up close to the mill entrance—the trunk was open. From my vantage point, I couldn't see whether he was loading or unloading the vehicle. Convinced that he was up to no good, I pulled into the driveway and exited my Renault. Ashford jumped out after me, taking off in pursuit of a group of rooks and jackdaws that made a clamoring exodus when the car door slammed.

Pointing to the No Trespassing sign, Dan said, "Don't you understand English? It's not safe to be around an abandoned building." Then he lowered the trunk lid and walked to the front of his car. "Why are you here? Have you learned something about Paul?" He folded his arms over his chest, studied my face, and waited for an answer.

"No, I haven't." In turn, I scrutinized his face and pointed toward the trunk. "I'm curious. If the mill is shut down, what are you doing here?"

"That's none of your business," he replied.

"If it has anything to do with Paul, I want to know."

"It has nothing to do with him," he said, his voice rising higher with each word.

"He believed in you." My voice lowered as I spoke each word. "I don't. You're hiding something. Is it in the mill?" I took a step toward the entrance.

His arms dropped to his sides as he moved forward, blocking my way. "There's nothing here that concerns Paul, you, or anyone else for that matter," he said. "I wish the lot of ye would disappear, once and for all." With that, he turned back toward his car. When he reached the driver's door, he glanced at me and said, "If you can't find what happened to Paul without sticking your nose into my business, maybe you should quit." Then, he got in and sped away.

I waited until his car rounded the bend in the road, then I ran toward the mill entrance and tried the door handle. It was locked. Most of the windows were covered over with plywood, but I was able to peek through one where part of the board was broken off. All I could see was a table littered with a variety of knives and blades. Sawdust lay in scattered piles on the floor. I could make out some footprints. It all looked like what one would expect from a shuttered business. Nothing seemed suspicious *except* for the door lock, which was shiny, new, stainless steel, and required a card key for access—no chance of finding a key under a rock or buried in the dirt nearby. Then, when I turned to leave, I spotted the video camera mounted in the eave over the door. Unless someone were looking for it, it would go unnoticed. Still convinced Dan was up to something, I decided to talk to Ben. First, though, I'd take another look around Rose Cottage. I called for Ashford, but as usual, he'd disappeared. Taking one last scan of the area, I got into my car and drove to the cottage.

∼

I ARRIVED TO FIND SEVERAL VEHICLES, INCLUDING A WHITE PANEL van with government plates, located along the side of the road. I parked mine, jumped out, and walked toward the crowd gathered outside the cottage's gate. I wasn't surprised to see Dan among the onlookers.

Moving beyond the group of gawkers, I strode up to Ted, who stood just on the other side of the gate. There I saw the mounds of earth, piled to the side of a four-foot-deep hole in the cottage grounds.

"Take it easy with that dirt, lads," Ted said. "It's valuable."

The three men, working with shovels to transfer the dirt to a wheelbarrow and then to a large plastic container, continued with their task.

"I guess you've confirmed there's gold here," I said.

"Aye, it's fairly dense in this particular area. We're moving what we've dug up to Dublin." Ted paused to ask everyone to step back as another worker arrived to hoist the first of the plastic containers over to the back of the government van.

"I called the garda and asked for assistance. I can't let anyone near this place or take any of the soil, for that matter."

Just then, a police car cruised to a stop. Two officers stepped out and began shepherding everyone on their way, including Dan. As he got back into his car, he glanced over his shoulder to look at me. His eyes narrowed. His lips pressed into a thin line. Then, he nodded, slammed the door, and drove away.

∼

I HEADED BACK TO CONG AND ANN RYAN'S REAL ESTATE OFFICE. It was time to put more pressure on her regarding the lie she'd been spewing about Paul. I felt like I'd hit the jackpot when I walked into her office and found not only Ann but Luke and

Leonard there as well. The first thing I noticed was the sheaves of paper that Leonard quickly folded up.

"We are busy here, Miss O'Brien. Sorry, but I don't have time to speak with you." Ann Ryan rose from her desk and tried to usher me back through the doorway.

"I'm not budging until you answer my questions," I replied. "You are using the Irish succession laws to get control of Happy Trails." I didn't really know but seeing them together like this brought it all into focus for me. I turned to Leonard. "Let me see those papers. I'll bet they are for some big development scheme you've all cooked up."

Before Leonard could reply, Luke's voice blasted through the office. "You are some crazy Yank, coming in here and demanding information from us. Who do you think you are?"

Faced with Luke's anger, I almost turned and ran out, but I stood my ground. "I don't believe for one second that Paul committed suicide. Happy Trails, Jane Doherty, and maybe Rose Cottage are at the center of this whole tragic end to Paul's life. Now, are you in on this land scheme with these two or not?"

"I only want to expand my stud farm. And Happy Trails should by rights belong to me. Don't try to get in my way, any of you," he shouted and stormed out of the building, slamming the door behind him.

"My son was always excitable, Miss O'Brien, but he'll calm down in time." Ann Ryan's eyes narrowed as she looked between Leonard and me. "I know how this looks, but you've got this, us, all wrong. We want to preserve the land. We're just trying to help Dan."

"Yes, that's right," Leonard chimed in.

"Is that so?" I would have laughed in his face but for the fact that Paul would never laugh again. "Is Dan in on this family venture? Is that why Jane is dead?"

Leonard glanced from me to his sister's face, his own a

mirror of uncertainty. Then he shrugged. "I'm just trying to help my sister. We grew up here. We have a right to see that things stay in our family."

Based upon our confrontation in Dublin, I knew he was a coward, so I stepped closer to him and said, "Is that why you followed me in Dublin? Is that why you've been stalking Evelyn Cosgrove?" I didn't have any proof that he had anything to do with Evelyn's disappearance, but my gut told me I was right. Instead of answering, Leonard shuffled his feet and stepped back.

"Admit that you've been following her." I stepped forward again in an effort to press Leonard into confessing.

His face crumpled along with his body as he slumped into one of the office chairs. "Okay, I admit I've been hanging around the area. It's just that she and that Dr. O'Dowd are so secretive. I couldn't get a word out of them about the dig site." He looked up at his sister with tears in his eyes. "I've only been trying to help Ann. I wouldn't have done anything to Evelyn. I just wanted to be able to provide Ann with information."

Ann's manicured hands waved her brother off like a gnat before she said, "I know what's best for Dan. He doesn't need to be in on all my thinking. He can fetch loads of money with the land the mill and Rose Cottage stand on. It would be nice to see a development of single-family homes there."

I figured I was right then about the papers Leonard tried to hide and why Ann had been busy courting Dan, but they hadn't answered all my questions. "What about Happy Trails? Are you working with Luke to get control of the stud farm?"

"No, that's between my son and Pat O'Malley. And as you witnessed, I don't get in Luke's way when he's angry. And you shouldn't either, Miss O'Brien," Ann replied. "Besides, he doesn't need my help. He'll win in the end."

"So, you killed Jane and then Paul to get control of Dan and his property," I accused them.

Ann laughed. "Don't be ridiculous. Once the government finishes up at the cottage, Dan will sell. I didn't need to get rid of Jane or Paul, Miss O'Brien. They did a good job of doing that themselves. Now, please leave. My brother and I have business to attend to." Then she turned her back to me and held her hand out to Leonard for the papers, which he passed to her.

Anger surged through me. How could these manipulative, greedy people still be walking around free? The police, as usual, seemed to be doing nothing. I followed Luke's example and slammed the office door as I left.

I WALKED TOWARD BEN'S PLACE. MAYBE HE'D HAVE SOME INSIGHT into where the police were in the investigation into Jane's and Paul's deaths. The lights were on in the shop, but I didn't see Ben. The door was unlocked, so I stepped inside and then checked the time. He should be here. Voices emanated from somewhere behind his desk. Moving toward that area, I noticed a curtain hanging over a door. I pulled the curtain aside and tapped on the door. When no one answered, I opened the door and ventured across the threshold of what looked like a storage area that led to the building's back exit. Ben sat, with his back to me, on the floor, rummaging through a box of books. When he didn't look up from his task, I walked over to him. "Do you have time for lunch?" I asked.

"What the heck!" He dropped the book he was holding onto the floor, jumped to his feet, and wiped his hands on his jeans. "You could give a fellow a heart attack, sneaking up on him like that."

"Sorry, but I didn't know what else to do. You were so intent." I looked around at what seemed like a mountain of boxes, spilling over with books. "You really love what you do, don't you?"

"Aye, it's my passion." He glanced at the back door, then bent to close the lid on the cardboard box. "And thankfully, I make a good living at it." He shook his head and continued. "You know, Paul was one of my best customers. He was always looking for another history book about an esoteric subject. Ah, well. Did I hear you ask about lunch? If so, the answer is yes. I'm famished. Let's go." He pointed at the door back into the shop, leading the way to his desk, where he picked up a ring of keys. "Anyway, what are you doing back in Cong?"

"I've just come from Rose Cottage. Ted's there with a crew. He confirmed the presence of gold ore. Lots of it from the looks of the amount of dirt they were carting off." I paused to run my hand along one of the bookshelves, its contents covered in leather. "I can't help but wonder if the gold has anything to do with Jane and Paul's deaths."

"That's actually a valid point. Hold on a minute. I've been moving books from Jake's library to the shop. I saw a book on the shelf that Paul was interested in at one point." Ben walked over to where I stood, but just as he reached forward, his phone rang. Glancing at the digital display, he held up his hand. "Hold on; I'll have to take this." He walked back into the storage area, closing the door behind him.

While I waited, I browsed the shelf he'd pointed at. Several of the book titles referenced the geography and topography of ancient ruins. Wondering if any mentioned Cong, I chose one entitled, *A Topographical Dictionary of Ireland*. I opened it, intending to look at the table of contents and index. Instead, a blank piece of paper fluttered onto the floor. Curious, I picked it up. Just a placeholder I guessed, but it did bring to mind Paul's supposed suicide note, the Dear Jake note I'd found, and the note Paul had found in his mother's jacket pocket about meeting someone in the woods near the priest hole.

"Righto, the book I mentioned is here somewhere." Ben's words interrupted my thoughts.

"It's okay." I waved my hand toward the shop entrance. "I'm starving. Let's eat now. Besides, I have to be back in French Hill for a call later this afternoon," I said, noting the time on my iPhone.

We walked across the street to The Quiet Man Café in silence. After we both ordered, I debated whether to tell Ben about the discussion I'd had with Ann Ryan and her brother. First, though, I wanted to know more about Paul's interest in the geology of the area. It seemed just too coincidental that Paul had perused a book on topography when gold was found at Rose Cottage.

After the server disappeared into the kitchen to place our order, I restarted our earlier conversation. "You were saying that Paul was researching the local topography."

"Yes, and don't ask me why. He never talked about his research much." Ben paused to load up his mug of tea with several teaspoons of sugar. "Do you think he knew about the ore? He'd been palling around with Evie a lot in the last few months."

"Paul didn't say anything to me." For a few seconds, I doubted Paul's honesty but dismissed the thought with a shrug. At that moment, the server appeared with our food. In between taking bites of our sandwiches, we continued to discuss the activity at Rose Cottage.

"You told me you hadn't seen Evelyn for months? Is that true?" I asked.

"Why would I lie? We were close once, but then Paul came into her orbit, and she dropped me." Ben's eyes widened, and his teeth clenched before he continued. "She didn't have much use for me, I guess. Too boring!"

"Well, without Paul and Evelyn, I have no way of knowing how much they knew about the ore. Besides, I don't think gold fever murdered Jane and Paul. I think something else is going on. Something closer to home."

"Like what?" Ben asked.

Moving my empty plate to the side, I told him about the conversation at Ann Ryan's real estate office. "Do you know about their scheme?" I asked at the end of my recap.

Ben's eyes narrowed. "Is this why you invited me to lunch?" The words escaped his clenched jaw in a whisper.

"I'm sorry. I have to ask. I just can't ignore the facts."

"What does a land grab scheme have to do with anything?" he countered.

"I don't know yet. But Luke was there too. And Ann seems convinced he'll win his case for Happy Trails. Ben, I saw your mother this morning, and she looked somewhat distraught. This fight for the farm seems to be taking its toll. Don't you think you should try to get to the bottom of what's going on around here?"

Ben's shoulders slumped, and a sigh escaped through his lips. Then he said, "I don't know what to do."

"Ben, a murderer is walking around Cong. You have to talk to the police. Paul showed me a note which he found in his mother's jacket about meeting someone in the woods. He gave that note to the police. Then, there's the note I found from Jane to Jake. I showed it to you, and later on, I gave it to Paul. He said he'd give it to the police, but I don't know if he followed through with them. Someone, and *I don't think it's me,* has to talk to the police. The truth about everything has to come out."

"Why? So my mother can be dragged through the mud? If the garda are doing their job, they'll figure out that Dan killed Jane and—I wouldn't be surprised—his own son." Ben pushed his plate aside, clutched his tea mug with both hands, and leaned forward. "My mother and Jake built a life here. That so-called letter doesn't change anything."

I didn't agree. I remembered the first night I'd seen Dan and Jane—the nasty backbiting and fighting. Of course, then, I hadn't known who they were or that Jane wouldn't be alive the next day. For once, I wanted the police to be involved. And they needed to see that letter if they hadn't already, and they needed to know about Leonard Ryan skulking around Cong.

"If you don't tell the police, I will," I stated.

"You can forget that. I'm not going to betray Jake and my mother." Ben's face flushed red from his cheeks to the whites of his eyes. "You have no right to cast aspersions on the dead. And, my mother has the right not to have her memories stomped into the ground." Ben looked around for the server and signaled for our check. "You'll have to find another way, Miss O'Brien." With that, he rose, threw some euros onto the table, and left the restaurant.

Now what? I couldn't go to the police; they'd already warned me to stay away. Why had Paul asked me to back off investigating his mother's death? Did he suspect Dan? I knew too well the pain associated with the secrets people we love keep from us. No matter how many times I looked at what had happened, I always came back to only one way forward—to confront Dan. But not today. I'd had enough. Exhausted, frustrated, whatever I wanted to call how I felt, I didn't have another argument with anyone in me. I also had to find Ashford before heading back to French Hill. I left the restaurant thinking about Paul, Dan, Jane, Pat, and Jake. Financial infidelity, gold fever, or greed? In the minds of certain people, either one or all of these provided a powerful motivation for murder.

CHAPTER 35

When I exited the restaurant, Ashford sat on the sidewalk. I began walking to where I'd left my car, expecting him to follow. Instead, he alternated between spinning around in circles, pushing his nose against the backs of my knees, and herding me toward the walking path. It was getting dark. Glancing at my phone, I was surprised to see it was almost 4:00 p.m. Ashford nudged me again. I relented, retrieved my sneakers from the car, and began the walk along the path toward the chateau, where I'd found Jane's body.

Along the way, I picked up a branch for Ashford to retrieve and return. The mindless, meditative back and forth ceased when his bark pierced the air. Then, he proceeded to run into the woods, pushing through the brambles and vegetation. *What now?* I squared my shoulders and turned toward the direction I'd last seen his tail—no sign of him, no barking, nothing. I continued walking.

"Damn dog!" The abrupt shout was followed by its owner, Dan Doherty, as he burst through the tangled undergrowth. The canvas bag slung over his shoulder, whatever it contained, clinked with every step he took. I froze in place, wondering if I should announce my presence. Curiosity, however, took the upper hand. I remained stationary. If he didn't see me, I'd follow him and determine once and for all what game he was playing.

I watched him scramble across the path and disappear into the woods on the opposite side. Glad that I'd donned sneakers, I tiptoed behind him, following the clanking sack. The path twisted and undulated, teeming with gnarled roots, damp mossy rocks, and dead leaf detritus. I grasped bone-thin tree trunks for support as I continued to pick my way forward. Suddenly, the path opened up to the waters of Lough Corrib. Several rowboats, tethered to the boathouse's dock, bobbed in the water. The letters "AC" along with a number stood out against what looked like fresh paint on each boat. The numbers started with one and ended with six. I counted five boats—number four was missing. Danger signs, warning against swimming and disclaiming responsibility, hung from the side of the building. I stopped. Dan stood on the dock where, one by one, he extracted the bag's contents—lantern, hammer, and what looked like several pans—placing them into the floor of one of the boats.

Striding across the short expanse of sand, strewn with broken shells, pebbles, and rocks, I called him out. "Dan Doherty." For a moment, he froze, his head rising from his task. He looked out over the choppy, gray-green water. Realizing the gusting wind carried my voice out over the riled surf, I shouted again. "Dan Doherty."

This time, he turned his gaze toward the shore. Seeing me step onto the weaving dock, he pivoted toward the boat, placed one foot in, and reached to unwind the rope from its mooring.

"Stop," I demanded. "I thought you wanted to help Paul."

He removed his foot from the boat, squared his shoulders, and faced me. Close up now, I recognized the materials lying in the boat's bow—prospector's pick, gold pans, and sieves. It all began to fall into place.

"You've been mining gold at Rose Cottage," I said.

He turned his gaze from me to look out over the water before responding, "Aye, I have. That property is mine. I have the right to do whatever I want with it."

"Did Paul know?" I asked.

"Not in the beginning, but he sussed it out," Dan shouted over the sound of the wind.

Why hadn't Paul said anything to me? And if he thought his father was up to no good, why had Paul asked me to clear his father's name? "When did he find out?" I demanded.

"That letter you gave to him came between us. He confronted me—the day you found his body."

Dan's eyes filled with water. I assumed the wind, not tears, was the cause. From what I'd seen of his behavior, I didn't think he had sympathy for anyone but himself.

"Was the letter true? Was Jake going to leave Pat for Jane?" I asked. Combined with the fight I'd witnessed in the pub, Dan had plenty of motive to kill Jane.

He laughed. "I doubt it. She still loved me. I could do anything. She always came back to me. But Paul, he was upset about everything—the money I owed the bank, my relationship with Ann Ryan. He blamed himself for not paying more attention to what was going on around him."

"What about the gold?"

"Jane copped on to my, let me call it, financial situation. She refused to help me. I was going to lose everything. When I discovered the gold, I realized I had a way out. I thought I'd really struck it rich."

"You're not making sense. The government owns whatever ore is on that property. Is your ego so big you think you're invincible from the law?"

"I'd already siphoned off enough before the government came into the picture. I'm going to be a wealthy man."

"Did Paul know?"

"Not until that day. We had a terrible row. He said he was going to the police with the letter. I tried to stop him, but he wouldn't listen. Dan's body slumped as if the words or increased winds deflated the bluster I'd noted in our earlier meeting.

At least that explained Paul's panic when I'd spoken to him on the phone about the engineer getting involved. He was worried about his father's guilt. But it still didn't explain why Jane or Paul was murdered.

"What is your relationship with Ann?" I asked.

"Any relationship we have is purely business."

"So, you're in on the land development plan she has for your property?" I watched his face for his reaction.

No one could have faked the surprise that flashed across his face. "That's my land. Nobody has a right to tell me what to do with it," he shouted. Maybe my assumption that Ann and Dan were in cahoots about the land was incorrect. She was just playing Dan along until she got the development deal.

"What are you planning now?" I asked, nodding toward the boat and the tools within.

"I'm dumping them out in the center of the lake. The water is meters deep out there. Nobody will be any the wiser." Suddenly, his body posture changed. He raised his chin and glared down at me through narrowed eyes. "Except for you. The nosy American. Now, you know my secret. What are you going to do about it?"

I glanced around, noting how alone we were. My eyes scanned the dock for a defensive weapon while I stalled for time. "How long have you been digging up around the cottage?" I asked.

"I'd just started when that damn Evelyn came back to town and happened to identify the cottage as the site of an ancient ruin." The words roared from his lips.

Dr. O'Dowd had said she knew where Evelyn was, but I still

didn't like what I heard. "So, you stalked her instead? Maybe crept around the woods or her house in order to scare her?" Although Leonard had already admitted his part in shadowing Evelyn, it didn't mean Dan hadn't done something similar.

His laugh echoed across the expanse of water. "Maybe the Rose Cottage ghost frightened her."

"Ghost?" I asked. My eyes scanned the shoreline for a broken tree limb, anything that might be used as a weapon. The ring buoy looked new but was mounted on a galvanized steel structure several yards away. From the look of Dan's physical condition, I realized he might be as agile as I was. I didn't know if I'd reach the buoy in time. I kept looking for a weapon.

"You know, the reported haunting." He pointed to the lantern. "You'd be surprised what a lantern, a sheet, and pushing people into wells and such does for keeping people away." Again, the laugh was interspersed with heavy breathing. "Works much better than a No Trespassing sign."

"You're willing to go that far? Pushing people into wells?" I grew angry at the realization. "*Like me.*"

"Evelyn did me a big favor," he said, looking at his manicured fingers. "The dig camouflaged what I was doing at night." He flexed his hands. Then his eyes returned to my face. "That is until you showed up—bringing that engineer Ted and the rest of the bloody government into town."

"What about Paul? Did you push him to his death?" The words spewed from my throat in an angry torrent.

Dan didn't reply.

I took a deep breath. "Did you kill your wife and your son?" I asked.

Still, no reply.

Around us, the sky grew darker. The lake boiled from the kicking wind. The rain plastered my skin and clothes. In the absence of a handy defensive weapon, I made a quick decision. I'd have to outrun him. The wooden planks linking the dock to the boat were narrow and wet. They also looked slippery. I was confident I'd outpace him if I could get a decent head start. Then, without warning, he broke the silence.

"Do you know the legend called the Lake of the Hounds?" he asked. He looked out over the water. When he returned his gaze to me, tears trickled down his cheeks.

I didn't point out that the legend was associated with Lough Conn, which was miles away. I assumed his guilt had taken control of his emotions and rational mind. So much so, he seemed to have lost his sense of place. I focused on Paul. "Paul loved you," I said. "He never stopped believing in you." My words appeared to break him down further. The tears created rivulets in his face. I continued. "Did you even listen to him? He wanted to prove your innocence!"

"This is all my doing," Dan confessed. "I've always believed you only win if you break the rules. I broke the rules, and now I've lost my wife and my son." Then, he continued his recitation. "The mythical hunter-warrior, Finn McCool's dog, Conn, chased a wild boar for days. According to the legend, water poured from the boar's feet, creating this lake. The boar swam back to land, but Conn drowned." Shaking his head as if in regret, Dan wiped the tears from his face. "Aye, I've been chasing the gold. And now I've lost my wife and my son. I loved them, him..."

"Are you okay?" Someone's voice interrupted.

Dan stopped speaking. I glanced toward the beach, where Ben stood, his eyes shifting between Dan and me.

Relief flooded through my body.

"I thought I heard voices," Ben said. His eyes continued to take in the scene. "What are you two doing out here? Met Eireann's posted a storm warning. It's best to get away from the water."

Ben walked toward the boat ramp. Before Dan could regain his composure, my eyes sought Ben's. Then, I explained, "I'm going to need your help. Dan's just been telling me about the gold at Rose Cottage and how much he loved Paul."

"Oh." Ben nodded in agreement. "I've suspected Dan was up to something nefarious at Rose Cottage for quite some time. I just didn't know what he was doing. I shouldn't have, but I said something to Paul. He didn't believe me when I mentioned I'd seen Dan around the cottage at night. Several times, after I'd closed up shop, I'd spot him digging around the cottage as I drove home to Happy Trails."

"Dan, I want to help you," I said. "Paul asked me to help you. Let's talk to the police. Ben and I will go with you."

"No." Dan's tortured cry rose on the wind.

The waves battered the boat's moorings, and the ramp's rocking increased. Dan lost his footing and dropped to his knees. Ben, looking worried, crossed the remainder of the beach to arrive where I was riveted to the planks. I kept my eyes on Dan. "We're going to have to get him off this ramp soon," I said to Ben, hoping Dan didn't hear me over the sound of the wind.

Ben didn't answer. Instead, he walked to the boathouse wall, where a coiled yellow rope rested upon a hook. He took the rope in his hands. Then, he nodded at me to join him. We approached Dan.

"It's me, Dan. Ben. Paul's friend. Don't worry; we'll get this straightened out in no time."

"Ben..." Sobs erupted, shaking Dan's chest. "I didn't..."

"Here, give me your hand," Ben said. "I'm going to guide you toward the beach. It's getting wild out here."

The lake pounded the shoreline. The sun, a faint beacon, slid into the horizon. I wrapped my arms around my body to keep it from shivering in the frigid air. I hoped Ben could handle Dan in his current emotional state. He'd be difficult to budge without his cooperation. Dan lifted his eyes toward Ben, and Ben offered his hand. I held my breath. Ignoring him, Dan tried to push himself upright, unsuccessfully. He crumpled onto his knees again when the water slapped the dock. Finally, the wind seemed to knock any resistance out of him. He huddled on the dock, shaking like a mound of flesh and bones. Ben stepped closer and wrapped the rope around Dan's waist, securing him to the dock post. "That should hold him for now," Ben said.

"I'll call the police," I yelled over the wind and pulled my cell from its holster. Then, I turned toward the boathouse to shelter the phone from the lake's spray and typed in 112.

"Don't do that, or he'll be the next Doherty to die," Ben shouted. My fingers froze on the *send* button. I turned to see a gun—Dan's head in its sight. The pistol melded into Ben's hand, almost as if it had been there all along. Shaking my head in disbelief, I pulled my eyes from the weapon to Ben's face.

"What do you mean he'll be the next Doherty to die? I asked, stunned at what I had heard and was seeing.

"Throw that phone into the water," he commanded. His gun hand didn't waver.

There was no way I could take the weapon from him. It cost me everything to do it, but I tossed my lifeline to the world. It hit one of the ramp's posts and bounced onto the rocky shore, just out of reach of the water and my hand.

"Ben, what is going on here?"

Seemingly satisfied that I wouldn't be able to reach the phone, Ben answered my question. "I'm righting the scales of justice. Now, walk over here to me. Take your time. I wouldn't want you to fall into the water. Yet."

I gasped from the chills that shook my body. They weren't caused by the charged air but from his tone. He sounded like he was discussing a literary work. I took a slight step in his direction. I'd already exhausted the odds of finding a potential weapon. I closed the gap between us as the water surged over the ramp.

"You killed Paul and Jane," I stated. I didn't know what else to do. I'd hit the *send* button when I threw the phone. But I had no idea if I'd had a signal. I could only hope the call went through, and the operator could hear our conversation. Maybe I'd be able to keep him calm until help arrived. The only thing I knew was that I didn't want to die, and I wouldn't be responsible for Dan's death.

"Sure, I did. And I'd do it again," Ben laughed. "Actually, I'm about to perform an encore." With the gun still nestled against Dan's head, Ben's eyes bored into mine. "I want you to get into the boat," he ordered with a smile.

My blood froze. I took small steps past both men, keeping my eyes focused on Dan's face—trembling with fear, nostrils streaming mucus, lips pressed together in grim realization. When I reached the boat, Ben used his empty hand to test the rope that held Dan tied to the dock. Satisfied, Ben pivoted to face me. "That's right. Step into the boat," he directed.

Fear stung like a sharp needle, piercing every part of my body. "No, I won't. Not until I have some answers." I said. I stood still, my legs wide, my feet braced against the dock— keeping their hold on the wooden precipice atop the water. Maybe I was crazy, but I wasn't about to go down without a fight. "Was it the gold?" I asked.

"You haven't done very much reading, have you, Miss O'Brien?" Ben's words taunted me. "If you had, you'd know the Bible verse concerning the sins of the father."

"My church-going days ended years ago," I said.

"You should know it, Miss O'Brien. You've lived it. 'The sins of the fathers have consequences not only for themselves but also for their children.' You're searching for your mother, aren't you? Don't know anything about your father. That makes you one of us—the children who've had to pay for their parents' indiscretions."

I pretended to consider his words. "You're telling me, all of this, everything has to do with love triangles and affairs of your parents." My eyes swept the landscape behind him for the millionth time. Something. Anything. I had to save Dan and myself. I spread my arms wide as if to encompass the world around us in my grasp. The gun in his hand pressed deeper into Dan's temple.

"It's about truth, Miss O'Brien," Ben said. "And the truth is I need the money from the stud farm to keep my business going. Everything was all sealed and wrapped up with a beautiful bow. Jake bequeathed Happy Trails to my mother. But then I found the Dear Jake letter when I was cleaning out Jake's library."

For a moment, I didn't think I'd heard him correctly. *All of this because of Jane's ultimatum?* It didn't make sense to the rational side of my brain, but that's what I'd just heard Ben say.

"What does that have to do with the stud farm?" I asked.

"Jake and Pat weren't married. With this letter, Luke has a good shot at mucking things up."

I continued with my questions. "What does Paul have to do with any of this?"

"He put it all together when you gave him that letter. He was going to go to the police. Stupid Paul. He thought I'd want to go with him out of respect for our parents," Ben answered. "He should have stayed out of the way. He shouldn't have hired you. Enough. No more talk. Get into the boat."

I didn't think Ben would wait too much longer to kill Dan and me.

"Jake was the man in the woods, wasn't he?" I asked, stalling for more time.

"Paul figured it out. He realized Jake was the one arguing with Jane in the woods. Paul thought he was confiding in me. But I already knew about the affair." Ben laughed. "Paul was such a fool. He actually believed Ann might have killed Jane in a jealous rage over Dan. As if Ann were capable of anything that involves deep emotional involvement."

"What did Jane and Jake's affair have to do with anything? Why kill over it?" I asked.

"Because Luke was left completely out of his father's will. Luke wants to break the bequest Jake made to Pat. Luke can contest it, saying that Jake didn't fulfill his responsibility to his own son. He's going to claim that Jake was seeing other women —that my mother shouldn't be entitled to anything because Jake and Pat weren't married—that blood comes first." The words erupted from Ben's mouth in a wail like the myth's banshee cry. "I had to kill Jane. I couldn't have her telling anyone about the affair. But then Paul told me he had that stupid Dear Jake letter. I had to kill him; that's all—and then destroy the letter once and for all." Ben laughed maniacally.

"But Luke knows about the affair. Dan told him. So do Ann and Pat. How do you plan to make this all work?" I asked.

"Without documentation, there won't be any tangible proof of the affair. And, loose ends can always be snipped." His hand gripped the gun, knuckles white with tension. The wind rested for a few moments, making it easy to hear his whispered, "Get into the boat, or I'll just end it now."

I looked at Dan, but his eyes were squeezed tight. He was of no help.

"So...I get into the boat. Then what?" I asked. "I don't think you're going to be able to move Dan."

Never taking his eyes from me, Ben pulled on the rope around Dan's body.

"I don't have to move him. Once you've been neutralized, I'll shoot Dan, untie him, and call the garda." His voice grew louder with each word. "I'll be the hero—say that I found Dan here standing over your body. I tried to stop him, but he turned the gun on himself. Just look at him, a whimpering mess. This will put an end to everything—Luke and his nuisance suit about the will. Finally, Happy Trails and the money will be my mother's and mine. Rightfully so." Ben laughed.

The wind roared back, carrying his laugh above the tree line, reverberating around us. A slight movement along the beach caught my eye. Hoping for someone, anyone, who'd decided to take a walk in the storm, I swept my eyes to the ground, not wanting to alert Ben. When I glanced up again, I saw a lone figure on the beach. Ashford.

No, go back. My mind screamed the words, but I didn't utter them. I'd rather die than see him die. I got into the boat. The waves lapped against the dock posts, ticking off time like a bomb waiting to detonate.

Ashford crouched as he moved across the sand. When he arrived at the water's edge, he laid down. His head rested on his front paws. I glanced out over the lake, hoping my movement would keep Ben from seeing the dog. But I needn't have bothered; Ben was focused on the task at hand.

"Not to worry, Miss O'Brien. It will be quick." He shifted his weight to position his body in my direction, the gun hand raised.

At that moment, Ashford drew himself up into a streamlined mass and hurtled across the dock. His snarls pierced the air. His bared teeth sank into Ben's arm. As Ashford growled and bit, Ben tried to curl up into a ball. As he fell, the gun spun across the wooden planks, off the edge of the dock, and into the lake's frigid water.

I climbed out of the boat and scrambled into the shallow water to retrieve my phone from the rocky shore. I called the police. Then, I stood guard over Dan—still enmeshed in rope. Ashford, his body draped over Ben's, snarled each time he moved.

CHAPTER 36

Ben confessed to it all—finding the Dear Jake letter, learning that Luke contested the will, worrying that Pat would lose the farm, and thus Ben's access to the money keeping the bookstore afloat. But of course, that wasn't the end —lives were disrupted.

Trying to get back into Aunt Georgina's good graces, Jimmy called to tell her he'd sold his partnership in Jane's fitness center to Sarah. But Jimmy's attempt at reconciliation with Aunt Georgina went nowhere—the relationship was over.

After Paul's funeral service in Lisloughry Cemetery, where he was buried next to his mother, the police arrested Dan on charges related to the illegal mining activities and for pushing me into the cave. Ann got her wish—Rose Cottage and the mill were for sale to raise money for Dan's defense fund. Luke backed away from his suit against Pat; instead, selling his stud farm to her. Then he left Ireland for Ocala, Florida, and a new start in the horse breeding business. Ben's Rarities was put on the auction block. Pat visited her son in prison as often as she could get away from her duties at Happy Trails.

We sometimes have a false notion that our life is normal, but when the truth becomes known, there are a variety of emotions—tremendous conflicts such as anger, guilt by association, disbelief, and denial. There are two sides to every person. In some cases, one side may be a murderer, a liar, or a cheater. The other side is a loving, intelligent person. Ben loved Jake and his mother. He loved his life. What part did the transgressions of the parents play in the events that led to Paul's death, Luke's anger, and Ben's turn to murder?

I thought of my own parents, the father I'd never known, my mother's cheerfulness and care. What didn't I know? What kind of person had my father been? What part had their errors played in their lives? In my life? Perhaps the answer lay somewhere on Achill Island—I hoped so.

Aunt Georgina's arrival at my kitchen door pushed my thoughts aside. She placed one of her homemade brown breads onto the table. My mouth watered, and my lips turned up in a smile.

I filled the electric kettle, put some mugs on the table, and took a variety of tea bags from the canister. While my mouth enjoyed the taste of the butter and jam slathered on a thick slice of bread, Georgina asked about my plans.

"Well," Aunt Georgina said, "when are you planning to drive to Achill?"

I rose from the table to retrieve the list from my purse. Taking the paper from me, Aunt Georgina perused it. When she finished, she tilted her head and turned her eyes to me. My stomach clenched at the tears that threatened to overflow onto her cheeks.

"Star, I can't imagine what it must have been like for you." She reached across the table to take both of my hands in hers.

"I know, Aunt Georgina. I know." I fought back the tears that threatened to erupt and instead smiled at her—boundless energy, empathy, and loving spirit.

Not one to wallow in pity or emotional outbursts, she continued. "The weather forecast is nasty at the moment. I wouldn't delay too long. Sometimes Achill's power is out for days after a strong storm."

Dropping my hands back to the table, I reached for my iPhone and studied its lime green case before I answered, "No, I won't be heading to Achill anytime soon. I have to return to the States for a few weeks. The Consulting Detective is working on a case that demands my presence. At least for a week or two. The client only wants to deal with me at this point." I sipped my tea as I reexamined the list of names that now lay on the table between us.

"The situation in Ridgewood is pressing. I have to choose between addressing the concerns of a long-time client or following up on these names right now. I have to choose the option that is the least destructive to my business—Ellie and Phillie depend on me."

"Is there anything I can do while you are away?"

"Yes, actually, I'd like you to follow up with someone for me," I said. "I never had a chance to tell you that Bridgett Sumner called me."

"That's nice. I've heard some good things about Michael's artwork. It's a pity he died before success found him."

"Yes, Bridgett mentioned that, but she also wanted me to know about a woman named Maggie O'Malley Hanlon, who lives in Achill. According to Bridgett, this woman remembers a house fire that killed everyone but a daughter. Going out there might be a long shot, but maybe you could go see this Hanlon woman while I'm gone."

"Of course, I'll go, loveen. Don't you worry; I'll take care of finding out what I can while you're gone. And what do you plan to do with Ashford?" Aunt Georgina asked. "I take it no one has claimed him."

"No. The Ashford Castle staff have been wonderful about posting information on their social media and within the resort about a missing border collie. But no one has come forward."

As I stroked his ears, he studied my face. Then, he gave me a wet lick on my cheek. Glancing at Aunt Georgina, I confessed that because he was an orphan, I'd decided to keep him.

"Jesus, Mary, and Saint Joseph, girl. How do you expect to do that with having to go to the States for a few weeks?" She shook her head and tossed the ends of the extra-long peacock threaded silk scarf that encircled her neck behind her.

Before I answered, I picked up a slice of brown bread and broke it into small pieces, which I shared with Ashford. "Oh, well, I thought I'd ask Lorcan to mind him while I'm gone."

"Lorcan?" Aunt Georgina pushed her tea mug around on the table. "Have you spoken to him about this?"

"No, but I plan to ask him before I leave. I don't think he'll mind. He's a dog person. He's already taken Ashford with him on his consultations and site visits. Ashford likes him, and I know I can trust Lorcan."

"Is that so? Now, tell me. Is it Ashford who trusts Lorcan or Star?" Georgina's eyes probed my face while she waited for an answer.

"You're not getting me to admit anything, Georgina. Besides, Lorcan never seems busy—not with the way he's always showing up at inopportune times."

"You haven't spoken?" For once, Aunt Georgina seemed at a loss for words as she pursed her lips.

"No, we haven't. Why? What's up?"

"Well..." Aunt Georgina's voice trailed off just as Ashford leaped from the floor with a bark. The kitchen door opened, and Lorcan entered. *When did he begin thinking he could just walk in without knocking first?*

"Lorcan, we were just talking about you. I was about to tell Star your news."

"What news?" I asked.

Lorcan smiled, sat down, and reached for a slice of brown bread. The man was infuriating—why was he always so calm?

And why did he think he could appropriate the last slice of brown bread?

"What news?" I repeated.

"Are you okay?" he asked.

"Of course, I am. Why wouldn't I be?" I replied as I sat straighter in my chair. I couldn't help but notice how his thick blond hair brushed against the top of his shirt collar. Like I said —exasperating.

"I was thinking," Lorcan said.

"Yes?"

"I'm sorry you haven't had time to follow up on what you found in the archives. You must be disappointed."

"Oh, I see. I thought you were referring to Ben's confession and arrest when you asked me if I was okay." I didn't want to talk about my mother with Lorcan—not now. His calmness, his kindness would unravel me in ways that I wouldn't be able to deal with.

"I saw Tom O'Shea in town, and he brought me up to speed on Ben and Dan. They'll pay for what they've done. Unfortunately, it's too late for Paul and his mother" – Lorcan's blue eyes held mine with his as he continued – "and for what almost happened to you."

"O'Shea?" I asked. "I'm not too confident the police will want to extract punishment for me. They resent my persistence —on both sides of the Atlantic."

Shaking his head in disagreement, Lorcan said, "That's changing. O'Shea just doesn't want a civilian interfering in garda affairs. He worries you may sustain serious injuries or worse one of these days, but he did admit that he admires your feistiness."

When Lorcan's lips turned up in a smile, I changed the subject. "Well, he won't have to worry about me for a few weeks. I was just telling Aunt Georgina that I have to return to the Consulting Detective about a project that's for my eyes only." Lorcan remained silent. "Anyway, since no one has claimed him, I've decided to keep Ashford. I was wondering if I could leave him with you while I'm away."

I grasped my iPhone as I waited for his response and the onset of butterflies swirling around my stomach to settle down. I'm not good at seeking help from anyone, and here I was asking Lorcan.

Ashford sat up on his hind legs and looked at both of us.

Lorcan picked a piece of brown bread from his plate and reached down to feed it to Ashford.

"Just tell her," Aunt Georgina said. She reached over and moved his plate, so he couldn't play with it any longer. "Before I do," she added.

"I'm sorry, Star, but I'm leaving for the United States tomorrow."

"You are?" The words caught in my throat. Here, I was beginning to depend on Lorcan, and he was about to leave. And what about Ashford?

"Yes. It's sudden. An unexpected issue with some airborne wind turbines on an energy project in Wyoming. It's my patent, and the engineers haven't been able to solve the issue."

Pilot, engineer, inventor. The person who had saved my life. But I just couldn't admit how much I liked Lorcan McHale.

"How long will you be gone?" was all I said.

"I'm not sure. It depends on the issue, the equipment, the weather—for as long as I'm needed."

I reached down to hug Ashford—my orphan dog—in an effort to hide my disappointment.

"Okay, I'll take Ashford while you're away, Star. Lord knows, I'll need the company with both of you gone to the States," said Aunt Georgina. Glancing at us, she stood up and headed toward the door. "I'll ring you later, Star, to arrange for a time to pick up Ashford."

As soon as the door closed behind Aunt Georgina, Lorcan

tilted his head and said, "I'm sorry I didn't get to fulfill my promise to take you to dinner."

"Dinner?" I asked. What else could I say? That I was sorry we wouldn't be spending any time together? It's not as if we were a couple or anything. I began clearing the dishes from the table. With my back turned to Lorcan, I looked through the tiny window over the sink at the green fields, the trees that ringed the garden, and the French Hill monument that kept watch over the area. At that moment, I realized just how much I'd grown to love this place.

"Star..." Lorcan interrupted my thoughts.

"Oh, yeah, I remember now..." I wanted to stop him before he said anything that caused my eyes to well up with tears. I turned from the sink and said, "Maybe next time. Now" – I looked around the kitchen before I turned my eyes to meet his – "I have to get ready to leave."

For a moment, I thought he looked disappointed before he unwound his frame from his chair and walked to the door.

"Goodbye, Star. Safe travels." He bent down to rest his hand on Ashford's head and then was gone.

Ashford's eyes appeared moist when he looked up as if to ask, *What's wrong?*

"Oh, Ashford, it's me, not you."

As I finished tidying up the kitchen, I thought about the obelisk at Ashford Castle and the words that Lady Ardilaun had inscribed there upon the death of her husband: *Rien ne m'est plus; Plus ne m'est rien.* Translated these words mean *Nothing remains to me any longer, anything that remains means nothing.* I grieved for all I'd loved and lost, for the feelings of warmth and friendship that I hadn't been able to reveal to Lorcan. Some people questioned where their fears came from, but I knew where mine came from. And I wasn't giving up. I wasn't putting any of it aside—the search for my mother, the love I felt for Aunt Georgina, Ellie, Phillie, Skipper, Ashford, the respect I'd developed for Lorcan, the sense of belonging I had when I was in this place—everything, all of it, meant something to me.

Just then, the landline rang.

"Hi, Ellie. Is everything all set?" I asked. Silence greeted me. Had the connection dropped? "Ellie?" I repeated.

"I'm sorry. I must have rung the wrong number. I'm calling to speak with Star O'Brien. Sorry to have bothered you."

"Yes, I'm Star O'Brien. I was expecting a call from someone else. Anyway, how can I help you?" As I waited for the caller to respond, I glanced at my iPhone, wondering if I had time for a walk before packing up.

"My name is Evelyn Cosgrove."

ABOUT THE AUTHOR

MARTHA M. GEANEY is the author of the highly praised non-fiction, women's leadership book, *Bring Your Spirit to Work: One Woman at a Time*. She is also the author of the Star O'Brien fiction series, which is set in the west of Ireland. Martha was born in New York City but lived in New Jersey, beginning at the age of eight. In 2017, Martha and her partner, Bill, moved to Florida, where she  enjoys cooking, reading, swimming, and her Schipperke puppy, Turlough.

Before turning to indie writing, Martha was a teacher, management consultant, university professor, and the dean of a business college. It was her leadership experience as a management consultant and her research for her doctorate that prompted Martha to write a self-help book for women who aspire to leadership roles.

Martha's passion for Ireland began when she made her first trip, at the age of four, to County Mayo, the birthplace of her mother, and County Cork, the birthplace of her father. She returned to Ireland again at the age of sixteen to attend a boarding school in Castlebar, County Mayo, for two years. Since then, Martha has visited her cousins and friends in

Ireland for more than thirty-five years. It is her love for the people, the country, and all its beauty that inspired her to create a mystery and suspense series set in Ireland about an amateur detective, Star O'Brien, who is an American.

Martha is currently working on her third Star O'Brien novel.

AND A FINAL NOTE FROM MARTHA—

Thank you for reading *Death at Ashford Castle* and for following along with Star as she unravels the mysteries of her life. If you have time, please leave a review on Amazon or Goodreads. You can also like my Facebook author page at *https://www.facebook.com/mgeaneyauthor*.

And if you have questions or feedback that you'd like to share, please contact me at www.martha-geaney.com. I'd love to respond to your comments.

Made in the USA
Coppell, TX
13 March 2021

51699608R00144